THE BRADDOCK BOYS: BRENT

AND

THE BRADDOCK BOYS: TRAVIS

BY
KIMBERLY RAYE

Dear Reader,

I'm thrilled to be back with another book in my latest vampire series for the Blaze line! Brent Braddock is the badass of the Braddock Brothers and, of course, one hot-looking cowboy. Once the most ruthless hired gun in Texas, he's now a modern-day bodyguard for the rich and dangerous. He's also wild and reckless and he *never* plays by the rules.

Abigail Trent, on the other hand, has lived every day of her life by a very strict set of rules. As a training commander for an elite special-ops team of navy SEALs, she's had to lose all the "girl stuff" and toughen up in order to claw her way up the career ladder and win the respect of her male peers. While she doesn't regret her choice, she can't help but wonder what it would be like to unleash the wild woman inside her just once.

She soon realizes that once won't be enough, however, when she comes face-to-face with Brent. Abby wants more. She wants forever.

I hope you enjoy the latest in the Braddock Brothers series! I love to hear from readers. You can visit me online at www.kimberlyraye.com or write to me c/o Harlequin Books, 225 Duncan Mill Road, Toronto, Ontario M3B 3K9, Canada.

Much love from deep in the heart!

Kimberly Raye

All th... ...imag... ...ation of
the aut... ...ie name
or nan... ...iown or
unkno... ...to the author, and all the incidents are pure invention.

All R... ...e or in
part in... ...arlequin
Enterp... ...eof may
not be... ...ronic or
mecha... ...an i... ...rmation
retriev... ...or otherwise, without the written... ...iblisher.

This b... ...trade or
otherw... ...he prior
conser... ...that in
which... ...ondition
being...

® and ™ are trademarks owned and used by the trademark owner and/or its
licensee. Trademarks marked with ® are registered with the United Kingdom
Patent Office and/or the Office for Harmonisation in the Internal Market and
in other countries.

First published in Great Britain 2011
by Mills & Boon, an imprint of Harlequin (UK) Limited,
Eton House, 18-24 Paradise Road, Richmond, Surrey TW9 1SR

© Kimberly Groff 2010

ISBN: 978 0 263 88076 2

14-0911

Harlequin (UK) policy is to use papers that are natural, renewable and
recyclable products and made from wood grown in sustainable forests. The
logging and manufacturing processes conform to the legal environmental
regulations of the country of origin.

Printed and bound in Spain
by Blackprint CPI, Barcelona

THE BRADDOCK BOYS: BRENT

BY
KIMBERLY RAYE

Bestselling author **Kimberly Raye** started her first novel in school and has been writing ever since. To date, she's published more than fifty novels, two of them prestigious RITA® Award nominees. She's also been nominated by *RT Book Reviews* for several Reviewers' Choice awards, as well as a career achievement award. Currently she is writing a romantic vampire mystery series for Ballantine Books that is in development with ABC for a television pilot. She also writes steamy contemporary reads for the Blaze line. Kim lives deep in the heart of the Texas Hill Country with her very own cowboy, Curt, and their young children. She's an avid reader who loves Diet Dr. Pepper, chocolate, Toby Keith, chocolate, alpha males *(especially* vampires) and chocolate. Kim also loves to hear from readers. You can visit her online at www.kimberlyraye.com

This book is dedicated to my mother.
Sometimes when life doesn't turn out as planned,
the only thing we can do is hang on for the ride.
I know it's been bumpy, but keep
hanging on for me,
I love you!

1

BRENT BRADDOCK HAD NEVER been the type of man to beat around the bush when it came to something he wanted. He was straightforward. Determined. Persistent.

One hundred and fifty years as a vampire who fed off both blood and sex hadn't changed him much.

While the average bloodsucker tried to curb the lust with a little roll in the hay, Brent preferred going straight for the jugular, no pun intended.

Not that he didn't like sex.

He *loved* it, and he sure as shootin' fired off a round whenever possible. Once upon a time, he'd been one of the fastest guns in the Confederacy and the most precise. Now he called himself a bodyguard and offered his skills to the highest bidder, which meant he spent a great deal of time in the big cities.

New York. Chicago. L.A. Prime hunting ground when it came to getting down and dirty. He could fall into bed with the prettiest filly around and never run the risk of seeing her again.

But this was small town central.

If he bedded a woman tonight, he was sure to bump into her again and again before he said goodbye to this map dot. While she might not remember him thanks to his vamp mojo, he would remember her. Worse, she would become more than a face. And that he didn't like.

He didn't want to know that she'd been voted Most Popular back in high school or that her dad owned the local feed store or that she went to the VFW Hall every Thursday night for spaghetti dinner. He didn't want to know her, period.

Knowing made it harder to turn his back and walk away.

And Brent Braddock *always* walked away.

"I didn't sign up for this," muttered the woman who pushed through the rear Exit of the Dairy Freeze. "I'm a waitress not a bus boy. I do tables, not trash."

The door creaked shut behind her, muffling the whir of a shake machine and the *hisss* and *poppp*! of a burger grill. June bugs bumped against the single bulb that burned near the back door.

She wore a white button up blouse with her name embroidered in pink across the right pocket, white shorts and a pair of white sneakers. Her breaths echoed in his ears and he tuned in to the steady thump of her pulse.

A knife twisted inside of him and his muscles clenched. Heat hummed the length of his spine. His hunger stirred. He watched as she dumped an empty banana crate near the dumpster a few feet away from where he stood in the shadows.

She started to turn, but then her gaze hooked on him and she started. "Holy Toledo," she touched a hand to her chest, "you scared me." She eyed him. "We don't allow customers out back."

"I'm not a customer."

"Then what are you doing here?"

"Waiting." His words slid into her ears and just like that, her annoyance faded and her interest piqued.

Her brow smoothed and her eyes sparked. "For who?"

"Who do you think?" He stared deep into her eyes and tuned into the rush of feelings bombarding her. Her anxiety because she was only one of two carhops on duty on a busy Friday night—the other was old lady Dolly who waited tables about as fast as a Thanksgiving turkey sharpened his own ax. Her anger because she'd spotted her ex, aka The

Rat Bastard, having a banana split with some tramp named Bernice. Her insecurity because she should have remembered to put on a swipe of lipstick before taking out the trash.

Talk about stinking rotten luck.

In the six years since she'd graduated high school, she'd spent a fortune trying every dating service known to mankind only to meet Mr. Tall, Dark and Yummy on her way to the f-ing dumpster.

She licked her lips and tried to think of something witty to say. "Why don't you come around front? I'll bring you one of our new Fat Cow burgers. It's a double decker with bacon and three slices of cheese. It sounds like a heart attack just waiting to happen, but it's really awesome. Especially with our double deluxe strawberry malt—"

"I don't want a hamburger."

"Then what do you want? If it's French fries, I could definitely make that happen—"

"You," he murmured again, but this time he made sure she got his meaning loud and clear. "I want *you*." He held her stare and willed away everything except the passion bubbling inside her. "Don't talk." He fed her lust with his own until her cheeks flushed. "Don't think." Her breaths quickened. Her eyes sparked. "Just feel."

The clenching inside your body.

The wetness between your legs.
The heat licking at your skin.

He sent the silent messages and her gaze smoldered. Her hands trembled as she stared back up at him, her expression slightly bewildered. Then a light bulb seemed to go off and suddenly she knew exactly what he wanted. Her eyes sparkled as she slid the buttons free on her blouse. The material parted, revealing a white lace bra. She popped the front clasp and pulled the cups apart. Her breasts sprang free. Her nipples pebbled at the instant rush of air.

His gaze fixed on a faint blue vein barely visible beneath her translucent skin. Her heartbeat drummed in his ears, the sound as intoxicating as the ripe smell that spiraled into his nostrils. His gut tightened and his desperation stirred and then everything faded into a sweet red rush.

He leaned her back over his arm, opened his mouth wide and sank his fangs deep into the flesh just to the right of her nipple.

Soft skin cushioned his lips and liquid heat spurted into his mouth. His fangs tingled and his entire body convulsed. He drew on her harder, deeper, her essence tunneling down his throat and warming him from the inside out. She trembled and gasped and he knew she felt the pleasure as keenly as he did.

The satisfaction.

It rolled through him after several delicious seconds and the tightness clenching his muscles started to ease. The fist in his gut loosened and suddenly he didn't hurt so much.

He indulged for a few delicious seconds before sanity sent up a red flag and a loud *Enough*! The beast was sated.

For now.

Easing the pressure, he retracted his fangs. He licked the tiny prick points, savoring the last few drops before leaning back. He caught her gaze and willed her to forget everything.

No tall, dark cowboy lurking in the alley behind the Dairy Freeze.

No uncontrollable lust urging her to strip down.

No fangs sinking into her breast.

Nothing but a sweet, intoxicating orgasm brought on by a very delicious daydream.

He pulled her blouse together. His fingertips lingered at one ripe nipple before he pulled away, buttoned her up and sent her back inside to finish her shift.

After that, he turned on his heel and did what he'd been doing for the past century and a half, ever since he'd been turned into a vampire on that fateful night so long ago—Brent Braddock walked away and never looked back.

2

"WHAT CAN I DO you for, sugar?" asked an ancient woman wearing a white button-up blouse, white polyester slacks and a pink apron.

"I'll have a double chocolate malt." Abigail Trent gave the hand-held plastic menu another once-over. "With extra whipped cream."

Dolly—according to the name embroidered in hot pink on her left pocket—pushed up her cat's eye glasses. "You sure about that?" She gave a pointed stare at Abigail's plain black combat boots before shifting up, over a pair of worn Levis, to her *Go Navy* hoodie. "We've got some nice fruit smoothies, sugar. Why don't you have one of those?" The old woman winked. "Half the calories."

Abby ignored the pinch to her ego and held tight to her resolve. "I'd rather have a malt."

Dolly wiggled her carefully penciled in eyebrows as if she were about to dangle a carrot. "We've got fresh mango banana."

"I don't like bananas."

"Strawberry Kiwi."

"I don't like kiwi."

Dolly gave her another once over. "You know, sugar, you're not half bad. What I can see, that is. If I were you, I'd definitely lose that there Unibomber look you got goin' for yourself. Especially if you want to rope a cowboy."

Abby narrowed her gaze at the presumptuous woman. "Do I know you?"

"The name's Dolly Cook and the real question is, do *I* know *you*?" She waved a crippled hand. "See, I know everybody in this town. Been working here for the past forty-eight years since me and my husband opened up the place. He passed on about five years ago, God rest his soul. My son took over the kitchen on account of the arthritis in my hands makes it impossible to grip a spatula. Luckily, it ain't spread to my feet and I can still walk up a storm." She indicated the white orthopedic shoes that she wore. "I handle the tables on account of I have a crackerjack memory and don't need to write anything down." She narrowed her gaze. "I ain't never seen you here before. You're new in town." Dolly arched a white brow. "Visiting family?" Abigail shook her head and the old woman added, "Looking for a job?"

Abby shook her head. "A person."

"Just what I thought." She waved a hand. "We get it all the time, what with the divorce rate sky high and the number of good men dropping faster than the stock market on a bad day. Why, women drive in from at least a dozen counties to scope out the local pickins. It's closer than driving to San Antonio or Austin and there's a lot less traffic, lemme tell ya."

"I'm not here looking for—"

"'Course when they realize the women around here are just as desperate," she went on before Abby could finish, "they usually end up heading for the city. Take that group over there." She let her gaze shift to a nearby table full of women nursing glasses of pink froth. "They'll load up on strawberry smoothies and then head for the honky tonk out on Route 9. When they strike out there—and they will strike out on account of every man this side of the Guadalupe will be over at the VFW for poker night—they'll head for Austin. They might have better luck there, but I wouldn't put my money on it. A good man is hard to find these days." Her gaze shifted back to Abby. "Sugar, if you want to lasso yourself a decent cowboy, you need to give yourself every advantage. That means ditching the fatty malt."

"I'm not trying to lasso a cowboy."

"Sugar, you can deny it all you want. But I see what's right in front of me. You've got desperate, hopeful and horny written all over your face. You're looking for a man, all right."

Yeah, she was. But it wasn't what Dolly thought.

Command Master Chief Petty Officer Abigail Trent wasn't looking for just any man. She was hot on the trail of *her* man, aka Rayne Montana, the best of an elite group of Navy Seals that Abby had hand-picked and trained herself. He'd gone AWOL two weeks ago in the mountains outside of Afghanistan.

Her first thought was that he'd gotten himself killed. But they'd yet to recover a body. If he'd been kidnapped (her second thought), his abductors would have contacted the Navy to bargain a trade for one of their own by now.

The MPs had come to the conclusion that he'd snapped from the pressure and bailed. They were in the process of tracking a credit card trail from Afghanistan to Switzerland.

But Rayne was too smart to leave such obvious clues. Even more, he was too good to cut and run. Too loyal. Too trustworthy. Like Abby, he'd been career military. Married to his job. Proud of each and every operation. He took his duty seriously. He wouldn't have abandoned a mission and compromised his entire unit unless he'd had no other choice.

Unless he was in serious trouble.

Despite what the higher ups were saying.

They were blaming Abby. They were convinced he'd cracked and that she'd been remiss and failed to notice. She'd been the Officer in Charge. The sole person responsible for the success of the mission and the safety of each man involved. It had been her duty to bring everyone home. To account for each and every man in her unit.

And that's what she intended to do.

Abby had let the MPs go on their wild goose chase while she'd taken a two week leave and hopped a plane for Rayne's hometown. It was Psych 101. When people were scared, they often gravitated back to the familiar. And if there was one thing Abby knew, Rayne Montana had to be scared. Fear was the only thing that would have pulled him away from the military.

And kept him away.

At least that was her latest theory and the one that had brought her to Skull Creek, Texas, to see if maybe, just maybe she could find a clue as to his whereabouts. Maybe he'd reached out to an old friend. Called them up. Paid them a visit. Sent them a letter. An e-mail. A text. *Something.*

She'd driven into town just a half hour ago and now she was here at the local drive-in, the only place open past sundown on a Friday night.

Located on the outskirts of town, the Dairy Freeze was the quintessential small town scene and the exact opposite of the various cities where her father had been stationed while she'd been growing up. Twelve of them to be exact, in as many years. He'd been a leading Naval recruitment officer back then, a job that had demanded constant travel and so they'd moved regularly. But while the address had changed, the atmosphere hadn't. Crowded. Noisy. Impersonal.

This place was crowded and noisy, too, but it was different. People knew each other. They smiled. They talked. Her gaze shifted to the cluster of round wrought iron tables that sat in front of a sliding order-up window. At one table, a busy mother handed out ice cream cones to a group of messy youngsters. At the next, an elderly couple drank root beer floats, shared an order of onion rings and offered up a stack of napkins when one of the kids dumped his ice cream in his lap. Next to them a cluster of teen-age boys in high school letter jackets and cowboy boots mingled with a handful of girls from a nearby car. Rows of drive-up stalls, filled with everything from pick-up trucks to mini-vans, lined either side of the busy courtyard area. People rolled down their windows and chatted with whoever sat next to them while the latest George Strait song drifted from the outdoor speakers. The smell of chili cheese fries and sugary sweet soft serve filled the air and stirred a strange sense of longing.

For food, of course.

Abigail had been living on powdered milk and beef jerky in the mountains outside of Kabul for the past six months. She certainly wasn't feeling suddenly hollow because the entire scene reminded her of her late mother and the one visit she'd paid to her grandparents when she'd been five.

She pushed aside the strange sense of melancholy and steeled herself as she faced Dolly.

"Thanks for the advice, but I'd rather have the malt." Words to live by as far as Abigail was concerned. Men were distracting. She'd learned that firsthand back in high school when she'd almost thrown away a full ride to the Naval Academy for one measly date with the captain of the hockey team. She'd lusted after him for months, dreamt about him, penciled his name on her notebook. He'd been so perfect and she'd wanted him so much. Enough to miss her application interview in favor of getting her hair done for the first—and only—time to try to impress him.

A wasted effort because the Hockey Hunk had stood her up for the head cheerleader. A girl who wore short skirts and high heels and lots of makeup. Luckily Abby had had a perfect record and so the acceptance board had rescheduled her interview and given her one more chance.

She'd realized then and there that she simply couldn't compete when it came to all the girlie stuff. Her hair would never curl quite as much and her body didn't fill out the sexy clothes quite as well. She'd also vowed to never let a man make a fool of her ever again. While she went out every now and then (she was a grown woman with needs, after all), she didn't let herself get emotionally involved. She didn't sit around dreaming of a big wedding or a happily ever after. She was living her dream—to stand on her own feet, command her own unit and serve her country.

She was good at it. She liked it. Even if it was a little lonely every now and then.

"Oh, and add a double chili dog to that," she added, eager to ignore the sudden tightening in her gut. Real food hadn't been the only thing she'd done without all those months in Afghanistan. It had been over eleven since she'd been with a man and she needed a really good orgasm in a really bad way. Not that a man was required in order to have one, but vibrators had yet to become standard issue special ops gear and so she'd been forced to leave her deluxe model Big Man at home. Since she didn't fraternize with her men and in-field operations didn't permit time or energy for fooling around, she'd done without. Add the fact that Rayne was missing, and her superiors were holding her personally responsible to the mix, and she was definitely feeling some major frustration.

"Add a double order of chili cheese fries to that, too," she told Dolly.

"Whatever you say." The old woman pursed her lips. "Damned young folks. Never listen to one iota of advice." She turned and waddled toward the glass door that led inside.

"With extra cheese," Abigail called after her before turning her attention to her surroundings.

She wasn't asking any questions yet. She'd come off a hellacious flight and she was tired. Which meant that tonight was all about doing a little recon and memorizing the lay of the land while she ate her first decent meal in ages. Then she would check into the nearest motel, plan her strategy for tomorrow's Q & A and get a good night's rest in a real bed.

She did a quick visual assessment, noting the faces and the cars and the details. She was good with details. It was one thing that made her a top notch commanding officer. That, and her instincts. She could assess a situation in the blink of an eye and note any threats, and then she could take the appropriate action. Deploy. Advance. Flank.

Run!

The warning echoed the moment she spotted the cowboy who rounded the side of the building. He made his way toward a beat-up 1967 Chevy Camaro parked near the road.

A pair of black jeans outlined his long, muscular legs. A black button-down shirt, the tails un-tucked, framed his broad shoulders. His sleeves were rolled up to his elbows to reveal the detailed image of a six shooter that had been tattooed on the inside of his left forearm. He wore a black Stetson tipped low on his head, shrouding the upper part of his face.

While he fit with the locals—he certainly looked the part with his boots and Stetson—he didn't *fit*.

She tried to picture him swapping stories at the local feed store or hanging out here at the Dairy Freeze, and she couldn't. His entire persona seemed much too intense, too detached, too mysterious for a small town like Skull Creek.

Too sexy.

The thought struck as her gaze hooked on his sensual mouth. An unexpected visual struck—of that mouth pressed to her throat—and her nipples snapped to attention. Need sliced through her, sharp and swift, and her stomach hollowed out.

As if he sensed her reaction, he turned. He tipped the brim of his hat back and the light illuminated his high cheekbones and sculpted nose. A fierce green gaze blazed across the distance between them and collided with hers.

Her breath caught and her heart paused. It was a crazy reaction for a soldier who made it her business to feel nothing and stay focused.

But for the next few, frantic heartbeats, her brain seemed to scramble and she forgot everything except him and the way he looked at her. Into her. As if he could see past the thick outer exterior, to the soft, vulnerable woman beneath.

As if that woman even existed.

She didn't.

Abigail had accepted that fact a long time ago when she'd failed so miserably with Hockey Hunk. Three hours in Chicago's top salon hadn't been enough to transform her from a pudgy tomboy into a desirable woman.

She'd still been too stocky, too shapeless, too ballsy.

Then and now.

But that was okay. She was a commanding officer, not a Hooters girl. She didn't need that kind of superficial attention. She needed respect.

Well, that and a really rocking orgasm to ease her current nerves.

His gaze swept her from head to toe and stripped away every scrap of clothing. Anticipation zapped her and the air bolted from her lungs.

He grinned then and she had the unnerving thought that he knew her frustration. That he knew *her*.

She stiffened and put up the invisible barricade vital to a special ops soldier. No expression. No emotion. Nothing. Just name, rank and serial number.

His gaze widened and surprise flashed in the bright green depths. At least she thought it was surprise. But then he turned, the car door opened and he disappeared inside. The engine caught.

A rush of panic bolted through her and she pushed to her feet.

Because Abigal Trent didn't waste her time thinking and analyzing. She was a field operative. Paid to trust her gut and act on it. And her gut told her something wasn't right.

He wasn't right.

He was hiding something, and there was only one way to find out exactly what that was, and whether or not it had anything to do with her latest mission. There was always the possibility and with her reputation hanging in the balance, she wasn't leaving any stone unturned.

Abby headed for her rental car and took off after him.

3

SHE WAS FOLLOWING HIM.

He knew it even before he saw the blaze of head-lights in his rearview mirror. He felt her. He'd felt her the first moment she'd spotted him.

Her piqued interest. Her pulse-pounding lust. Her surprise. She'd never reacted so fast, so fierce to any member of the opposite sex and it had freaked her out.

He knew the feeling.

It didn't matter that he'd sucked down enough blood to last him several days. His gaze had met hers and bam, the hunger had sliced through him, cutting him to the quick and scattering his common sense. In an instant, he'd wanted to forget everything—partic-ularly the all-important fact that his youngest brother Cody was waiting for him, along with the computer genius that was going to help him track down his sister-in-law. That's why he was still stuck in this hole-in-the-wall. He needed a lead on Rose and her whereabouts. Once he had enough information, he would hit the road and find her. After he watched his youngest brother tie the knot next week, that is.

Then he would uncover the truth behind the tragedy that destroyed his family and his home one hundred and fifty years ago.

He could still see the flames on that fateful night. Smell the sharp scent of smoke and decay and death.

The Braddock Boys had ridden into the chaos together. Brothers who'd vowed to watch out for each other. A pact they'd made as kids when their father had abandoned them to ride off after some saloon whore. Lyle Braddock had died in a bar fight not long after, and not one of his boys had mourned him. They'd been too busy taking care of each other to worry over the no-good sonofabitch and the fact that he'd never been much of a father figure.

When Cody had up and left to join the Confederate cause, Brent and his brothers had ridden along to keep an eye on him. They'd seized supplies and helped Confederate troops and made a name for themselves as the most notorious raiding group the Union army had ever seen. They'd sure-as-shootin' been a major pain-in-the-ass to Quantrill and his boys.

But then the war had ended, the South had lost, and the Braddocks had headed home.

They'd arrived to find the entire ranch—the main house, the barn, the outbuildings—consumed by flames. The herd had been scattered. And what was left of his family? Gone.

Dead.

A nightmare. That's what Brent had thought as he'd leapt off his horse and tried to save what he could, who he could. The whole scene had seemed so surreal. The dead bodies, most burned beyond recognition, stretched out here and there——his mother, the half dozen hired hands, the ranch foreman, Colton's wife Rose, their six year-old son. But then reality had hit along with a very real crack to the back of his skull. He and his brothers had been attacked from behind, each picked off one-by-one, and left to die.

They would have been six feet under for sure if not for Garret Sawyer. Garret was the creative genius behind Skull Creek Choppers, the fastest growing custom motorcycle manufacturer in the South. He was also the two hundred year old vampire who'd turned the Braddock Brothers that night and given them a second chance at life.

At vengeance.

Up until two weeks ago, Brent and the rest of the Braddocks had blamed Garret for the massacre. They'd been hellbent on finding him and doling out justice. Cody had been the lucky one who'd tracked him to Skull Creek first. Only, it had turned out that Garret had been innocent. He'd arrived after the attack and done all he could to save the brothers who'd been just this side of death. Garret had given them his blood and brought them over in the nick of time, but he'd been too late to save anyone else. Or so they'd thought. But Garret had revealed that he'd also turned a wounded couple he'd found several miles away. The vampire had assumed they were victims of an Indian attack and so he'd done what he could to help—he'd given them his blood the moment they'd taken their last breaths.

A man and a woman.

Rose.

After all this time, she was still alive. Still out there somewhere. A vampire.

While Brent had no idea what had happened that night—if she'd been an innocent victim or a cold, calculated murderess who'd orchestrated the massacre and sacrificed her own son—or who the man was that had been with her, he knew that she knew.

She held all the answers and he wouldn't stop until he'd found her.

All the more reason to forget the damned ache in his gut, hit the gas and lose the woman trailing him.

Cody was waiting.

Even more, Dillon Cash was waiting. Dillon was the one doing the research on Rose, compiling information and trying to come up with a lead. He needed to get his ass in gear and head over to Dillon's.

At the same time, he couldn't shake the curiosity that churned inside him. Particularly since he had no clue who the woman was or what she wanted from him.

Nothing. Nada. Zip.

Which didn't make a damned bit of sense because he was a friggin' *vampire*. When it came to the opposite sex, he read every thought, anticipated every move. There were no surprises.

Until now.

Until her.

Sure, he'd connected with her initially like he did with all humans. He'd seen her initial reaction—the surprise, the lust, the longing. But then her expression had closed like a window slamming shut and he hadn't been able to pick up anything else.

No name.

No background.

No intentions.

One hundred and fifty years and he'd *always* been able to read a woman's thoughts. But damned if this one hadn't shut him out. A fact that made him almost as hard as the lusty beast that lived and breathed inside of him.

He was intrigued. Aroused. Hungry.

And while the last thing Brent needed to do was waste his time with confrontations, suddenly it was the only thing he wanted to do.

He eased off the gas, pulled onto the side of the road and climbed out of the car.

This was not good.

The warning screamed in Abigail's head the minute she pulled up behind the Camaro.

Her headlights sliced through the darkness, illuminating the abandoned car. Her gaze shifted to the pastureland that stretched for miles on either side of the road. He was nowhere in sight. No shadowy figure fleeing in the moonlight or trucking down the road. Which meant that while the car appeared abandoned, it wasn't.

Fear made her heart pump faster and she drew on it. Despite what most people thought, fear could be good. It motivated people, kept their senses heightened and sharp. Most of all, it fed the survival instinct. The key was not to let fear get the upper hand and interfere with brain function. It was all about breathing and thinking. Abigail had learned that during her first special ops mission in Iraq. She'd been cornered by a small group of insurgents who would have captured her had she given in to the gripping terror in the pit of her stomach. The visions of interrogation and torture and death. But instead of the outcome, she'd focused on the moment. On thinking of a way to get to the knife in her boot. Plotting a line of attack. Finding a means of escape.

The fear had turned to power then and she'd made it out alive.

She forced another deep breath and stared at the car in front of her, her gaze searching for some sign that he was still in it. He had to be.

Her gut tightened, her instincts screaming yet again that something wasn't right. Why would he hide unless he had something to hide? She killed her engine, leaving the headlights blazing, and climbed from behind the wheel.

A few seconds later, she eased up beside the car, every nerve in her body on high alert as she slid along the sleek finish and stalled just shy of the door. Her gaze sliced to the right, through the window and the thick darkness to find…

Nothing.

He wasn't sprawled on the front seat or hunkered in the miniscule space in the back.

The Camaro was empty.

Impossible.

She whirled, drinking in the surrounding countryside. She'd been all of twenty seconds behind him. No way could he have crossed the wide open pasture in that short amount of time. Not flat out running. Not even hauling it on a four-wheeler.

Her mind raced as her attention shifted back to the muscle car. Her gaze dropped to the foot of space between the bottom of the car and the ground. It wasn't enough to accommodate a man of his size. At the same time, she'd seen seven men stuff themselves into a crawlspace the size of a single shower stall to escape capture. Desperation was the mother of the impossible.

"You might as well come out." Abigail summoned her most commanding voice. "I know you're under there."

"Actually," the deep, timbre of his voice slithered into her ear a heartbeat before she felt his presence, "I'm out here." A hand touched her shoulder. "Right behind you."

4

SHE WHIRLED AND STARED up at him with blue eyes so clear and vivid that he should have been able to see everything going on in her head. She was startled. That's all he got before the window slammed shut and he was pushed out.

For the first time, he found himself stuck noticing her features. The sparkle of her eyes. The fullness of her cheeks. The smattering of freckles on the bridge of her nose.

Cute.

But Brent didn't do cute. Even more, he didn't do locals. So what if she had the bluest eyes he'd ever seen and a pink, pouty mouth that inspired the most wicked thoughts? He wasn't interested. No sir.

Her lips parted and the faintest intake of breath echoed in his super sensitive ears.

The sound echoed in his head, rumbled down his spine and made a bee-line straight to his cock.

Okay, so he *was* interested. But he knew it wasn't the lust that drew him. He couldn't help but wonder what was going on behind her closed expression, and how she managed it in the first place. No woman had ever shut him out before.

Except his new sister-in-law, that is. But Brent had always figured that had something to do with the fact that she'd been sucking face with his brother. She and Cody had exchanged blood and so she shared his strength. Translation? She wasn't susceptible to another vampire's influence.

But this woman didn't draw her strength from another bloodsucker. It was all her own and damned if that fact didn't turn him on in a major way.

She hadn't had sex in a really long time.

It wasn't a truth he read in her gaze. Rather one that he gauged in her reaction. The stiffening of her body, the rapid in and out of her breaths, the frantic pulse beating at the base of her neck.

He stiffened. "Why are you following me?"

"Don't flatter yourself. I was taking a drive and I saw your car on the side of the road. I thought you might have broken down."

"I saw you back at the Dairy Freeze."

"I like to drive after I eat. It helps the digestion."

She killed the eye contact and cast a glance at his car. "So what's up?" She rounded the front end and started to lift the hood. "Did you overheat?"

He rested a hand atop the metal and pushed it back down with a loud *whackkkk!* "You're good."

"What's that supposed to mean?"

"You don't even blink."

"I'm afraid I don't know what you're talking about."

"You're feeding me a load of bullshit and most people blink when they do that. But you haven't batted an eye."

"Maybe that's because I'm not lying."

"Or maybe," he rounded the car and stepped up to her, "you're just really, really good at it."

Abby had the sudden urge to step back. He was too close and he smelled too good and she was too freaked out by both. Particularly since she didn't get freaked out. Ever. She kept her cool. Her focus. Her objective. Always.

Until now.

Until him.

"What are you really doing out here?" His deep voice slid into her ears and made her heart beat that much faster.

Her hands trembled and she stiffened, determined

to get a grip and keep her mind on her mission. "I'm looking for a man."

He regarded her for a few frantic heartbeats before a grin tugged at the corner of his mouth. "That much I can help you with." His meaning hit and a wave of heat swept through her.

"That's not what I meant." She licked her suddenly dry lips. "I'm looking for a specific man."

"For a specific purpose?" He arched an eyebrow and her heart paused. He was playing with her. She could see it in his eyes and hear it in the deep timbre of his voice. "I'm a jack of all trades. Maybe I can help you out."

Yeah, baby.

She ignored the frantic cry of her hormones and tried to remember the details of the story she'd worked out on the drive from San Antonio to Skull Creek. "I'm looking for my ex-boyfriend. We broke up last month and he moved back here. I think." She didn't sound half as convincing, but then that was the point. To play the sad, confused, pathetic ex-girlfriend and get the locals to talk to her. "One of his relatives passed on and left him quite a bit of money but the estate lawyer can't seem to locate him."

Something sparked in his gaze. "So you're not from here?"

She shook her head. "I've got a place in Chicago, but I don't see it much. My job keeps me busy."

Sales. That's what she was going to say when he asked what she did for a living. She'd been through enough interrogations to know that that was the next logical question.

"So what is it you're after? A piece of the money, or do you still have a thing for him?"

"Sales."

"Excuse me?"

Yeah, excuse me? Let him ask the question before you answer, dumbass. What are you thinking?

But she wasn't thinking. Standing there, with the moonlight spilling down around them and his scent filling her nostrils, the only thing she could do was feel. The sweat trickling between her shoulder blades. The awareness rippling up and down her spine. The hollowness between her legs.

"That's what I do for a living," she blurted. "In case you were wondering."

"I wasn't. So are you going to answer the question? Money? Revenge? Which is it?"

"Closure. Our break-up was really abrupt. He moved out with no warning and the only thing I got was a text message saying goodbye. I figured if I came here to tell him about the inheritance, it would give us a chance to talk about things." When he gave her a doubtful look, she added, "You wouldn't understand. It's a girl thing." Or so she'd heard. She'd never been much of a "girl". Not in the way she acted—no strutting her stuff or wowing men or texting her BFF about her latest conquest—and certainly not in the way she looked—no skimpy clothes or make-up or lacey panties. That truth had always been something she'd been proud of.

But staring up into his gaze, she found herself wishing she'd put on something—anything—besides baggy jeans and a hoodie.

"So what's his name?"

"Who?"

"The ex-boyfriend?"

"Rayne." She stared deep into his eyes, searching for some spark of recognition. "Rayne Montana. Do you know him?"

"Can't say that I do. I'm just passing through myself. I'm visiting my brother and his wife. In fact," he glanced at his watch, "I'm running late. I was supposed to meet them fifteen minutes ago."

She tried to ignore the sudden disappointment that washed through her. "Sorry about the misunderstanding." She started to dart past him, but he caught her arm before he could think better of it.

His fingertips seemed to tingle, sending shock

waves through her. Her stomach hollowed out and her nipples pebbled.

"No bother." His gaze pushed into hers. "So what does he look like?"

She glanced up from the point of contact. "Who?"

"The boyfriend."

"Ex-boyfriend." She wasn't sure why she felt the need to correct him except that she'd always been a stickler for facts. It certainly had nothing to do with the fact that she didn't want him to think she was actually attached. As if he'd even be interested.

But that was the thing. Despite her hoodie and baggy jeans and regulation cotton underpants, he did look interested. His gaze gleamed with a dozen wicked thoughts and she couldn't help herself.

"We're not together anymore."

"I sort of figured that's what *ex* meant."

"He's a little over six feet," she rushed on, eager to ignore the heat creeping into her cheeks. Blushing? She didn't blush. She didn't stammer. She didn't act like a freakin' idiot. "Short, dark hair. Very fit. Scar on his left bicep."

"If I see anyone that fits the description, I'll send them your way. By the way, what's your name?"

"Abby. Abby Trent. Yours?"

"Brent Braddock."

"Nice to meet you, Brent."

"My pleasure."

The last word conjured all sorts of images as Abby climbed into her car and headed back to the Skull Creek Inn, and straight into a cold shower.

Because the last thing Abby intended was to get side-tracked by a man. She had a job to do and she fully intended to stay on course.

No matter how much she suddenly wanted to take the nearest Exit to Sexville.

5

"I'D ALMOST GIVEN UP on you," Cody said when Brent finally walked into *Mary Sue's Wedding Nirvana*. *Mary Sue's* was the one and only bridal shop and tuxedo rental in Skull Creek and the last place Brent wanted to be at the moment.

His pulse pounded and his muscles clenched. He was wired. Desperate. Hungry.

"You were supposed to be here a half hour ago." Cody stood to the left near a small sitting area. He worked at the buttons on his white tuxedo shirt. "All the other guys have gone and left."

"Sorry to miss the party but I had something I had to deal with." Brent sank down into one of the leather chairs and tried to ignore his brother's curious gaze.

Cody arched an eyebrow. "Something or some-one?"

"Does it matter?"

"No, it's just that you might want to watch yourself around here. It's a small town. A safe town. The last thing we need are rumors flying." He finished the buttons and shrugged on the black jacket. He turned towards Brent. "What do you think?"

"I'm glad you're the one getting married and not me."

"It's not so bad." He flexed and the fabric pulled and tugged. "Granted it's not nearly as comfortable as a T-shirt and jeans, but I've suffered through worse. Speaking of which, the offer still stands. We'd really love to have you in the wedding."

"I'm not really a wedding kind of guy. Love and marriage and forever and ever…" He gave a shudder. "Not my thing."

"You don't have to marry anyone. You'll just be standing up with me."

"Maybe next time."

"There won't be a next time." Cody looked so certain that Brent almost believed him.

He might have if not for the all important fact that his brother was a friggin' *vampire*. Translation? Temporary. Things might be picture perfect now, but it wouldn't last. While Miranda herself seemed cool with it, there were others who wouldn't be so accepting. Someone would eventually find out that there were bloodsuckers living in Skull Creek and then all hell would break loose. It always did.

Brent had learned that firsthand and it was a lesson he didn't intend to forget. He'd barely gotten out of Jamison, Texas, without being staked, and all because he'd been stupid enough to fall in love. Or at least he'd thought it was love. It had been early on, right after he'd been turned. He'd been desperate for his life back. For a sense of normalcy. And then he'd met Lila. She'd been pretty and sweet and just like *that* he'd been able to see the two of them settling down and living happily ever after.

A stupid fantasy. That's all it had been. He'd needed to feel like a man again, just a man, and she'd wanted someone to take care of her. The minute she'd seen the truth, she'd turned on him and run back to her family. Her father had told the entire town. They'd come for him then. Captured him. Tortured him.

They'd known he was a bloodsucker with the strength of ten men. But there'd been five times that many. They'd overpowered him, chained him up, beat him. They'd been ready to stake him, too, but he'd managed to work his hand free just in time. He'd made it out, but barely. He wasn't risking his afterlife or his heart ever again.

Love—if there even was such a thing—sucked, no pun intended, and nothing good could come of it.

Not for Brent.

And certainly not for Cody.

His brother might be playing at normal now, but he wasn't. He never would be and eventually the shit would hit the fan and he would have to leave.

"I've got Dillon compiling a list of all the Rose Braddocks in the United States," Brent told him, determined to pull him onto a safer subject. One he could actually do something about. "Once he's done, I'll start checking them out."

"Before the wedding?"

Cody looked so nervous for a split second that Brent couldn't help himself. "I'll be there next Saturday for the ceremony, I just can't promise anything else."

"You can't or you won't?"

"What difference does it make?" He shrugged. "So what's with the blue? I thought most tuxedos were black?"

"Miranda likes blue. She says it brings out the blue in my eyes."

Brent grinned. "You're worse off than I thought, little bro."

"Yeah," Cody admitted, but there was none of the surprise or worry Brent would have expected at such an admission. His brother actually looked happy. "The house is almost done." When Brent turned a questioning look on Cody, he added, "The one I've been building for the past six months? The one I've told you about a dozen times? My wedding gift to Miranda?" Brent shrugged and Cody added, "They just put the floors in yesterday. There are still a few minor things left to do like the phone jacks and the cable hookup, but for the most part it's finished. I spent the day out there yesterday to make sure everything got done."

"With workers in and out?"

"There's a basement that locks from the inside. The workers only have access to the front door." His gaze met Brent's. "If you need a place to crash, I keep a key stashed near the front porch that unlocks the basement. You could camp out until the wedding."

"The motel's just fine."

"I'd really like you to take a look and tell me what you think about the place."

"Does it matter what I think?"

"No," his brother said in all honesty, "but I'd still like you to see it. It's out off old Farm Road 86, about six miles past the turn-off. We could head over after this and I could show you around."

Brent shook his head. "I'm meeting Dillon. So do you have a guest list?" he asked, suddenly eager to ease the flash of disappointment in his brother's gaze. Cody's expression quickly shifted into surprise, and Brent added, "Just because I'm not your best man doesn't mean I can't throw you a bachelor party."

"You don't have to—"

"Just hand it over. A week from tonight. Mark your calendar." He took the paper Cody pulled from his pocket and shoved it into his jeans. Pushing to his feet, he said, "I gotta go."

"I was thinking you might want to stop off after you swing by Dillon's and hang out with me and Miranda. I know she would love it. She wants to get to know you."

"Dillon has a lot leads. It might take a while."

Cody looked ready to argue, but then he shrugged. "Keep me posted."

Brent nodded and walked out of the bridal shop.

Ten minutes later, he pulled into the parking lot of a renovated service station with a neon blue sign that read *Skull Creek Choppers* gleaming in the front glass window. It was the last place he would expect to find a nest of vampires, but then that was the point. The place was ultra small town with its antique gas pumps and old-fashioned *Goo Goo Clusters* sign. Unassuming. Inconspicuous.

Safe.

For now, Brent reminded himself. It wouldn't last. It never lasted.

He rang the buzzer on the high tech security pad sitting next to the door. A split-second later, a lock released and the door opened. He walked into the small room that housed the office portion of the motorcycle manufacture. A tall, muscular man sat in front of a state-of-the-art computer system. He didn't glance up. He didn't have to.

Dillon Cash was a computer guru and the third member of the infamous trio that made up Skull Creek Choppers. He worked with Jake McCall and Garrett Sawyer, both vampires and geniuses when it came to chopper design and construction. Brent had never ridden one of their bikes because he was more of a muscle car kind of guy, but he'd admired their designs more than once.

"So what's up?" he asked Dillon. "Did you find anything specific?"

"Not yet, but I've posted several comments on the different vampire blogs out there detailing Rose and her physical description. It's a long shot, but it worked once before when we were looking for Garrett's maker." He handed over a list of different blog sites. "I'll be keeping an eye on the comments, but you might want to check things out to. That way if anyone posts anything that sounds familiar to you, you can let me know. In the meantime, I did a search for every Rose Braddock in the continental United States."

"And?"

"There are over three hundred of them. I ruled some out based on background, birth certificates, etc., which leaves one hundred and thirty-six possibilities. That is, if she's even using her same name." Dillon handed over a print-out. "I'm doing more detailed searches to narrow it down, but it's going to take time. Speaking of which," he glanced at his watch, "I've got to run. I printed out the various blogs I commented on if you want to monitor them yourself. You might recognize something familiar. Meanwhile, we bide our time and keep looking."

"What's the hurry?"

"It's date night. If I'm late, she'll kill me." He grinned. "Again."

"Damn straight I will." The comment came from the attractive blonde who appeared in the doorway. Brent caught her gaze, but he couldn't read anything behind the twinkle in her eyes.

She came up to Dillon and slid an arm around him. "We need to hurry. The movie starts in five minutes." Her gaze met Brent's. "How's the search going?"

"It's going."

"Keep the faith. If she's out there, Dillon will find her." She smiled up at Dillon. "He found Garrett's maker."

"That's what I've been told. Thanks, man."

"Don't mention it," Dillon said.

"Do you have a girlfriend?" the female vampire asked point-blank.

"Excuse me?"

"Do you have a girlfriend?"

"I don't do girlfriends."

"Ahh," a knowing gleam lit her eyes, "a boyfriend then."

"I don't have a boyfriend either."

She shrugged. "Give it some time. You'll meet Mr. Right soon."

"I'm not gay."

"A player?"

"Something like that."

"Is it?" She leveled an intense stare at him. "Something like that? Because if not and you're a halfway decent guy who's just a little shy, I've got a really great girl I'd like you to meet."

"Meg," Dillon warned, "you promised you wouldn't play Cupid."

"I'm not playing Cupid. It's just that I hired this new girl at the dress shop and she doesn't know very many people in town. I'm guessing Brent here doesn't either and nobody should be alone on a Friday night." Her gaze shifted to Brent. "My friend's name is Daphne. She's really anxious to meet a good guy."

His gut tightened and a frown pulled at his mouth. "I'm not a guy."

"I know what you are."

"Then you'll understand when I say thanks, but no thanks." He nodded at Dillon and then he turned and walked out because the last thing Brent Braddock needed was a fix-up.

He could get his own friggin' date. If he wanted one, which he most certainly did not. He didn't need company, he needed to feed again. Maybe then he could stop thinking about Abby and how badly he'd wanted to press her up against his car and feel her curves up close and personal.

His groin twisted, pressing against his jeans as he walked out of the shop. Hell, he still wanted to, a feeling that intensified when he pulled up at the Skull Creek Inn and saw her car sitting in the parking lot.

His stomach hollowed out and he sat there for a few minutes, staring, wanting.

What the hell was she doing here?

But he already knew. They were smack dab in the middle of small town central. Skull Creek wasn't exactly a tourist mecca which meant the Skull Creek Inn was it when it came to motels. Damn straight she'd be here.

But understanding it didn't make it any easier to swallow. He needed to stop thinking about her and with this new turn of events, he wasn't placing any bets on that possibility. He stiffened as he caught sight of her through the lobby window. His muscles clenched and electricity sizzled up his spine. Anticipation coiled inside him and his gut contracted.

His fangs tingled as he watched her follow Winona down the concrete walkway toward his room. They stopped just one door shy and Winona shoved the key into the lock.

No way. No friggin' way.

Even as the thought struck, Winona pushed open the door and led Abby inside. A switch clicked and yellow light spilled through the slats of the shade that covered the room's one and only window. He caught a glimpse of Abby, her eyes sparkling and her lips slightly parted, before the shade closed. The air conditioning unit groaned and started chugging away, keeping time with the frantic race of adrenalin through his veins.

She'd checked into the room right next to his. Forget pushing her out of his head and avoiding her for the next few weeks. He was sure to run into her again. That and there was no escaping the fact that he was a vampire. Meaning, despite sheetrock and tacky wallpaper, he would be able to hear her. Smell her. Feel her. Want her.

Like hell.

He keyed the ignition, shoved the car into reverse and peeled out of the parking lot. And then he headed for his brother's place.

6

THE FAMILIAR ROAR of an engine echoed in Abby's ears and awareness rippled through her. She glanced at the motel room door and fought down the sudden urge to haul it open and see who was outside.

But she already knew.

The notion struck and she quickly pushed it aside. Just because the engine was loud, didn't mean it belonged to a '67 Camaro. That was her own wishful thinking caused by deprived hormones and a desperate lack of sleep.

She gave herself a mental shake and forced her attention back to the old woman standing in front of her.

"...looks like you got lucky tonight." Winona Adkins wore a blue and orange flower print dress, a pair of sagging knee-high panty-hose and white orthopedic shoes. "This is the only room we have open on account of the rodeo is in town, so we upgraded you. This here's the executive suite."

Abby glanced around the ancient room, from the king-sized bed covered with a faded patchwork quilt, to the scarred hardwood floor and the worn nightstand. It was old, but clean. "*Executive* as in minibar?" She'd left her chili dog behind to race after Brent and her stomach was none too happy.

"A full bathroom. All our rooms have a toilet and sink only, but you got the whole enchilada."

Abby thought of a hot shower and how long it had been since she'd felt such a luxury. "Even better."

"The only thing wrong with it is the air conditioner." She motioned to the window unit that made a slow, churning noise. "It's low on Freon, but Jimmy Joe Mercer can't get out here to fix it 'til next week on account of he's fishing at the coast. In the meantime, you'll have to make do with the ceiling fan until another room opens up."

"It'll be fine." She'd done a seven month tou in Iraq. A little Texas heat certainly didn't scare her.

"Maid service is around noon," Winona went on, "but not after two on account of I never miss Dr. Phil." She set the keycard on the nightstand and motioned to a red plastic bucket. "Ice machine's in the lobby and there's a snack machine right next to it.

We also put in a washer and dryer just down the hall if you want to do any personal laundry. But don't go overstuffing the drum 'cause Merle—he's the only washer repairman in town—is with Jimmy Joe." She nailed Abby with a stare. "And don't go stuffing no unmentionables down the toilet either 'cause they talked Lewis Thalman—he's the local plumber—into going with 'em."

"I promise to be very careful."

"We also offer free muffins every morning." Winona rounded the bed. Wrinkled hands reached for the comforter and folded down the edges. "But you have to get to the lobby before eight if you want the blueberry ones 'cause that's my Eldin's favorite. He's my grandson." She smoothed the blankets and shot a glance at Abby's ringless finger. "He's single, you know. Makes a decent living managing this place for my daughter who moved to Port Aransas with her husband last year. He's got nice eyes, all his own teeth, and his plumbing works like clockwork."

"All the qualities any woman could want in a man."

"Exactly." Winona gave her a sly grin. "I could introduce the two of you when he gets back from Bingo."

"Thanks for the offer, but I'm afraid I already have a boyfriend," she blurted, remembering the lie she'd told Brent Braddock. "I mean, we broke up, but I'm hoping things might still work out."

Instead of giving her a skeptical look, Winona smiled. "Well, what do you know?" She pulled a business card from her pocket and handed it to Abby. "This just might be your lucky day."

Abby stared at the card and a bolt of shock ripped through her. A purple penis, complete with a top hat and eyes, danced across the white vellum. Beneath the image, Winona's name blazed in neon purple letters, followed by the title *Pleasure Consultant*.

O-kay.

"I got an official degree and everything on-line at PleasureConsultants.com," Winona rushed on. "I help women by teaching 'em how to keep the sparks flyin' in their relationships. Host a class right here in the motel lobby every Tuesday night. First one is free, but then you got to pay per lesson like everybody else. This week we're doing *BJ Techniques That Don't End in a Trip to the ER*. It's all about watching the teeth, you know. That, or you can just take 'em out first."

"I really hate to miss that," *not*, "but I'm only in town for a few days."

"That's what they all say." Winona waved a hand. "Don't you worry. I've seen more than one guest add a few days to their trip once they see me in action on

the motel's informational channel." At Abby's surprised look, she added, "It's a small town, sugar, not
Mars. We got cable, too. 'Course, the reception ain't
all that great on account of we're still using rabbit
ears on our sets." She motioned toward the 22-inch
TV that sat in the corner. "You have to stand near the
window and hold a coat hanger if you want to get rid
of the snow. But that's just for HBO. The informational channel comes directly from Eldin's computer
in the lobby, so the picture is crystal clear."

"You have your own podcast?"

"It's pre-recorded. We ain't figured out how to
do a live one just yet. But my Eldin signed up for
one of those on-line video editing courses last year.
Took bits and pieces of all my classes for the past
six months and put them together on one DVD that
runs every hour along with check-out instructions,
lobby hours and a listing of local attractions. There's
a bake sale over at the Lion's Club tomorrow. Got the
best German Chocolate cake around. I'm thinking
I'll pick up a few for Tuesday night's class."

Sex *and* cake. It didn't get much better than that.

Winona waddled over to a nearby closet and pulled
a few extra blankets from the top shelf. She set them
on a small chair before flashing Abby a narrowed
gaze. "But just 'cause I believe couples should have
plenty of sex, doesn't mean I ain't a decent, God-

fearing woman. This here's a respectable establishment." She wagged an arthritic finger. "We don't allow no parties or loud music or carrying on. And we surely don't allow no swearing or cussing." She turned toward the door. "Unless you're telling off old Zeke Mitchell from the gas station next door," she paused, hand on the knob. "Why, he sneaks over here every morning to snag our newspaper while my Eldin is picking up muffins at the bakery. Talk about a cheap SOB." The click of the latch punctuated the statement. Hinges creaked. Shoes squeaked. And Winona was gone.

Abby blinked and stared at the piece of vellum in her hand. Thanks to the military, she'd been all over the world. She'd seen it all—power hungry czars, crazed dictators, brutal extremists.

But she could honestly say she'd never, ever seen a seventy-something-year-old pleasure consultant with a dancing penis business card.

Tonight was definitely a first.

In more ways than one.

The thought struck and Brent's image walked into her head. Her stomach hollowed out and she remembered the intense desire she'd felt when she'd stared into his eyes. The overwhelming urge to forget everything—her duty, her plan, her objective—and act on it.

She'd wanted to.

She still did.

Electricity hummed over her skin and her nerves buzzed. She felt antsy. Wired. This close to the edge. As if something was about to happen and she was counting down the seconds.

She shook aside the strange sensation and headed for the bathroom. A shower and a good night's sleep would fix everything. Her muscles would relax. The exhaustion would take over. And then Brent Braddock would be history.

That's what she told herself, but the minute the warm water hit her skin, her senses fired fully to life. The hot rivulets streamed over her flesh and she started to tingle in all the right places. Or rather, the wrong places given her current situation and the fact that she couldn't afford to lose her focus. Her thighs clenched. Her nipples tightened.

Don't think. Just go through the motions and get the job done.

She reached for the soap. The ripe strawberry scent spiraled through her nostrils and the pink lather tickled the insides of her fingers. She slid the soap back into the tray and ran her soapy hands up and down her arms. Over her shoulders. Between her breasts. Down the planes of her stomach and lower. Until she reached the fleshy mound between her legs.

Her hands trembled and she twisted the tap. Cold water blasted over her, killing the sensations. There. That was better. Bearable.

She stood under the icy spray for several minutes, until her heartbeat slowed and her determination returned full force. She could do this. She could push him out of her mind and concentrate on her mission. She could.

Turning off the water, she reached for a towel and padded into the bedroom. She pulled on a tank top and panties, killed the lights and climbed between the sheets. She closed her eyes and tuned in to the slow groan of the air conditioner. It whined and sputtered, spitting out lukewarm air that soon had her kicking off the covers.

Laying there, she stared at the ceiling fan and tried to ignore the tickle of perspiration that slid down her temples, the undersides of her breasts. A fine sheen soon covered her skin and her breaths grew frequent and more shallow until she just couldn't seem to get enough air.

Crazy.

She'd been stranded in the middle of a desert in the high heat of day before and never felt this feverish. But tonight was different. An edge hung in the air. Expectancy twisted her stomach tight. The stifling atmosphere closed in, pressing down and suffocating her.

She pushed to her feet, hauled on a pair of shorts and grabbed the ice bucket. She'd done hot before, but this was ridiculous.

Then again, the temperature had nothing to do with the failing air conditioner and everything to do with the Camaro parked in front of the motel.

She came up short in the open doorway and stared at the familiar black muscle car sitting next to her rental. She hadn't heard him pull in because she'd probably been fighting her hormones in the shower, but it didn't change the fact that he was here. And that on a deeper level, she'd been completely aware of his presence.

That's why she'd been so restless.

So needy.

So hot.

She drew in as much oxygen as she could gather, steeled herself and hooked a left down the walkway toward the front office. A few minutes later, she arrived back in her room with a bucket full of ice. She fought the split-second urge to knock on his door before rushing inside her own and slamming and locking it behind her. Grabbing a plastic cup, she made herself a glass of ice water and chugged every last drop. She twisted the temperature knob on the air unit down as far as it would go, opened up the few windows that ran on the back wall and stretched out on top of the sheets. Closing her eyes, she concentrated on the coolness that lingered in her mouth and pictured herself on a snowy mountaintop in Afghanistan. Freezing and miserable and sweaty.

Wait a second.

There'd been no sweating on that mountaintop. No buzzing nerves. No tingling nipples. She'd been this close to freezing to death and her only thought had been survival.

Not him and the way his lips tugged slightly more at the right corner of his mouth when he smiled or the way his eyes glittered so brightly whenever they snagged on her mouth.

Survival, she reminded herself. Think chattering teeth and numb fingers and tingling toes—

Bam!

The slam of a door shattered her thoughts. Her breath caught and every nerve jumped to awareness. Her ears tuned to the steady thud of footsteps. The creak of a mattress. A radio flicked on and Tim McGraw started singing about bad boys and good men and, well, the *last* thing she needed to think about was either one.

Brent Braddock was back and he was right next door.

7

JUST BREATHE. She forced her eyes shut and did a deep breathing exercise to soothe her jumpiness. She'd learned the technique to deal with the extreme pressure of being in the field and it had always worked every time.

Until now.

With the song playing and the occasional *thud* and *creak* from next door, she couldn't seem to slow her lungs enough to relax. Not when she kept picturing him stretched out naked on the bed. His tanned body dark and sensual against the paleness of the sheets. His muscles tight and bulging with sexual tension. His eyes blazing with—

She sat up and killed the image. With trembling hands, she reached for the remote and hit the ON button. Winona's voice crackled over the speaker, drowning out the sounds drifting from next door. She cranked up the volume as loud as it could go.

"...when a marriage gets a little stale, it's time for fantasy role play to spice things up. There ain't a woman alive who doesn't go all weak in the knees when she thinks about being captured by a pirate or forced into submission by a high falutin' sheik. It's the same for a man. While he would never nail a real milkmaid, especially since the only one around here has a mustache and goes by the name of Hank, he still entertains the fantasy every now and then. Not about Hank, but about his woman. He'd like to see her in a short skirt and little suspenders. That, or he'd like to see her as a sexy nurse or a gypsy or one of them there hot-to-trot flight attendants. So let's get busy, ladies. Dress up, turn him on and help him land that plane right smack dab down the center of that runway..."

Abby had a quick visual of herself clad in a flight attendant's outfit sitting astride a very sexy Captain Brent and her thighs clenched. The temperature seemed to kick up a few blazing degrees and she reached for the glass of ice sitting on the nightstand.

She grabbed an ice cube and touched it to her lips. Icy liquid drizzled down the corner of her mouth, winding a path down her neck. She slid the cube down over her chin, to the pounding pulse beat. The hard chunk felt cool and soothing. *Cool*, as in the opposite of hot. If she could just focus on the sensation, she might be able to forget the fire burning her up from the inside out.

Moving the ice even lower, she slid it over her collarbone, down between her breasts. The frigid touch grazed the tip of one nipple and she stiffened. Electricity zipped up her spine and a gasp caught on her lips. Her skin grew tighter. Itchier. Hotter.

This was definitely not helping.

No, there was only one thing that would help ease her frustrated hormones—sating said hormones. Not that she was about to knock on Brent's door and ask for a quickie. Hardly. While her body might crave him, the reality was that she could handle this all by herself. She'd done it before and it made the morning after a lot less complicated.

One orgasm coming right up!

She grabbed another piece of ice and touched it to the quivering bud of her clit. Hunger spurted through her and her nerves hummed. The air seemed to shimmer and her heart started to pound. She slid the hard coolness along the length of her hot slit. The ice melted against her blazing flesh, drip-dropping between her fingers and gliding down her palm as she moved back and forth. The coldness quickly disappeared, until only her fingertips rasped the swollen flesh.

She didn't meant to fantasize about him, but she couldn't help herself. Through a haze of pleasure she saw him standing there wearing nothing but a pair of jeans and a hungry expression.

Watching.

Waiting.

The notion sent a rush of excitement through her and she slid a finger inside her drenched heat. Her body clenched and she moved her hips, riding the sensation, drawing it deeper until her breath quickened and a cry worked its way up her throat. The room seemed to explode in a burst of color as she arched, holding on to the feeling for a long, brilliant moment.

"Beautiful."

The deep, familiar voice slid into her ears and jerked her back to reality. Her eyes snapped open, and that's when she realized that it wasn't just her erotic imagination at work.

Brent Braddock stood, live and in color, at the foot of her bed.

She blinked, but he didn't disappear. Shock ripped through her and she bolted to a sitting position. Scrambling for the sheet, she stuffed it under each arm. "What are you doing here?" she blurted, her heart pounding out of her chest.

"Enjoying the view." The deep, seductive voice whispered through her head so clear and distinct that she could have sworn he spoke the words.

He didn't. The only movement of his mouth was the faintest crook of a grin. Slow. Subtle. Sexy.

Her heart skipped its next beat.

"I heard a scream," he finally murmured. "I thought you might need help."

"I stubbed my toe." It wasn't the most original lie, but it was the best she could do with him standing so close and staring so intently. "It hurt, so I yelped."

His brows drew together. "It didn't sound like a yelp. It sounded like a full-fledged—"

"How did you get in here?" she cut in, eager to distract herself from the heat creeping up her spine. "I locked the door."

"You must have made a mistake." He shrugged. "It opened right up."

Her mind did a quick rewind. She felt the metal against her fingers. Heard the click of the deadbolt. "I don't make those kinds of mistakes."

"There's a first for everything." He cocked an eyebrow. "How else would I be here?"

He had a point. He couldn't very well have slipped through the keyhole. He was six foot plus of solid, hunky muscle. Half-naked and devastatingly handsome.

Half-naked and devastatingly sexy.

He wore only a pair of faded jeans. Muscle sculpted his chest and arms. Slave band tattoos, the pattern dark and intricate, circled each bicep. Hair sprinkled his chest from nipple to nipple before funneling into a silky swirl that followed a decadent path that bisected a very impressive six pack before disappearing beneath the waistband of his jeans. A frayed rip in the denim gave her a sneak peak of one muscular thigh dusted with hair.

She had the sudden image of that thigh flush against hers, his body pressing her down into the mattress, his lips eating at hers, and her mouth went dry.

"Let me take a look at your toe." His deep voice pushed into her head and snatched her back to reality and the all important fact that she was naked beneath the sheet and he was still standing there. His pale green eyes darkened to an impenetrable jade and her stomach hollowed out. "To see how badly you're hurt."

She pulled her knees up to her chest beneath the sheet and tucked the cotton more securely under each arm. "It's fine. Really. No permanent damage." She summoned a smile and tried to ignore the urge to jump up and pull him down onto the bed with her. "Thanks for checking on me."

"Anytime."

The word held a wealth of meaning and lingered in her head long after the door closed behind him.

As if he really and truly wanted her as badly as she wanted him.

He didn't.

She knew that.

She'd always known that when it came to men.

She was a plain cookie in a bakery full of chunky decadence. And no man in his right mind would sink his teeth into the ho-hum sugar variety when he could have quarter-size pieces of melt-in-your-mouth chocolate or M & Ms or peanut butter. It just didn't happen that way. Men didn't lust after her. Or flirt. Or send suggestive signals.

Especially men like Brent Braddock. He was way out of her league with his smoking body and his raw sensuality. No way was she reading his signals correctly.

At the same time, that's what she did. She read people for a living and assessed every situation. It was her job and she was good at it. Even more, she didn't make careless mistakes.

He wanted her. He really and truly *wanted* her.

And she wanted him.

A truth that had her powering on the TV again, desperate for a distraction.

"It's all about dressing for success, Ladies." Winona stared back at her from the television screen.

It was the last thing she needed to watch, but she found herself tuning in anyway for lack of anything better.

At least that's what she told herself.

"If you want your man to notice you, you have to go the extra mile," Winona went on. "And if you want him to *really* notice you, you need to do it with the minimum amount of clothing because men like to see skin. Lots and lots of skin. And a slutty pair of high heels don't hurt none either. We've got several shops right here in Skull Creek where you can buy a decent pair of tramp shoes…"

Winona droned on about the need for high heels and how they made the legs look longer and the boobs look bigger. It was nothing Abby hadn't heard before in the girls' locker room back in high school. Of course, she'd never had such an interesting visual to go with the gossip (namely Winona parading around in a pair of silver sandals with blinking red lights on the toes). Yes, she'd heard it over and over, but she'd never tried it.

Not then and certainly not now. She was fine with

her life. Fulfilled. She didn't need sexy clothes. Or sexy men. Or another orgasm.

She needed to find Rayne. End of story.

That's why she'd come here in the first place. To find her man.

Her man. Not just any man. And certainly not one as hot and sexy as Brent Braddock. She didn't need that kind of distraction right now.

Even if she suddenly wanted one.

Letting loose a deep sigh, she kicked off the covers, forced her eyes shut and settled in for the longest, most restless night of her life.

8

IT WAS THE EARLY hours of the morning and Brent was doing his damnedest to shut out the sounds coming from the next room and forget the woman stretched out on the bed. He wasn't thinking about her. He was sleeping. Right here. Right now.

He clamped his eyes shut and punched at his pillow. *Sleep.* The silent command echoed in his head, quickly drowned out by a soft sigh and the rustle of sheets.

He turned onto his opposite side, punched at the pillow and tried again.

Ka-thunk, ka-thunk, ka-thunk…

The steady beat slid into his ears, a soft, subtle sound that kept time with his own heartbeat.

Shit.

He turned onto his back and stared at the ceiling.

Instead of seeing the white plaster, he saw Abby. Her long, loose hair draped over the pillow. Her knees parted. Her skin covered with a fine sheen of sweat. Her lips parted on a gasp. Her hands working at the ice.

His groin clenched and he damned himself a thousand times for going over there in the first place.

He'd tried to resist. He'd turned on the radio to drown out the noise, taken a cold shower, given himself a great big mental kick in the ass and climbed into bed determined to sleep.

But then he'd heard her sharp intake of breath and the bubble of a gasp as she'd touched the ice to her skin, and he'd stopped thinking altogether. The rule about not being able to enter a dwelling unless invited didn't apply to motels or other public establishments where people came and went and so, in a flash, he'd been at the foot of her bed. Watching. Wanting.

Holy shit.

He knew better. He'd always known better and so he kept his distance whenever he settled in any one place. No getting to know anyone. No making friends.

It wasn't a reality he liked, but it was the way things were and he was used to it.

Hell, he *liked* it.

He'd learned the hard way with Lila. They'd had plans that had all gone to hell in a handbasket because of what he'd become. She'd turned on him and he'd had to run for his life.

He'd learned at that moment that the less he knew, the less he cared, the easier it was to leave.

And leaving was inevitable.

As soon as the thought struck, he thought of Cody and Miranda and the new house his brother had just built.

A friggin' idiot. That's what Cody was, chasing some ridiculous happily ever after. Brent knew firsthand that it wouldn't work. He'd almost been killed that night Lila had turned on him. While the scars had faded, the memory of each lash was as vivid as if it had happened yesterday. Sure vampires healed rapidly, but they still felt pain. More intensely than most because their senses were so heightened.

Settling down was a bad idea. Getting attached to one woman was even worse. And building a friggin' house? Talk about jumping off the deep end.

He told himself that as he listened to the soft sounds of Abby's breathing. Winona's voice played in the background, but it was Abby he heard. The slide of skin across the sheets. The soft in and out of each breath. The occasional gasp when Winona said something particularly shocking.

The noises vibrated in the air, brushed across his skin and stirred his already aroused body until his fangs tingled and his dick throbbed and he reached his limit. Pushing to his feet, he pulled on a T-shirt, hauled on his boots and grabbed his keys.

He meant to drive around and clear his head. That was it. Just some blessed distance to regain his perspective. But then he saw the turn off for Farm Road 86 and he couldn't help himself. He hung a left and drove a few miles until he saw an old cattle guard on his right. He bounced over the metal and headed down the dirt road. Pasture stretched endlessly to his left and his right and he punched the gas harder. Gravel and dirt flew in his rearview mirror and the wind rushed through the open windows.

By the time he spotted the two-story ranch house, he'd worked off enough tension that he could actually think. Pulling up in front, he killed the engine and climbed out.

A construction dumpster sat off to the right and a pile of dirt to the left. The driveway had yet to be poured, but otherwise the house was just about finished. The outside was a combination of white hill country rock and tan stucco. A massive porch stretched the full length of the first floor. It was the kind of house made for lots of kids and big Christmases and Sunday barbecues.

Not that Cody could have any of that. His little brother was pretending. Setting himself up for heartache.

Brent walked the perimeter of the massive house before he wound up back in front. True to Cody's word, he'd left a key stashed under a rock to the right of the porch. Sliding the metal into the lock, Brent turned the doorknob and walked into the large entryway. He went from room to room, his boots echoing on the hardwood floor and bouncing off the walls.

With every modern convenience, vaulted ceilings and granite countertops, it was nothing like the old ranch house where they'd grown up so long ago.

At the same time, it felt exactly the same. Warmth radiated from the vanilla colored walls and embraced him, and as he walked from room to room, he didn't feel so cold.

Cody had been right.

It was nice.

It was home.

The minute the thought struck, he kicked it right back out. He'd lost his home a long time ago. His family. Even though his brothers were still around, things were different. They were different. The relationship, the closeness, the family bond they'd had,

had all been shattered. They were all on their own now. Alone.

Just the way he liked it.

He flipped off the lights and darkness smothered the strange sense of melancholy that had slipped through him. His vision sharpened and focused and he walked down the main hallway, through the kitchen until he found the door leading to the basement.

A few seconds later, he collapsed on the cot that had been set up underground for the times when Cody must have pulled an all-nighter to finish the house in time. The quiet settled around him as he closed his eyes and he welcomed a wave of relief.

Better. Much better.

He didn't have to hear her every sigh or smell the sweet scent of her shampoo or imagine what she looked like stretched out on the bed, or how easy it would be to barge into her room and take what he so desperately wanted.

He'd come close. Dangerously close.

Never again.

From this moment on, he was thinking with his head, not his cock, and keeping his distance the way he always did.

He could get by on blood alone. He didn't *need* to have sex with Abby. The damned trouble of it all was that it was the one thing he *wanted*. The only thing.

And he knew deep down that his lust would eventually win out. And all hell would break loose when it did.

THE LAST THING Abby needed was a pair of high heels.

She told herself that the next morning as she stood outside of *The Sweet Stuff*. It was one of the clothing stores Winona had mentioned in her infomercial about dressing for sexcess. Not that Abby needed sexcess.

The only thing she really needed was to buy a decent outfit that made her look like the jilted girlfriend rather than—to quote Dolly—a Unibomber. With combat boots and dog tags, no one would buy that she could even attract a man, much less that she'd had a bonafide relationship with one. Particularly Rayne Montana. He'd been definite man candy.

To other women, of course. She'd always been so focused on work that she hadn't spared him much attention. There'd been no chemistry. No instant *wow* like she felt with Brent.

Her memory stirred and she saw him standing at the foot of the bed. Definite wow.

Not that it mattered. She was on a mission and priority number one was finding Rayne.

He was hot which meant he would have settled down with an equally hot woman. Hence the outfit change.

Still, she wasn't buying a pair of high heels or strappy sandals or stiletto boots with studs. A pair of flip flops or ballet flats would work just fine.

There was no reason to go overboard even if she did sort of like the silver lace up high heel sandals in the front window. If she'd been in the market for slut shoes, they would have made the top of her list. But slutty and feminine were two different things. One attracted a man and the other screamed *trust me, I'm a poor jilted female*.

Since she was, in fact, playing the jilted female, she wasn't trying to attract anyone. She didn't have time to play dress up for some man, even if she'd liked the way a certain man had looked at her last night when he'd stood at the foot of her bed.

As if he'd wanted to lay her down and love her within an inch of her life.

The heat of the moment.

That's what she'd decided.

Any man would have been turned on by a nearly naked female masturbating with ice. It wasn't because Brent actually liked her.

It didn't matter. That's what she'd realized last night. It had felt good to feel desired. To feel beautiful. She'd felt both for those few moments when he'd looked at her. She'd felt like a woman and she'd liked it. A lot.

Not enough to think that Hockey Guy was a fluke. She knew she wasn't cut out to prance around in high heels and dresses in the real world. It wasn't who she really was. It never would be.

But for a little while?

Her gaze went to the silver sandals and the red dress on display just above it. Both definitely screamed *I have a vagina and I know how to use it.* She couldn't help but wonder how Brent would look at her if she wore something like that. The same way he'd looked at her last night? Would he be turned on enough to actually touch her this time? Kiss her?

She entertained the possibility all of five seconds before drop-kicking it back out. She had work to do. She had two weeks to find Rayne or her butt was going in the frying pan. Her future was at stake, and she'd always put her career over her own needs.

Her mind made up, she drew a deep breath and pushed open the door.

9

AN HOUR LATER, Abby walked out of the clothing shop wearing a brand new outfit with two extra bags on her arms. Plenty to tide her over for the next few days while she tracked down Rayne. A pair of silver ballet flats clung to her feet and a pink sundress the sales clerk had insisted complimented her complexion swirled around her knees.

While she'd never been much for pink, she had to admit that it did give her cheeks some color. And the cut wasn't so bad either. The bodice hugged her chest and actually made her look a cup size larger. The skirt itself flowed over her hips, disguising their fullness and making her look as if she had a waist. She had the fleeting thought that she'd been missing out all these years in her combat boots and baggy fatigues.

But then a strap crept down her shoulder, reminding her that her body just wasn't made for all this girl stuff. She hiked the cotton back up, tightened her grip on her bags and headed for the rental car that sat parked at a nearby curb.

It was a typical Saturday morning on Main Street and people walked to and fro. Two old men sat outside of the diner working on a crossword puzzle. A girl scout stood on the corner selling cookies. Tossing her bags into the trunk, she locked up the car and headed for the pharmacy that stood next to the clothing shop. It was time to get to work.

Pushing through the glass double doors, she scoped out the interior. An old-fashioned soda fountain sat off to the right. Red stools lined the counter that spanned the length of the wall. Straight ahead, a tall man with a shiny bald head and a white lab coat worked behind a clear plastic partition. A fifty-something brunette with a ten-gallon hairdo worked the small counter in front of him. She wore a similar white lab coat, a pair of rhinestone-studded cat's eye glasses and a pen tucked behind one ear.

Abby walked up as she keyed in a prescription for the customer in front of her.

"I'm tellin' you, Charmaine, we don't sell nothin' like that. This here's a pharmacy. We got your usual sundries, but you'll need to go on-line to one of them sex shops if you want a vibrator."

"I don't want a vibrator. I'm interested in a hand-held massager." The customer rubbed at her neck. "For stiff muscles. The doc says it'll help even more than the pain medicine. You sure you don't have one stashed in the back?"

The clerk shook her head. "We ain't had none since Maybelle Dupree gave herself a bad burn last year, if you know what I mean. Elmer," she pointed to the white lab coat-clad man who stood in the back measuring out a bottle of pills, "refused to stock any-more of 'em. Says he ain't setting himself up for a lawsuit because half the women in this town are un-dersexed and don't know how to read the operating instructions. It said plain as day right there on the label—For External Use Only. Why, she had to go to the emergency room and everything."

"I heard about that," Charmaine said. "Heard tell it took three doctors and a nurse to dislodge the thing."

"It was four," the clerk corrected, "and I heard there's still a piece missing."

"No wonder she looked so happy when I saw her dancing at the VFW hall last week."

"Ain't that the truth." The clerk nodded, hand-ing over the prescription and the woman's change. "I heard Doo or Dye is offering massages now. Got one of the hair stylists doin' it in between the perms and the colors. You ought to check that out." The clerk turned her attention to Abby. "Name?"

"Abby. Abby Trenton."

"Trenton with a T," the woman murmured as she turned toward the massive drawers that lined the wall. "I'm afraid it's not here. When did you drop it off, hon?"

"I didn't. I'm not here for a prescription." She pasted on her most hopeful expression. "I was hoping I could ask you a few questions."

"Elmer," the woman called over her shoulder. "Better get that space cleaned up back there. The Feds are here again."

"I'm not a government official."

One perfectly penciled eyebrow shot up. "Not even the IRS?"

"No."

"Jimmy Jo's Detective Agency? Landsakes, I told Elmer not to go off meeting that redhead from the diner for lunch. Pauline's on to you," she called over her shoulder to the man behind the glass partition. "I knew it was only a matter of time."

"We're just friends," Elmer called out as he filled a plastic container with tiny white pills. "She likes to play dominoes."

"I'm not a detective," Abby told the clerk. "I'm a receptionist. From out of town. I'm here looking for an ex-boyfriend of mine. His name is Rayne Montana."

The woman's gaze went wide with excitement. "You're Rayne's girlfriend?"

"Do you know him?"

"Everybody knows him, honey. He grew up around here. Lived his whole life just up the road."

"What about recently?"

"Sure enough. He's been living out at his grandma's place just over the railroad tracks. At least, he was. I ain't seen him around for the past few weeks. Not since he left on his honeymoon."

Abby had anticipated a lot of scenarios, but this hadn't been one of them. "He's married? Are you sure?"

"Didn't watch 'em tie the knot myself—they kept it small with friends and family only—but Milly Haskins heard about it from Darlene Chapin who heard from Ethel McIntosh who heard from her daughter, who's a waitress at the bar where Lucy— that's his wife—works. Said it was a nice little ceremony—rose petals down the aisle, huge flower sprays on every row, violin music and everything."

"*Married?*" She tried to digest the turn of events. He'd gone AWOL and endangered everyone in their unit to come home and get *married*? He'd never even had a girlfriend to Abby's knowledge. Sure, he'd mentioned an old high school flame once or twice, but there'd been no letters from home. No trips back for the holidays. He'd always spent any time on leave volunteering for extra assignments. Keeping busy. Filling the void because he'd had no family to return to. No home.

Abby knew the feeling because she'd done the same. With her father gone, she'd had no one to share the holidays with. Even before, they'd never celebrated much. No big turkey. No massive tree. No presents.

Her father had believed in discipline and structure and self-sacrifice. There'd been no rushing down the stairs on Christmas morning. No rummaging through the stockings. No giggling and laughing over turkey.

Not that she'd wanted those things. Okay, maybe she had once or twice, but the bottom line is that she'd been fine without them. She was fine now. And Rayne had been, as well. Or so she'd thought.

"You're sure we're talking about the same Rayne Montana?"

"Trust me. We ain't got an overabundance of 'em around here. He's spoken for, sugar. So if I was you, I'd head back home and forget all about him."

"I can't do that."

The clerk arched an eyebrow and her eyes danced with excitement. "You ain't knocked up are you?"

"Of course not."

The excitement disappeared. "Then go home, get even and forget all about him. That's what I did with Harley. He's my ex. Broke up with me on the one year anniversary of our first date. Instead of showing up at my house with an engagement ring, he showed up with Ellen Carlysle. Told me they were running away together to Del Rio and that he wanted his pearl handle hunting knife back on account of they were going hog hunting together. I slammed the door in his face, put the knife up on eBay and then gave specific measurements of his privates on my Facebook page. Length *and* diameter. Then I headed down to the VFW Hall and found myself a new man, and that's all she wrote." She wiggled her ring finger. "Been married for over six months now." She leveled a stare at Abby. "Forget about him, sugar."

"You don't happen to know where he went, do you?"

"Bermuda, I think. Or maybe it was Bali. Either way, there's no sense running after him. He'll be home by next Saturday. His wife starts summer classes at Travis County Community College the following Monday. She's studying to be an interior designer. Good looking little thing." When she realized what she'd said, she added, "Not as good looking as you, hon. You're much prettier." She swept a gaze over Abby. "I like the pink."

A rush of warmth swept through Abby. A crazy reaction considering she felt about as comfortable as a stuffed sausage. But she went a little warm inside nonetheless and for a split-second, she forgot all about Rayne and her desperation to find him. She thought about Brent and the fire in his eyes and she found herself wondering what he would think about the pink.

Not that it mattered. He wouldn't even see her in it for that matter, since she fully intended to stay as far away from him as possible while she was in Skull Creek. She didn't need the distraction. She needed to concentrate on Rayne.

He'd left the unit for a woman.

As simple as the truth was, it only made the situation that much more complicated. It just didn't add up. It would have been easy for him to leave the military with an honorable discharge rather than risk his reputation by running off. He could have left after his last tour to settle down and start a family rather than re-enlisting, which he'd done three times.

He didn't have to risk a court marshal.

But he'd done just that. He'd gone AWOL and

jeopardized his mission, not to mention his unit. Just like that.

Because of a woman?

The question dogged her as she headed down to the corner diner. It didn't make any sense. A dedicated soldier would never do such a thing and Rayne had been one of the most dedicated. There had to be more to it.

Not that it mattered.

She was here to find him, haul him back and clear her reputation. Not uncover his motives. The MPs could take care of the hows and whys.

She was here to bring him back, period.

Which was exactly what she fully intended to do once he came back. And he would come back. He had a wife now. A family. A home.

A pang of envy rushed through her before she managed to remind herself that she'd never been cut out for the home and hearth thing. She didn't cook. She didn't clean. She didn't stay in any one place for more than a few months. Her job didn't permit it, and her job was everything.

"You're military," her dad had always told her. *"It's in your blood. It's who you are. No sense denying fate."*

He'd been right. The one time she'd tried to change her life, to put on makeup and dress up and be a normal sixteen-year-old girl, Hockey Hunk had laughed in her face.

Abby ignored the strange sense of regret that rushed through her and pushed through the doorway of the diner. She spent the next hour eating chicken fried steak and verifying the clerk's story. Rayne Montana had, according to Doris the waitress and Monty the cook and Ellen and Irma from the Ladies Auxiliary, gotten married in a small, private ceremony two weeks ago to a woman named Lucy Rivers. They'd left on a vacation to the Bahamas/Bermuda/Bala/fill-in-your-favorite-vacation-spot-that-started-with-a-B. While no one knew exactly where they'd gone, everyone said the same thing—they would be back in time for Lucy to start classes the following week.

It was Saturday and Rayne was expected to return home a week from today, which meant the only thing for Abby to do was bide her time and wait.

While she was relieved that she'd found him, she couldn't shake the restlessness that settled in the pit of her stomach and followed her around for the rest of the day as she scoped out Rayne's old house and visited the bar where Lucy Rivers worked.

A crazy feeling because she'd done more than her share of surveillance over the years. She'd killed endless hours waiting for the right moment to strike.

She'd spent one hundred and sixty-three days down in Guatemala watching the entrance to a cantina, day in and day out, and she hadn't felt nearly the anxiety she felt when she finally made her way back to the motel.

She pulled up next to Brent's Camaro and awareness skittered up and down her spine.

Her knuckles brushed the smooth black finish as she angled between the cars and headed for her motel room. Her hands trembled as she slid her key into the lock and opened her door. Her ears tuned, listening for any sounds, but the only thing she heard was the hum of the air conditioner and the click of her own doorknob.

She tossed her keys aside, flipped on the TV and watched as Winona waltzed around a brass stripper pole and demonstrated proper hand technique when doing a spin. The sight was frightening (we're talking a seventy-something-year-old woman), yet oddly fascinating at the same time. Abby had never actually seen a stripper pole, nor did she know what to do with one. Five minutes with Winona and she felt as if she could grab hold and work it out. She envisioned Brent parked in a chair, watching intently as she strolled back and forth in front of him wearing a racy outfit and sky-high heels. She dropped pieces here and there, teasing him, tempting him.

It was the craziest fantasy because Abby didn't do either when it came to men. But she wanted to.

The realization hit her as she heard the shower turn on next door. The pipes grumbled and the water rushed and she knew that Brent was about to climb in.

Her hands trembled and her nipples pressed tightly against the bodice of the sundress. But she didn't just crave an orgasm. She craved the warmth that had rushed through her last night when she'd become aware that he was standing there, looking at her, wanting her.

The surge of feminine power.

The certainty deep inside that she was every bit the woman she tried so hard to hide.

Just a woman.

Soft and feminine and sexy and vulnerable.

That's how she felt when he looked at her. And while she couldn't afford to feel that way in her daily life—her survival in the field relied on the respect of her men and the power of her authority—she had to admit that it was kind of nice.

For now.

She felt like a beautiful, desirable woman when Brent looked at her and that's what she found herself wanting to feel again. Not just the sweet rush of warmth when she came, but the certainty that he wanted her and only her at that moment.

She had no illusions that he felt more. He didn't really know her. He thought she was the poor, jilted girlfriend, not some ball buster with the military. Should he learn the truth, she had no doubt that he would turn and walk away just like every other man in her past.

Men were intimidated by her. They always had been and they always would be.

But not Brent.

Not yet.

While she wasn't fool enough to think the feeling would last—once he realized the truth about her, he would run the other way like every other man in her past—there suddenly seemed nothing wrong with playing dress up and indulging her feminine side in the meantime.

She reached for one of the shopping bags and pulled out the silver strappy heels and the tight red dress she'd bought on a whim. Her memory stirred and she saw herself standing on the doorstep watching Hockey Hunk leave with the head cheerleader. It had been the most humiliating moment of her life.

Because she'd put her heart on her sleeve.

She hadn't just liked Hockey Hunk. She'd loved him. After months of sitting across from him during tutoring sessions, rooting for him at every game, sharing her lunch on those days when he forgot his, she'd been head over heels for him.

This was different.

This was sex.

And so she didn't have to worry about making a fool of herself. She would be the one walking away this time.

A thrill rushed through her as she ran her hands over the stretchy fabric. It was nothing like anything she would ever wear in real life.

Which was the point entirely.

To abandon her tomboy image and be the woman she'd never allowed herself to be. She was through wondering what it felt like to dress up and tempt a man.

She was going to experience it firsthand.

Starting now.

10

THIS WAS *NOT* GOOD.

The thought struck even before Abby knocked on Brent's door. He knew it the moment she made up her mind to stop resisting and give in to the lust that burned inside of her. It was a knowledge that had nothing to do with his heightened vampire senses and everything to do with the awareness that sizzled in the air around him. The expectancy that settled in his gut. As if something monumental was about to happen and it was just a matter of time.

The feeling dogged him while he finished up his shower. Then a knock sounded on his door, confirming his worst suspicions. His heart skipped a beat as he stepped out of the shower. His hand trembled as he reached for a towel. Excitement zipped up and down his spine and he stiffened.

The last thing he wanted was to see Abby on his doorstep. He needed distance. Safety.

He wiped at the water dripping from his face and knotted the towel at his waist. Another knock sounded and his muscles clenched.

He wasn't going to answer. That's what he told himself. He would pretend to be asleep and slip out once she'd given up.

But then she knocked again and he caught a deep whiff of her sweet shampoo. He reached for the knob.

"Yeah?" He hauled open the door and got the surprise of his afterlife.

She looked nothing like the Plain Jane woman who'd followed him from the Dairy Freeze and everything like the woman he'd glimpsed last night in her bedroom. Sexy. Seductive. Irresistible.

Her dress was short and tight, cut down to there and up to here. Red spandex hugged her voluptuous curves and left little to the imagination. And where there wasn't shiny red fabric, there was skin. Lots and lots of soft, supple, tempting flesh that made his mouth water and his pulse race.

He didn't mean to stare. He meant to play it cool, to close the door and ignore her, but he couldn't help himself.

His gaze shifted up before sweeping back down

and pausing several places in between. The smooth column of her throat. The frantic beat of her pulse. The bare curve of her shoulder. The deep swell of her luscious breasts. The press of her ripe nipples against the thin material that barely passed for a dress. The flare of her hips. The long, bare legs that seemed to go on and on.

"I hope I didn't wake you up," she murmured, only the faintest tremble in her voice giving away that she might be the slightest bit nervous.

"I was in the shower."

"I see that."

And so could he. For a split-second, her guard faltered and he read the thoughts that raced inside her pretty little head. Her gaze drew him in and suddenly he was right there, seeing through her eyes, feeling what she felt, wanting what she wanted.

He'd been partially hidden behind the door when he'd first answered her knock, but he was completely visible now. Visible and nearly naked, with only a towel slung low on his lean hips and water beading on his dark skin.

Nearly naked and oh so close.

She could feel the heat coming off him, smell the enticing aroma of clean soap and virile male. She took a deep breath as her eyes drank in the sight of him. The white cotton wrapped around his lean waist

*was in stark contrast to his tanned muscle. Broad
shoulders framed a hard, sinewy chest sprinkled with
dark hair that tapered to a slim line and disappeared
beneath the towel's edge. The same hair covered the
length of his powerful thighs and calves. He was
every bit as hot as she remembered and she gave
herself a great big mental kick in the ass for not
acting on her feelings sooner.*

She wanted him.

*Her body clenched and wetness rushed between
her legs. She should have reached for him last night,
pulled him down, invited him in. She'd held back.
She was still holding back, but not because she was
afraid. She wanted to fulfill her deepest fantasies.
To tempt him with her body and lure him with her
smile. She wanted him so hot that he couldn't keep
his hands off her. She wanted him to throw her on
the bed and strip her bare and lick her from head to
toe—*

"What do you want?" he blurted, killing the vivid
image.

His groin tightened and he stepped back behind
the door again, desperate for a barrier between them.
Something to keep him from reaching out and pulling
her inside the room. He was close. Too close. The
hunger pushed and pulled inside of him and he knew
he wouldn't last five seconds if she kept looking at

him with such passion in her eyes. And he had to last. He didn't do sex. And he certainly didn't do it with the locals.

Then again, she wasn't actually a local. She was temporary. In town in search of her ex. Or so she said.

She was lying. Even more, she was good at lying, at masking her feelings, which made him all the more suspicious of her. She wasn't who she pretended to be.

Not that it mattered.

Regardless of who she was or why she was here, she wasn't from Skull Creek. She was temporary. She wouldn't be hanging around next week. Or next month. Or next year. And he wouldn't have to face her again should he come back and visit Cody. So why shouldn't he take her up on what she was so obviously offering?

At the same time, there was just something about her that made him wary. The fact that she wasn't easily influenced by him bothered him to no end. He couldn't bend her to his will, otherwise she would turn and walk away right now.

Walk.

He stared deep into her eyes and sent the silent command, but she simply batted her eyelashes, her gaze hopeful, hungry.

She was stronger than any other woman he'd ever known. Different. Dangerous.

To his resolve. His peace of mind. His heart.

When the last thought struck, he drop-kicked it back out. That was the last thing he had to worry about. He didn't stick around long enough for his heart to get involved. He kept his distance and took his sustenance only when he needed it.

His dick throbbed, reminding him that the one thing he needed right now was a warm, lush woman.

The woman standing before him.

"I really have to go," he murmured. "I've got someone waiting on me."

"Oh." Disappointment flashed in her gaze and he couldn't help himself.

"My brother," he heard himself blurt. *What the hell?* He didn't explain. Even more, he didn't talk. *Just shut up and let her think the worst. Even more, shut the door right friggin' now before you do something you'll really regret.* "He's getting married next Saturday and tonight's the shower. It's a couples' shower," he explained. "Not that I'm a part of a couple. But it's for men and women and I'm family so I have to go."

"Oh." The disappointment faded in a rush of relief. She smiled. "Where are they getting married?"

"A friend of ours has a ranch outside of town. The wedding is there, but the shower is at Darlington House. It's this old restored mansion over on Main, near the town square. It used to be the home of Sam Black, the founder of Skull Creek, but now it's a historic landmark. They give tours and use it for special events. Weddings. Receptions. Anniversary parties."

"Showers," she added. She smiled and his chest tightened. "What about afterward? We could meet up later." She looked so hopeful that he almost agreed.

Almost.

But Brent had been resisting the lust for sex that burned inside of him far too long to give in so easily. Sex was off limits while he was in Skull Creek. It was a vow he'd made when Cody had asked him to stick around, one he intended to keep. It would be hard enough to leave his brother when all was said and done. He wasn't adding a woman to the list.

"I'm busy later," he murmured. And then he closed the door before he did something really stupid like pull her close, sinking his fangs into her sweet neck and his cock into her warm and willing body.

No sex, he reminded himself. Even more, no blood and sex. That was a double whammy. A sure-fire way to find himself in a heap of trouble.

Having sex with her would be bad enough. But having sex with her *and* drinking her blood? That would tie him to her emotionally. He would be able to hear her thoughts, feel her feelings, *know* her.

No way. No how. *Hell*, no.

Brent listened as her heels clicked back toward her room. The knob clicked. Hinges creaked. The door thudded shut and he welcomed a rush of relief.

But it was short-lived when he realized that all that separated them was measly sheetrock. His hands trembled and his body tightened and he pulled on his clothes with lightning speed. Snatching up his keys and his Stetson, he headed for his car, his gaze locked on the Camaro. He wasn't going to look toward her room. Or think about her and the way she'd looked in her tight red dress and sparkly shoes. Or the fact that he was so hard he could have cut diamonds at the moment.

Getting the hell out of there. That's all that was on his mind at the moment.

That and finding a little relief. No way would he make it fifteen minutes at the shower in his present state. He needed to sate the hunger deep in his belly. He needed calm. And he knew just how to get it.

He fired the engine, pulled out of the parking lot and headed to the Dairy Freeze for a quick bite.

HE COULDN'T DO IT.

Brent stared at the woman draped over his arm.

The waitress from the other night. Just as willing. Just as eager.

Her heartbeat echoed in his ears, begging for his fangs, but he couldn't seem to make himself do it. As hungry as he was, he wasn't hungry for this. For her.

"Please," she murmured, her gaze glazed with passion as she stared up at him. While she didn't consciously remember, her subconscious did and that's what was in control at the moment. She wanted the sweet release he'd given her the other night when he'd drank from her. The pleasure.

And he wanted Abby.

The truth thrummed through him and he released the woman. Buttoning her blouse back up, he stared deep into her eyes.

This was just another dream. Go back inside and forget all about it. About me.

For a split second, he wished he could turn the mind control on himself. He wanted to forget Abby and the way she'd looked in her red dress. The way she'd looked last night.

Even more, he wanted to forget the way she'd looked at him.

The desperation. The desire.

He'd had women want him before, but only because of what he was. Abby wasn't influenced by that. She was strong. Immune to his control. Unfazed by it.

Yet she still wanted him.

Of her own accord.

That's why he couldn't forget her. And that's why he bypassed the various couples clustered here and there in the main parlor and headed straight for the bar the moment he arrived at Darlington House.

"What's up with you?" Cody asked him when he cornered him later that night.

"I'm just having a drink."

"You don't drink. We don't drink." Vampires were more sensitive, which meant they not only saw and heard things that most people couldn't. They also felt things more intensely. Translation? Brent was a cheap drunk.

Usually.

Oddly enough, three glasses of Crown Royal still hadn't been enough to make Brent forget Abby and her sexy red dress.

"Slow down," Cody told him when he tossed down number four.

"Shouldn't you be helping your bride-to-be open gifts?" He motioned to Miranda who stood across the room, holding up yet another silver serving platter. "Don't these people realize you can't use that?"

"Some are humans and no, they don't realize it.

And they'd better not realize it." He gave Brent a warning look. "Take it easy, okay?"

"No problem." He waved the waiter off when he started to refill the glass and Cody looked relieved.

"So what did you think about the house?" When Brent tried to look puzzled, Cody grinned. "I know you stopped by. Nice, huh?"

"It's a house."

"Do you think she'll like it?"

"I think you should stop worrying about whether she likes it and start worrying over what you're going to do with seven Crockpots."

Cody glanced behind him in time to see Miranda unwrap the next present and his face fell. "Whatever happened to gift cards?" he muttered as he made his way back over to his fiancée.

Brent pushed away from the bar, said his goodbyes and slipped out before Cody got to the envelope he'd left on the table upon his arrival. Outside, he climbed into his car, hiked the windows down and spent the next half hour hauling ass down the interstate, feeling the wind whip at his skin. Hoping it would cool him down and ease the lust eating away inside of him.

No such luck.

He was still as hot, as horny as ever when he pulled into the parking lot later that night.

He killed the engine and sat there, staring through

the windshield at the closed curtains of her room. He knew he should go out to Cody's. He could sleep in his brother's basement tonight and save himself a night of tossing and turning and fantasizing.

At least that's what he told himself.

But deep down, he knew he was past the point of sleep. She was in his head, under his skin, and there was no escaping the picture she'd made on the bed with her legs spread, or on his doorstep wearing a racy red dress and eager smile.

It was crazy, but he couldn't decide which he liked better. He knew it should be the first, but as much as he'd liked seeing her naked body, he'd liked seeing her smile, too. The tilt of her full lips. The flash of uncertainty in her gaze, as if she wasn't half as daring as she pretended to be.

She wasn't, despite the fact that she'd pulled the curtains aside and was now standing in the window, staring at him.

Drive away.

The command echoed, but damned if he could make himself start the engine. Instead, he sat still and waited to see what she would do next.

11

HE'D TURNED HER DOWN.

The knowledge should have been enough to sway Abby from her current plan, but it wasn't.

She hadn't made it through boot camp and years of special training by being easily discouraged. When she made up her mind to do something, she did it.

Now was no different.

While Brent had turned her down, he hadn't wanted to turn her down. He'd wanted to reach out, pull her into his arms and kiss her senseless. She'd seen as much in the stiff set of his muscles. The flare of desire in his eyes. The tense set to his jaw. He'd wanted her, but he'd held back.

He was holding back now.

She watched as he sat behind the steering wheel,

his hands clenching the wheel, as if he couldn't quite decide what to do.

While he might not be able to make up his mind, she'd already made up hers. If putting on a sexy outfit hadn't been enough to push him past the point of no return, she would just have to try taking it off.

Slowly.

She leaned over and flipped on the ancient radio that sat on a nearby table. A turn of the knob and she cleared away the static and tuned in to a local country station. A twangy, sexy Big and Rich song filled her ears and she closed her eyes. The beat filled her head and thrummed through her body. She started to move her hips from side to side. Pushing her arms into the air, she slid her hands beneath her hair and lifted the weight, the same way she'd seen Winona demonstrate during her pole dancing snippet.

The realization that Brent was parked outside, watching her from his car made her heart pound and her blood race. Her body came alive, her nerves buzzing, and her movements grew more seductive as she listened to the lyrics about saving horses and riding cowboys.

She danced for the next few seconds, lost in the rhythm of the song and the seductive edge, until the music finally faded into a slow tune by Faith Hill and Tim McGraw.

Chancing a peek to see if Brent was still watching, she found the car empty. Disappointment rushed through her as she came to a dead stop and stared through the window. And then came the insecurity.

Maybe she'd read him wrong. Heaven knew it wouldn't be the first time. She'd been so convinced that Hockey Hunk had returned her feelings, so dead set in the notion that he loved her as desperately as she loved him that she'd poured out her feelings that night only to have them thrown back into her face.

There'd been no feelings involved now. Just lust. And pride.

She was such an idiot.

Then and now.

"Don't stop on my account." The deep, sultry voice brought her whirling around to find Brent standing in the corner of the room. His eyes gleamed. Tension held his body tight. His muscles bunched beneath his white T-shirt. Taut lines carved his face, making him seem harsh, fierce, predatory.

She glanced at the closed door. She hadn't heard it open. No footsteps. Nothing. It was as if he'd slid through the keyhole. "How did you get in here—" she started, but then he was right in front of her, his fingertip pressed to her lips.

"Don't talk," he murmured. "Just finish what you started."

Suddenly the specifics of how he'd gotten into her room ceased to matter. The only important thing was that he was there. Right in front of her. Watching again.

Waiting.

She licked her lips and touched a finger to her throat, to the frantic pounding of her pulse. Her hand lingered before she slid a finger to the edge of her dress, tracing the line where warm flesh met spandex before moving to the spaghetti strap.

Hooking her finger beneath, she slid the stretchy material down over her shoulder. She did the same with the other strap until the material caught only on her aroused nipples. She traced the indentation of one, fingering the peak until a gasp trembled from her lips.

Brent watched, his eyes dark and hooded and bright, bright blue—

Wait a second.

He didn't have blue eyes. He had green eyes. Vivid, grass-green eyes that made her think of lazy summer days and endless stretches of pasture. She blinked and sure enough, his eyes were green again.

Again? They were always green. You're so worked up that you're not thinking straight.

And how. Her hands trembled. Her body shook.

"More," he murmured, the one word throaty and raw and desperate.

A surge of feminine power went through her and she pushed the material down over her aroused nipples, to her waist. She eased it over her hips, her thighs, her knees, until it puddled around her ankles.

Leaning down, she grasped the edge of the dress and tried to step free. Her heel caught and she stumbled backward.

"Easy." Brent caught her, his strong, powerful hands steady on her arms.

Heat rushed to her cheeks, but he didn't seem the least put off by her clumsiness. His gaze smoldered. His touch lingered for a long moment, as if he hated to let her go.

He did.

He forced his hands away and stepped back to give her the floor again.

She drew a deep, shaky breath and watched the flare of desire in his eyes when her breasts lifted up and out. The sight fed her confidence and she reached for her front bra clasp. A twist of her fingers and the cups fell aside. Cool air slid over her bare breasts, but then his gaze chased away the sudden chill as quickly as it had come. Her heart pounded harder. Her blood rushed faster.

Just like that, a drop of sweat slid down her temple. She was hot. A feeling that had nothing to do with the failing air conditioner and everything to do with the fire that burned between them.

She touched the undersides of her breasts, cupping the soft mounds, weighing them and feeling the heat of her own touch for a long, delicious moment. All the while, she imagined that it was Brent touching her, searing her.

She skimmed her palms over her nipples, down the plane of her stomach, to the waistband of her panties. The moment she felt the soft cotton, doubt pushed past the desire drumming at her temples. She wore plain regulation panties without a hint of lace. No sequins. No beading. Nothing even remotely sexy.

When she'd bought the new clothes, why oh why hadn't she opted for new undies, too?

Because while she was, indeed, female, she didn't think like one. She thought in terms of comfort rather than appearance. Functionality rather than seduction.

Brent Braddock didn't seem to notice. He stared at her as if she wore the skimpiest thong. His gaze gleamed with excitement. Desperation. Hunger.

Impatience rushed through her, chasing away the insecurity and filling her with pure, raw need. A need she had to satisfy or else.

She pushed the panties down and toed them to the side. When she leaned down to work at the straps of the shoe, Brent's voice stopped her.

"Leave them on. They're sexy."

You're sexy.

His deep voice echoed in her head, but she didn't see his lips move. Before she could wonder about it, he leaned down and touched his lips to hers in a quick, hungry kiss that sent electricity zinging from the point of contact.

The sensation ended all too soon and he pulled away. Then he simply stood there. Staring at her. Waiting for more.

She quickly obliged. She touched the tip of one breast and circled before moving to the other. She rubbed her nipple and squeezed, making her own breath catch before she moved lower, over her belly button, her pelvis, to the damp, swollen flesh between her legs. She stroked herself and her nerves hummed. Another lingering stroke and she pushed deep inside her drenched flesh.

Pressure gripped her, so sweet and intense, and she gasped. She'd pleasured herself many times before, but it had never felt the way it did now. With Brent so close. So interested.

She fanned her fingers, pushing and wiggling until her body swayed from the desire gripping her.

But it wasn't enough. She wanted his fingers inside of her. His touch. Him.

And he wanted her.

"Just sex," he murmured, his gaze suddenly wary. "That's all this is. I don't want to date you or get to know you or listen to your life story. I'm not looking for a relationship."

"Neither am I." She closed the few inches that separated them. Staring up into his heated gaze, she murmured, "Your turn."

He hesitated a split-second and she feared he would turn and walk away, the way he'd done last night. And today.

Not this time.

Instead, he reached out and rasped one nipple with his knuckle. Pleasure bolted through her and she caught a gasp that bubbled from her lips.

He slid his arms around her and down the small of her back until he cupped her buttocks. As if she weighed nothing, he pulled her legs up on either side of him and lifted her. He settled her firmly against the rock-hard length barely contained by his zipper.

She wrapped her arms around his neck and lost herself to the delicious friction as he rocked her. The course material of his jeans rasped against her sensitive flesh, and pleasure rushed through her, igniting every nerve ending until her body glowed from the feel of his.

A day's growth of beard rubbed against the tender flesh of her neck, the slope of her breasts, chafing her and stirring her sensitive skin. He arched her backward, drew one swollen nipple into his mouth and sucked her so hard she almost fainted from the pleasure.

The sensation was both pleasure and pain as he suckled and nipped with his teeth. No man had ever done that and she arched as warmth gushed between her legs from the pure intensity.

Then he captured her lips in a kiss that sent her senses reeling. His tongue tangled with hers, delving and tasting until she could barely breathe.

He turned and she felt the mattress at her back. He leaned back and made quick work of his jeans until he stood before her wearing nothing but a look of pure intent.

She leaned up on her elbows as her gaze swept him from head to toe. Muscles carved his torso, from his bulging biceps and shoulders to his ripped abdomen. Dark, silky hair sprinkled his chest, narrowing to a tiny whorl of silk that bisected his abs before spreading into a soft nest that circled his sizeable erection. A drop of pearly liquid beaded on the plum-like head of his penis and she had the insane urge to lean forward and taste him.

Before she had the chance, he turned and retrieved a condom from his pocket.

He tore open the foil packet and rolled it down his hard length. Catching her bent knees in his hands, he parted her and gazed at the heart of her.

No man had ever looked at her so fiercely, so intently and a wave of doubt spiraled through her. She tried to close her legs.

"Don't be shy now. Not with me." His gaze caught and held hers. "Not ever with me."

She nodded and let herself open. He looked his fill, his gaze roving over her, his eyes flaring so hot and bright that she felt her own body temperature rise.

When she was this close to going up in flames, he leaned over her and plunged his hard, hot length inside, until flesh met flesh and he filled her completely.

The feeling took her breath away and her heart stopped for a long moment. She'd never felt as close to a man before.

Sure, she'd had sex. But it had always been swift and to the point. The primary goal? To get to the good stuff. The orgasm itself.

This was different. This *was* the good stuff. His

body flush against hers. His lips driving her insane. His hands roaming over her body. His erection rasping her tender insides.

He pushed himself an inch deeper before he started to withdraw. She clutched at his shoulders, desperate for more as he plunged back inside. In and out. Over and over. Until her nerves spun out of control.

Sensation snatched her up and whirled her around like a tornado. The air rushed from her lungs and the room started to spin.

He pushed deeper, harder, faster, until she couldn't take anymore. Pleasure crashed over her, turning her this way and that, spinning her faster than she'd ever thought possible in her wildest, most erotic fantasies.

This *was* a fantasy, she reminded herself even though it felt so incredibly real. The roughness of his skin, the power of his body, the possessiveness as he stared down at her and bucked into her one final time.

His back arched, his muscles strained. His eyes glittered, blazing a bright, brilliant purple—

She blinked and the vivid color faded into a sea of sparkling green. Confusion rushed through her, but then he rolled onto his back and pulled her flush against his side. His arms went around her and he held her tight, as if she were his one and only. His woman. And he never meant to let her go.

It was a crazy, hopelessly romantic thought. The kind straight out of a cheesy romance novel, but then that's what this was.

A fairytale.

A fantasy.

One that would end all too quickly once Rayne arrived in Skull Creek and she returned to her life.

It would be over all too soon, which was why she intended to relish every moment of what was happening right now.

She closed her eyes and snuggled deeper into his embrace.

12

WHAT THE HELL was he doing?

Not the sex part, of course. He knew why he'd done that. The moment he'd seen her dancing in the window, he'd known he couldn't resist any longer. Even more, he hadn't wanted to resist. While he'd yet to figure out Abby, he'd learned enough to know that she wasn't like one of the locals. There would be no seeing her day in and day out.

And since she was the only woman he couldn't read, he knew there would be no getting to know her. No real connection.

Just sex.

It made sense, which was why he'd given in last night.

That and one too many drinks.

So he didn't regret the sex part. It had been fantastic. Phenomenal.

It was the fact that she was curled up next to him sleeping like a baby that he was having trouble with.

That, and the fact that he liked it.

A helluva lot.

The realization struck and he stiffened. He slid away from her and threw his legs over the side of the bed. He was a vampire, for Christ's sake. He didn't cuddle. He had sex and drank blood and inspired fear in the heart of millions. He wasn't the cuddling type, and neither was she. He could tell by the way she rolled onto her back and threw her arms above her head that she wasn't used to sleeping with anyone.

Yet she'd fallen asleep in *his* arms as if it were the most natural thing in the world. As if she liked it. As if she liked him.

He ditched the thought. There was no *like* involved at all. They barely knew each other. He'd worn her out, soaked up her delicious energy. It made sense she would be exhausted to the point of falling asleep.

What didn't make sense was the fact that he still wanted her. He should have felt one hundred percent satisfied, his hunger sated.

He wasn't.

Staring at her spread out on the sheets, he wanted more than anything to climb back into bed with her. He wanted to see if she made the same noises if he licked her to the point of orgasm. If she would cry his name at the moment of release. If she would bury her head in his neck and fall fast asleep when they were done.

Crazy.

Sleeping wasn't on the list of possibilities with Abby. Nor was waking up with her or having breakfast or waltzing outside hand-in-hand in the bright light of day.

There was no morning after for Brent. He was a vampire, and so he gathered up his clothes and did what he'd been doing for the past one hundred and something years.

He turned his back and walked away.

ABBY LISTENED to the click of the door and the roar of his engine.

He was leaving.

That fact shouldn't have bothered her.

For one thing, she hated sleeping with anyone. She was a major bed hog and so it was better that he'd left before she'd had to fight him for the covers. Besides, sleeping wasn't part of her fantasy. It was all about unleashing her feminine wiles and she'd done so last night. Now it was time to get some much needed rest.

Then she could go for round two tonight.

And that was the problem in a nutshell.

She much preferred Brent not sticking around to see her in the bright light of day with major bedhead. Talk about blowing her newly found image.

At the same time, she wasn't nearly done building that image of herself as a desirable woman. She had several days left until Rayne came back and she had to return to her life, and she wanted to make the most of each. She certainly wasn't bummed because she'd thought for a split-second that Brent might actually like her. They didn't even know each other, and she fully intended to keep it that way.

No, it was time to move on. If she wanted to unleash her feminine side, she didn't have to do it with him.

There were plenty of men in Skull Creek. Granted, she might not have the same sizzling chemistry with any other man, but she was willing to give it a shot and test out a few more tidbits of wisdom courtesy of Winona and her infomercials.

Like the fact that men had a weakness for feet.

That's what Winona preached when Abby turned on the television set later that morning.

"Get a pedicure," the old woman was saying. "Clean up those tootsies and, if you're lucky, your man might take the hint and suck on a few."

It made sense and so Abby headed for the local hair salon to indulge in her first ever pedicure.

Because this fantasy wasn't about Brent. It was about Abby. About delving deep and living out her most erotic thoughts. It was about enjoying her femininity.

Even if it hurt like hell.

"Do you have to scrub so hard?" she asked the blonde who leaned over the footrest, a pumice stone in her hand and a determined look on her face.

"What on earth did you do? Walk across the Sahara barefoot? Your feet are as rough as horse hooves."

"Thanks for the boost to my confidence."

"Seriously. Haven't you ever heard of lotion?"

"I don't usually have time for lotion." Not in the military. She barely had time to snag a tube of Chapstick at the commissary in between field operations.

Until now.

She had five full days left to herself before the real world intruded. "I'd like a foot bath, too," she told the blonde. "And a paraffin wax. And a hot oil massage on the balls of my feet."

By the time she left the salon, she'd spent a hundred and fifty dollars and her feet looked ready for a flip flop commercial.

Instead of heading for the beach though, she hit the nearest bar and grill, determined to make the most of the time she had left. She wore a blue jean mini skirt, a white tank top with the phrase *Cowgirls Do It Better* spelled out in pink rhinestones and a pair of pink high heels.

Her outfit wasn't as flashy as the red dress last night, but it did spark some serious interest from the male clientale of Joe's Bar and Grill. A truth that fed her self-esteem and kept her from running back to the motel to see if Brent had returned.

This wasn't about turning on one man. It was about exercising her newfound feminine wiles and wowing them all.

And that's exactly what she intended to do.

SHE WASN'T IN her room.

Brent pulled into the parking lot and stared at the darkened window where Abby had put on her show the night before. Disappointment rushed through him. It was a crazy feeling because he surely hadn't expected her to be ready and waiting for him after he'd walked out on her this morning.

Any other woman, yes.

They would have been ready and waiting for him, desperate for a little more of his attention.

Not Abby. She wasn't the least bit fazed by his

vampire charisma. No sitting around, pining away. No meeting him at the door wearing nothing but Saran Wrap and a hopeful expression.

Instead, she was prowling the local bar.

The truth hit him when he turned the corner and saw her rental car parked in front of a neon Bud Light sign. It was a cause for celebration, right? The last thing he wanted was a woman getting hooked on him. But damned if he wasn't a little ticked off that she'd moved on quite so fast.

He frowned and an image rushed at him. He saw Abby stretched out on the bed, a smile curving her full lips as she reached out for another man.

Was she friggin' nuts?

His spot wasn't even cold and she was already looking for a replacement? Not that she would find one. Hell, no. What they had done last night had been one-of-a-kind. An experience she wouldn't be able to duplicate with just anyone.

On top of that, she wasn't the type of woman to sleep around. She wasn't nearly experienced enough to tell the good guys from the bad.

And you know this because…?

He'd seen the hesitation in her eyes, the awkwardness of her moves and the damned wonder on her face when she'd exploded around him. She wasn't nearly the wild and wicked woman she pretended to be and she was about to bite off more than she could chew if he didn't stop her.

He pulled up behind her, killed the engine and climbed out of the car.

"So you're from Charlotte?"

"Chicago," she told the cowboy sitting next to her. His name was Paul and he was more the drugstore variety than the real deal. He sold real estate during the day and bootscooted his way across the local honky tonks at night. He'd been on his way to the Cherry Creek Saloon when he'd decided to stop off for a drink. One look at Abby and he'd settled on the stool next to her and offered to buy her a drink.

She was on her second and doing her best not to notice the narrowness of his shoulders beneath the starched shirt. So what if he wasn't as muscular as Brent? He was still a decent guy. Even if he did smell like the fragrance section of a department store.

"So you've been in Skull Creek for two months now?" he asked.

"Two days."

"Oh, yeah." He grinned. "I knew that."

He did. She'd told him as much three times, along with the fact that she was from Chicago and she liked Italian food and her favorite color was red. But he'd been too distracted by her chest to pay much attention to anything she said.

Yeah, baby.

She'd wowed him to the point that he couldn't think straight, much less pay attention to what she was saying.

Score one for Abby the ultra femme.

At the same time, it would have been kind of nice if he had looked her in the eyes. At least once.

"That's a really nice shirt."

"You should know, buddy" came a deep, familiar voice. "You've been staring at it long enough."

Awareness sizzled up Abby's spine and she knew, even before she chanced a glance, that Brent Braddock stood directly behind her.

13

ABBY TWISTED TO SEE Brent, his gaze riveted on a surprised Paul. The cowboy's hat bobbed as he forced his attention from Abby's chest to the man standing behind her.

"Who are you?" Paul asked.

"Her bodyguard. Now get lost."

"But I coughed up the cash for two margaritas."

"You'll be coughing up your dinner if you don't slide off that barstool and start walking."

Brent didn't have to repeat himself. Paul hit his boots and retreated across the room to a redhead who stood near the jukebox. Strong fingers gripped Abby's arm and tugged her from her seat.

She shrugged away from Brent and faced off with him, her chin in the air. Her chest heaved from all the extra air she was forced to draw in because suddenly, she couldn't seem to get enough with him so close. "What are you doing?"

"Saving you from yourself."

"Thanks, but no thanks. I don't need a white knight."

"Do you know what that guy had in mind?"

She arched an eyebrow. "Sex?"

"Sex," he declared. She smiled and his gaze narrowed. "What are you? Some kind of nympho?"

"I'm a jilted woman who's trying to get over a bad relationship and have a little fun. I've got a week until my ex rolls back into town so I can tie up loose ends. I want to enjoy myself until then."

She could feel his gaze on her for a long moment. "Bullshit," he finally muttered.

"What's that supposed to mean?"

"It means that you're not a receptionist and you're not from Chicago and you sure as hell aren't trying to get over your ex."

"How do you know?"

He picked up the Driver's License sitting on the bar next to her margarita, which she'd handed over when she'd ordered. "Because this was issued in South Carolina, not Illinois."

"So? Maybe I spent most of my life in South Carolina and moved to Chicago just recently."

"Did you?"

"I thought you didn't want to know?" she countered. "Not me or my life history. Just sex, remember?"

He looked like he wanted to say something, but then his mouth clamped together and he signaled the waiter for a beer.

"So what's with Urban Cowboy over there? He doesn't seem like your type."

"You don't know my type. You don't know me," she reminded him.

He didn't say anything for a long moment. Instead, his gaze moved around the room, touching here and there, before zeroing in on her once again. "I know that guy lives with his mother and bums money off her to buy beer." When she arched an eyebrow, he shrugged. "It's a small town."

"Thanks for the warning, but I hadn't planned on marrying him. It's all about fun, remember. A week of it, to be exact." She still had five days left. A lifetime compared to her usual schedule.

A piddly amount when it came to the rest of her life.

She had to build enough memories to last. It was a realization she'd come to during her foot fest that day. Odds were she would never get the chance she had right now. No time to play dress up. To pretend to be something she wasn't. A lifetime and this was the first time she could really and truly enjoy herself. Once she dragged Rayne back to face charges and cleared her reputation, she would go back to doing what she did best—leading her men and running successful field ops.

In the meantime, she was going to make the most of her time in Skull Creek.

With or without Brent.

She glanced to the side and eyed him. He looked so handsome that she wanted to hop into his lap and do her own variation of the very detailed lap dance she'd seen Winona demonstrate. It was a wild, crazy impulse. One she never would have acted on in the real world.

She didn't act on it now, not with him sitting so close and staring at her as if she'd been caught with her hand in the cookie jar. He looked irritated. Jealous even and guilt spiraled through her.

Make-believe, she reminded herself. None of this was real. Not his concerned look or the strange possessiveness gleaming in his gaze.

But for a few seconds as they sat side by side, his thigh warm and strong against hers, it felt real. *He* felt real.

"You should be careful," he finally said. "You can't just go around picking up men. It's dangerous."

"Trust me, I can take care of myself."

"So sayeth every woman."

"I'm serious. I've got a black belt in Karate and years of hand-to-hand combat training," she blurted before she could stop herself. When he arched an eyebrow, she added, "My dad was career military. He taught me everything he knew." Martial Arts. Special Weapons. She could even arm wrestle.

Not that she told Brent that. She'd already admitted too much and he'd been more than clear that he didn't care.

But for someone who didn't give a crap he was being awfully nosy. The realization made her want to smile.

Silence settled around them as she sipped her margarita. His thigh brushed hers and her heart stuttered. So much for moving on to the next guy.

She still wanted this one. She just wasn't so sure he still wanted her. He was here, which said a lot. At the same time, he was also griping her out which didn't exactly spell out I-want-to-jump-your-bones.

"What branch of the Armed Forces is your dad in?" he asked after several seconds of silence ticked by. It was the last thing she expected from him. At the same time, he seemed eager for a distraction from the heat flowing between them.

She eyed him. "Are you sure you want to hear this?"

"No, but tell me anyway." *It's better than sitting here wondering how I'm going to keep my hands off you.*

The words whispered through her head and she couldn't help herself. She smiled.

Not because he'd actually said them. She knew it had to be her imagination at work. His lips hadn't so much as moved. At the same time, she had the strangest feeling that the ridiculous thought rang true.

"*Was.* He was a Navy recruiter. He passed away a few years ago from a heart attack."

"I'm sorry."

"Don't be. He died doing what he loved most— briefing new recruits."

He grinned and the pain that she always felt when she talked about her dad eased just a little. "Actually, he didn't die right away." She wasn't sure why she was telling him this. He hadn't asked and even if he had, she never talked about it. Not in the few years since he'd passed away and certainly not now, to a virtual stranger.

But he didn't feel like a stranger. There was something familiar about him. While she didn't know him from Adam, she had the absurd notion that he understood.

That he understood her loss because he'd faced his own.

"They took him to the hospital, but he didn't want to call me. He wasn't a very emotional man. I busted out crying when I scraped my knee once and he had a fit. Crying is for the weak and Trentons aren't weak, he always used to say. That was the first and last time I ever cried. I didn't even cry when they handed me his ashes. I should have." Her gaze riveted on a small drop of condensation that slid down the outside of her glass. "I should have cried, right?" The words tumbled past her lips. The accusation she'd felt every moment of every day. The sneaking suspicion that haunted her and reminded her that she was every bit the cold, emotionless person her father had once been. "Most people cry when they lose their dad." Except the cold, heartless ones.

"Trentons don't cry," her father had said. *"They don't show weakness and they don't act silly over some boy and they don't jeopardize their entire future to go to some silly prom. Suck it up, girl. You're a Trenton."*

And so she had. She'd sucked it up and buried her feelings to the point that she'd stopped thinking she even had any. And then her father had died, and his death had proved as much.

"My father always wanted me to be tough. I guess he finally got his wish."

"He doesn't sound like much of a father."

"He wasn't. He was strict and demanding and I think he always blamed me for my mother's death. She died when I was a few months old. She had diabetes and having me put too much of a strain on her system."

"It wasn't your fault."

She'd told herself as much many times in the past, but hearing him say it made her actually believe it.

"I lost my mother in a fire."

"And your dad?"

"I don't know. He left long before that and never looked back. It was just me and my brothers after that."

"How many brothers?"

When he hesitated, she added, "Come on. We're only talking. I promise I won't hold it against you later."

He arched an eyebrow. "Just sex?"

"Just great sex."

He grinned. "Three."

"I always wondered what it would be like to have brothers."

"You wouldn't be sitting here right now, that's for sure. No brother would stand by while his sister cruised a bar for strange men."

"Is that how you see me? Like a sister?"

"You're not my sister." His gaze caught and held

hers, as if he knew she needed to hear the words. "Not by a long shot."

Silence stretched between them once again, but it wasn't awkward this time. A sense of camaraderie wound between them, crossing the distance and killing the tension. A feeling that fed her courage and urged her to voice the one thought playing in her head. "You're right about me, you know."

"I'm always right, sugar."

A grin tugged at her lips before the expression faded into one of serious intent. "I don't do one night stands, but I meant it when I said I want to spend the next five days having some serious fun. Since we have great chemistry, it makes sense to have fun with you instead of bringing home a different cowboy every night. It would be just physical, of course. I'm really not looking for a relationship." Her gaze met his. "So how about it? Are you up for a repeat of last night?"

"Hardly." She frowned and a grin tugged at the corner of his mouth. "I was hoping it would be even better."

And then he grabbed her hand and led her out of the bar.

WHEN THEY ARRIVED back at the motel, Abby didn't waste any time on small talk. True to her word, she kept things strictly physical and stripped off her clothes. Once she'd shed everything, she reached for his T-shirt.

He lifted his arms and let her slide the cotton over his head. She backed him toward the bed then until the backs of his knees hit the mattress and he sat down on the edge.

Then she dropped to her knees and wedged herself between his legs as she leaned forward. Her lips closed over his right nipple. Her teeth caught him, her tongue flicking out to ply the nub.

"Holy hell," he ground out, his gaze fixed on her head as she suckled him. Her body wedged closer, pressing against his massive hard-on and his gut tightened. His pulse raced and he had the sudden image of her trailing her lips lower, unzipping his pants and taking him into her mouth.

Her moist red lips pressed against his skin and stirred the hunger. He could feel the need bubbling inside of her. He threaded his fingers through her hair, holding her close and soaking up the sweet heat.

But there was more. He felt his own lust building until he wanted nothing more than to haul her into his lap, press her back against the mattress and devour her ripe nipples. He wanted to spread her legs.

To slide into her. To sink his fangs into her sweet, delectable neck.

He wouldn't.

This was sex, he reminded himself, determined to stay focused. Even more, this was her show. He'd taken the lead last night, but it was her turn now.

She pulled back and stared up at him with heavy-lidded eyes. "Do you like that?"

He nodded and her slim fingers reached out to unfasten his jeans. "Do you like this?" Her knuckles grazed him as she worked the zipper over his hard length. His entire body trembled in anticipation. He tilted up just enough to let her pull his jeans and underwear down to his hips.

His penis jutted forward. The veins bulged, the skin slick and tight. A white drop beaded on the head and her gaze riveted on it. She licked at her bottom lip once, twice, and then she leaned forward. Her tongue flicked out and she lapped at his essence.

Electricity zapped him and his nerves started to tingle. She licked him from root to tip, making him burn hotter before drawing him into the wet heat of her mouth.

He closed his eyes as hunger sucker-punched him in the gut. His jaw ached and his fangs tingled. He knew she would see the truth if she glanced up at him and so he cradled her head, urging her to continue even though her mouth was pure torture.

He needed her to stop, but he couldn't stop her.

He didn't want to.

Pleasure drenched his body and he braced himself against coming right then and there. It wasn't about his own orgasm. That wasn't how it worked. He was the one who fed off of *her* excitement, her ecstasy. He didn't even have to come to feel satisfied.

But he wanted to.

He gathered his composure and forced his eyes open. Her silky hair trailed over his lap and he reached down, pushing the soft strands back so that he could see her face. He meant to pull her away, but he couldn't help himself. He watched as her red lips slid over his hard length. She suckled him, swirling her tongue around and around, pushing him closer to the brink. So close—

With a growl, he cupped her face and pushed her away. Her confused gaze collided with his. "Did I do something wrong?"

It was the perfect opportunity to kill the heat between them and say "Yes, you're not any good at oral sex."

But he couldn't bring himself to lie. Not with her looking so uncertain and so damned beautiful.

"You did everything just right." Satisfaction

beamed in her gaze and filled him with a strange sense of warmth.

She slid up his body and touched her lips to his.

He tasted his own essence and it stirred the beast that lived and breathed inside of him. His tongue tangled with hers and he deepened the kiss, wanting to consume her the way she'd consumed him only a few moments ago. The kiss was hot and wet and mesmerizing. So much more than ever before.

Because she was so much more.

He pushed aside the startling thought and reached for her hips, pulling her down onto his lap, and urging her legs up on either side of him.

He cupped her bottom and plunged into her slick flesh. Fire shot through him and thunder pounded in his ears. Finally her soft voice pushed past his sensual haze and he became aware of her hand splayed against his chest.

"We need protection," she breathed.

He wanted to tell her that he couldn't hurt her. That he would never hurt her because of what he was. But he'd vowed never to reveal himself to anyone ever again.

Keep quiet and keep moving. That had been his motto since Lila had turned on him.

Never again would he make that same mistake.

No matter how much he suddenly wanted to.

He withdrew and reached for his pants. A few seconds later, he retrieved a foil packet.

She took it from him, pulled out the contents and reached down between them. Her fingers brushed and stroked as she slid the condom over his throbbing length. And then she braced her hands against his chest and drew him deep into her body with one swift, downward motion.

The pleasure was so intense that a groan rumbled from deep in his throat. His entire body went rigid and he clenched his teeth to keep from closing his mouth over her neck and sinking his fangs into her as deep as his cock.

"Don't move." He held onto her sweet ass, his fingers pressing into her softness as he held her still and tried to gather his wits.

He had to think.

To stay in control.

He intended to, but then she arched her back, drawing him in deeper, and shot his intentions to hell and back. Pure pleasure washed over him and need pumped through his veins.

It was a feeling that intensified as she started to ride him, her body clasping his as she moved up and down, side to side. He braced his thighs, holding himself rigid as he massaged her buttocks and pressed hungry kisses to her throat. Her pulse beat against his lips and his throat went dry. His jaw ached.

He took every downward thrust, and met her with an upward plunge. Harder. Faster. Until she reached her breaking point. Her forehead wrinkled and her cheeks flushed and her lips parted. Her fingers dug into his shoulders.

He caught her fierce cry with his mouth and gathered her close as she shook, her climax crashing over her, drenching her and flowing into him from every point of contact. His cock deep inside her. His arms locked tight. Their bodies flush together.

Energy sizzled along his nerve endings and suddenly it was too much. He exploded, his own cry echoing in his ears, along with the frantic beat of her heart. His back arched and his vision clouded a bright brilliant purple.

Her gasp drew his attention and he realized all too late that she was staring smack dab at him. Into him. Shock twisted her features, but there was something else, as well. A strange sense of wonder that killed any fear and kept her gaze locked with his.

She stared at him, seeing him for what he was and the truth crystallized at that moment. Abby Trenton didn't just pose a threat to his existence.

With her sweet smile and her freckled nose and

her stubborn attitude, she posed a major threat to his heart. He'd never met a woman like her before.

And he never would again.

He knew it as he stared into her gaze. He also knew that he was falling in love with her and there wasn't a damned thing he could do to stop it.

14

SHE STARED AT HIM a moment longer before reality seemed to sink in and her eyes went wide. Fear rushed through her and blazed bright in her eyes. Suddenly, Brent forgot all about love and falling.

She'd seen him.

Holy shit, she'd *seen* him.

But he had an even bigger problem. His hunger stirred. His gut twisted and his body shook. He needed a drink. He needed her.

The truth pounded through his head and sent a rush of panic through him. He broke the contact between them, scrambling away. He stumbled to his feet and staggered backwards. His back came up hard against the opposite wall and he heard the crack of plaster. His stomach clenched and his muscles contorted. His mouth watered and his fangs ached. His gaze riveted on her lush body and an invisible hand tightened around him and squeezed.

Abby watched as Brent's eyes blazed a bright, furious red. His teeth pulled back and his fangs glittered and for a split-second, she wanted to rush over to him and give him what he so obviously needed.

Blood.

Her blood.

Denial rushed through her, along with fear. Not the fear of him, but of herself, her reaction. Because for a split second, against the better judgment she'd honed for months in the field, she'd wanted to help him. To reach out. To offer herself.

She still did.

She rushed hell for leather for the bathroom and tried to ignore the ridiculous notion. The door slammed and she flipped the lock.

He was a vampire.

A real, honest-to-goodness *vampire*.

She wouldn't have believed it if she hadn't seen it with her own eyes. Even now, she wasn't one hundred percent certain and her mind raced for a more plausible explanation. The margaritas. She'd had almost three. Translation? She was drunk. Hallucinating. That had to be it.

Why, this entire night was probably just a bad dream. A crazy nightmare wrought from too much alcohol and a lifetime of deprivation when it came to her sexuality. She'd buried her desires far too long and now everything was rushing to the surface, making her punchy and distorting her sense of reality.

That's what it was.

A nightmare.

One she would wake up from all too soon.

"We need to talk." His deep voice slid into her ears, pulling her back to reality and nailing home the truth—this wasn't her imagination. She felt the bare tile beneath her feet, the anxiety pressing down on her. "Please," he added.

So much desperation filled the one word and she almost opened the door. It wasn't a dream. Just a big misunderstanding. There were no such things as vampires. She was having a hallucination. A margarita induced hallucination. The next thing she knew, she would be seeing little green men in sombreros.

"I know this is a lot to grasp."

The air lodged in her chest as shock beat at her already numb brain. She rushed to the sink. Flipping on the faucet, she plunged her hands beneath the cool water and splashed some onto her face, as if she could wash away the images that rolled through her head.

"You're not a vampire," she heard herself say. "There's no such thing."

"There is," he said after a long moment, as if the

words were as hard to say as they were for her to hear. "I know it seems crazy, but it's true."

"A vampire? A real vampire?" She knew she sounded like a raving lunatic repeating herself, but she couldn't help it. She was trying to grasp the impossible and her brain just didn't want to accept it. "Vampires don't exist. Only on TV and in books. Not in real life."

"We exist," he said quietly. "I'm not allergic to garlic and crosses don't bother me, but I'm still a vampire. My senses are heightened and I can do things that most men only dream about. I'm strong and I can hear things. And when I look into someone's eyes I can see what they're thinking, too. Usually..." His voice trailed off for a long moment. "But not with you. For some reason, I can't see into your thoughts. Just the occasional glimpse. You're strong, Abby."

Which explained why she was cowering in the bathroom and clutching the edges of the sink like an idiot.

"I've never met a woman like you. You're different. Special."

It was an admission she'd hoped to hear her entire life. And while the circumstance wasn't one she would have predicted, a rush of satisfaction went through her anyway.

"You're smart and beautiful."

She stared at herself in the bathroom mirror and noted the flush to her cheeks. The sparkle in her eyes. She was different now. She felt it from the tips of her toes to her fingers.

"What did you do to me?"

"Nothing. It's just great sex. That's another perk of being a vampire. I'm pretty good in the sack."

"What else?" she heard herself. This was crazy. She should be crawling out the nearest window and running for help instead of playing twenty questions.

"I can see myself in a mirror like everyone else," he went on. "But that thing about bats is a myth. I can transform into other things if I want to, but it's usually more trouble than it's worth. I can levitate. And I have fangs."

Because he was a vampire. A night stalking, blood-drinking *vampire*.

Her memory raced and suddenly everything started to make sense. The sudden change of his eye color. The way he moved so swiftly and silently. His sudden appearance in her room that first night. His dark good looks and the dangerous pull that seemed to lure her closer against her better judgment.

An image rushed at her and she saw him, his fangs poised, his eyes glowing.

"You were going to bite me, weren't you?"

"I wanted to. I wanted it more than anything, but I wouldn't have done it. I didn't have to. I'd already fed."

"On who?"

"On you, Abby. Vampires don't just feed off of blood. We also crave energy. Sexual energy. Your orgasm fed me enough to curb my bloodlust." Silence settled as she tried to process everything he was saying. "Open the door. I promise I won't hurt you."

She wasn't sure why she believed him except that he'd had plenty of chances to turn her into a human Happy Meal if he'd wanted. The fact that he hadn't echoed through her and suddenly she wanted to flip the lock more than she wanted her next breath.

She wanted to know the truth about him. How long he'd been a vampire, who had turned him and why. She wanted to know everything and that need stirred her fear even more than the fact that he had actual *fangs*.

It was just sex, she reminded herself. She didn't want to know his background. His life. Him.

She just wanted a few wonderful memories to tide her over for the rest of her orderly, routine life.

Emotion push-pulled inside her and she shook her head frantically. This was too much. It was time to stop right now before she did the unthinkable.

She wasn't falling for him. She wasn't falling for anyone, man or vampire.

Never, ever again.

"Get out of here."

"You don't mean that."

"Get out right now before I call the cops."

Silence followed for several long seconds, as if he was trying to decide whether or not to believe her. He shouldn't have. She was bluffing, the same way she'd done time and time again on mission after mission. She knew how to persuade people. To survive.

That's what this was about. Survival. Of her body. Her heart.

Oh, no.

Panic rushed through her and the words tumbled out. "If you don't get out of here, I'm going to scream bloody murder. I mean it."

The thud of a door punctuated her sentence, and just like that he was gone.

She stood there for several long moments listening to the pounding of her own heart before she finally slid the lock aside. Sure enough, the bedroom was empty and a strange sense of loneliness swept over her.

She snatched up her clothes which lay in a heap where she'd left them. Her gaze shifted to Brent's T-shirt that still lay draped over the back of a nearby chair. Before she could stop herself, she reached for the soft cotton and slid it over her head. His scent filled her nostrils and she had the disturbing thought that she'd just lost the one thing that mattered most.

Nuts.

She hardly knew him. And he hardly knew her. They were virtual strangers.

So why did she feel so empty inside?

The question haunted her as she picked her way around the room, snatching up clothing and straightening the covers. Finally when there was nothing left to spend her energy on, she crawled into bed and burrowed beneath the covers.

And then, for the first time since she'd skinned her knee so very long ago, Abby Trenton started to cry.

15

SHE'D SEEN HIM.

She'd really and truly seen him.

Dread and denial whirled together to make his gut ache and his hands tremble. Sure, he knew that she'd glimpsed the truth a time or two when his control had slipped, but it had been so quick that she'd probably written it off as her imagination.

But this time she'd gotten a good, long look.

There were no excuses he could make. No escaping the truth.

He couldn't make her forget. Even though it was a trick of the trade, it didn't work with her. He'd tried it that first night when she'd followed him from the Dairy Freeze and it had been useless. She had a strong will. She knew how to conceal her thoughts and hide behind a mental barrier.

Bottom line, she knew how to keep him out of her head. So he was SOL. He couldn't make her forget all about him.

As depressing as the thought was, he found a small sense of solace in it. For the first time in his life, he didn't want a woman to forget him. He didn't want to blend into the background like a bad dream or vanish in a puff of smoke. He wanted to stand out. To have a permanent place in her memory. In her life.

He ignored the last thought and focused on gunning the engine of his Camaro. He needed to get out of here. To stop thinking and just drive.

He pulled out onto Main Street and headed for the city limits. It was time to pack up and leave. Dillon could text him any information that he might eventually uncover about his sister-in-law's whereabouts.

And Cody?

His brother would just have to get married without him. It wasn't like Brent was going to stand in as his best man. He'd made it clear that he didn't like weddings. Hell, he'd made it clear that he didn't want Cody to get married, period.

Impossible.

It would never work, no matter how much Cody wanted it to. He was too different from Miranda.

And if he turned her?

The possibility stuck in his head. One he'd never

considered because he'd never wanted to doom anyone to his same fate. He'd been a vampire over one hundred and fifty years and he'd never turned anyone.

And he never would.

Especially someone he loved.

It was hard enough living with the pain of rejection. But living with the knowledge that he'd destroyed someone's life? That he'd doomed them to a fate far worse than death?

Not no, but hell no. He wouldn't do it even if Abby begged him.

Not that she would. She feared him. She'd made it perfectly clear that she wanted nothing to do with him. She was probably on the phone at that moment, ranting about vampires and how he'd deceived her. And while he doubted anyone would believe her, particularly after she'd had a few drinks down at the local bar, he knew it was just a matter of time.

He gunned the engine and crossed the railroad tracks at the far edge of town. A turn to his left and he was heading for the Interstate, dead set on getting the hell out of town before people started to get suspicious.

They would. He had no doubt about that.

At the same time, he owed his brother a word of warning. Cody had told him not to get too close, but

Brent hadn't listened. While his gut told him that Abby wouldn't turn on him, he couldn't be sure. Not after the way she'd kicked him out. He picked up his cell phone and dialed.

"Meet me at the new house," he told Cody when his brother picked up on the third ring.

"What's wrong?"

"Just get in the car and drive. Fifteen minutes."

"WHAT'S GOING ON?"

Brent looked at his brother, not knowing quite what to say. "She knows."

"Who knows?"

"Abby."

"Abby who?"

"She's the woman I've been seeing for the past few days. She's new in town. She's here looking for Rayne."

That got Cody's attention. "Why would she be looking for Rayne?"

"She says she's a receptionist, but I think she's military." In fact, he knew she was military after their conversation last night. While she'd played it off as if it were only her background, the pieces had quickly fallen into place.

"We knew it was just a matter of time," Cody said. Rayne had married his sister-in-law a few weeks after being turned into a vampire in the mountains outside of Afghanistan. He'd been attacked and left to fend for himself.

Not knowing what else to do, he'd come home one last time before going on the run from the authorities and himself. He'd been a fledgling vampire. Scared of what he'd become. Fearful that he would hurt someone.

But he'd found a support system right here in Skull Creek with Cody and the handful of other vampires who'd taken up residence in the small town. They'd taught him to control the hunger, to feed it slowly so that it didn't devour him.

Still, the fact that he was coping didn't change the truth—he'd run away from the military and they'd all known it was just a matter of time before someone came looking for him.

They'd all believed it best to meet the threat head on, bending whoever showed up to their will so that they would forget all about Rayne and the fact that he was AWOL.

A plan that might have worked if anyone other than Abby Trenton had shown up.

She was stubborn.

Determined.

Sexy.

The thought struck and he stiffened. It didn't matter how sexy she was. It was over.

He was outta here.

"I'll call the others and see if we can't influence her and send her on her way."

"It won't work."

"How do you know?"

"Because I know. She's got a strong will and she's not easily influenced."

"She can't be that strong."

"Trust me, I've tried. She's not like everyone else. She won't bend. She's got the tenacity of a pit bull. No matter how much I stare into her eyes, I can't get her to listen to me."

Cody didn't say anything. He just stared at Brent long and hard before his face cracked into a smile and he started to laugh.

"What's wrong with you? Didn't you hear anything I said? She knows and she's going to blow the whistle on all of us. There's no way you can win in this situation. She's too stubborn."

"You're falling for her," Cody finally said once his laughter had died down. "Hook, line and sinker."

"Bullshit." There was no *falling* involved. He'd already fallen. Hard.

"You sure as hell are. She's gotten to you."

"She's going to tell the world we're vampires, little

brother. If you have half a brain you'll get the hell out of here before she does."

"I'm not leaving," Cody said after a long contemplative moment. "This is my home now. I won't give it up."

"You're crazy." Brent turned and started for his car.

"And you're scared."

The comment brought him to a dead stop. He turned on his brother. "What's that supposed to mean?"

"You're afraid to get close to anyone. Afraid they'll hurt you. Afraid they'll let you down. But that's no excuse to keep walking away from everything and everyone."

"I can do whatever the hell I want."

"True, but you'll always be alone if you do."

"Maybe I like being alone."

"And maybe you're full of shit. You're so used to running that you don't know how to stop. I know. I used to do a lot of running myself, always walking away when people got a little close and things got a little too intense. But then Miranda changed all that."

"She made you want to stick around," Brent murmured, remembering the push-pull of emotion he'd felt when he'd stood outside the bathroom door, trying to persuade Abby to open up. He hadn't wanted to leave.

No, for the first time in over one hundred years, he'd wanted to stay put.

"Are you kidding?" Cody smiled. "Miranda made me want to run for my afterlife. Faster, harder than ever before. That's how I knew she was the one. When a woman scares the bejesus out of you like that, she has to be something special." He let the statement hang between them for a long moment before he added, "You should try to talk to Abby."

"I already did that."

"So try again."

"And if she calls the cops?"

"Then you'll figure something out. We'll all figure something out. Together."

The offer was tempting, but Brent had been going it alone, relying on himself, his instincts, his desperation far too long to stop now.

He shook his head. "I can't take that chance. I won't. And if you have half a brain, you won't either. This situation is about to blow up." Then he turned and walked away.

"What about the wedding?" Cody called after him.

"I'm sorry," Brent muttered. And then he climbed into his car, gunned the engine, and left.

16

He was leaving.

That's what Brent told himself as he headed down the Interstate. If Cody had any sense of self-preservation, he would follow. But his little brother had gone off the deep end. Home. There was no such thing. There couldn't be. Not for them. They were vampires. Cold. Ruthless.

Scared.

Like hell. Brent wasn't scared. He was smart. He'd learned from his mistakes. It was all about survival. He wasn't running, he was staying alive. There was a difference, even if Cody was too damned lovestruck to see it. He would realize his mistake all too soon and it would be too late.

Not Brent.

He was going to stay one step ahead of the storm.

He was going to stay alive. Even if it meant being alone for the rest of his existence.

Lonely.

The truth struck and the weight of it pressed down on him. He realized then and there that he wasn't half as afraid of being strung up and left to fry in the hot sun as he was of never seeing Abby again.

That thought tore at him far worse than any horsewhip.

He wanted to fall asleep next to her and wake up with her every morning. He wanted her warm body cuddled up next to him and her sweet smile greeting him when he opened his eyes.

Even more, he wanted to pick her brain and find out more about her childhood, her life. He wanted to know and suddenly that thought wasn't half as frightening as the possibility that he might never know. He'd spent his entire afterlife keeping his distance because he thought it would make things easier when it was time to walk away.

It didn't make a bit of difference now. His chest ached and his throat burned.

He was walking away, running away, and it hurt like hell. Far more than anything he'd ever suffered before.

The realization hit him like a two-by-four and his stomach hollowed out. This was his greatest fear.

He wasn't afraid of being discovered. No, he was terrified at the thought of being ripped away from the one thing he wanted most—Abby. And he was doing it himself.

She doesn't want you, buddy.

Maybe not, but he wasn't going to add to the pain by putting more miles between them. She might not want him, but he was going back. He was going to face her and do everything in his power to show her how good they were together.

How good they could be.

And if she freaked and revealed his true identity?

It wouldn't matter. That pain was nothing compared to the thought of never seeing her again. Of giving up. Of not trying.

He hit the nearest Exit and made a U-turn, because Brent Braddock was through walking away.

It was time to stop running and start fighting.

HE WAS KNOCKING on her door again.

Abby listened to the familiar rap of knuckles and fought the urge to jump to her feet, haul open the door and throw her arms around Brent.

He was a vampire.

Even more, he was an annoying, persistent vampire who'd spent the past three days knocking on her door every night.

She hadn't answered, but that hadn't swayed him. She'd half-expected him to kick open the door or morph into a wisp of smoke and slide through the keyhole, but he'd done neither. He'd simply pulled up a chair and talked to her as if they were sitting face-to-face.

He told her about his childhood. About growing up with brothers and horses and lots and lots of cattle. He talked about the war and how he and his brothers had followed Cody to keep an eye on him. And he told her about the massacre and his suspicions that his sister-in-law had been involved somehow.

He told her about his life. And damned if she didn't have the urge to tell him about hers.

She didn't.

She didn't say a word because she knew that even if he'd changed his mind about the two of them getting to know each other, it still didn't make a difference.

It wasn't like they could have a future together.

She had to go back, to clear her name, to keep leading her unit and building her reputation and fighting for what she believed in. She'd worked too hard and sacrificed too much to give it all up to stay in Skull Creek with Brent Braddock.

No matter how much she suddenly wanted to.

So she kept her mouth shut and tried not to hang on his every word. During the day, she prowled the town and tried to keep herself busy. She got her hair done and did more shopping and tried to forget the man waiting back at the motel for her. But none of it was half as much fun as it should have been. Even Winona and her infomercials started to seem depressing. By the time Friday rolled around, Abby had all but given up on reveling in femininity.

Instead, she pulled on an old pair of sweats and a T-shirt and dove into a quart of chocolate ice cream. One more day, she reminded herself. One more day and Rayne would return. Then she would be out of here.

The thought wasn't nearly as comforting as it should have been and she devoured the carton in less than fifteen minutes. She was just reaching for another when she heard his voice.

"I know you love me."

She didn't say a word. She couldn't, due to the sudden lump in her throat.

She couldn't love him. And no way could he love her. They hardly knew each other.

The only trouble with that logic was that she'd gotten to know him over the past few days. Even more, the incredible sex between them had forged a connection. While he couldn't seem to breach her thoughts unless she wanted him to, she could breach his.

She'd discovered that much early this morning while she'd been lying in bed, trying to convince herself to get up and face another long day.

One minute she'd been staring at the ceiling and the next, she'd seen the blaze of fire. Heard the shouts. Smelled the smoke.

She'd seen inside of his head. His nightmare.

She'd felt every lash of the whip as it came down on his back and she'd felt the sting of betrayal. The hopelessness of being surrounded by so much hate. The loneliness of being a one hundred and fifty year old vampire and she'd understood.

Because she'd felt that same loneliness growing up with her father, moving from base to base, never really belonging. But wanting to. Wanting it so badly she could taste it.

The one time she'd taken a chance on easing that want, she'd been devastated.

Like her, Brent had wanted to fit in. To fall in love. To be normal. And so he'd taken a chance too.

And he'd been betrayed. Lila had turned her back on him. Walked away. Run away.

They had much more in common than just the sex.

They were cut from the same cloth, with the same hopes and dreams. The same fears.

"I'm leaving tonight," he said, through the door. "Dillon has a lead on a few women that fit Rose's description. I'm going to fly to New Mexico and check the first one out."

"What about your brother's wedding?" she heard herself ask. "Aren't you going to stay for that?"

"I'm not in much of a mood to celebrate. He'll do fine without me."

"But he's your brother."

"Yeah, well, life's tough. We all learn that sooner or later. I just wanted to let you know." He paused and then she heard the thud of his footsteps as he turned. "I'm sorry about everything."

Before she could stop herself, her hand went to the doorknob. She hauled open the door.

"Brent."

He turned at the sound of her voice. He wore faded jeans, a simple white T-shirt and a relieved expression.

"I know about Lila." She wasn't sure why she told him except that she'd been thinking about it all day. About him. His past. His pain. Her own. She knew he'd been trying to forge a connection with her the past few days and suddenly she wanted him to know that he'd done just that. "I saw her in your dream."

Confusion clouded his face and she wanted so much to reach out. But regardless of the fact that she understood him, that she loved him, she was still leaving. She'd worked too hard to get where she was. She couldn't just abandon it for a man.

Besides, he'd never asked her to. Sure, he'd stuck around but he'd never actually said the words.

Stay with me. Spend the rest of your life with me.

He wouldn't go that far because he was still scared.

"We're connected now. When I close my eyes and clear my head, I can hear what you're thinking. It's the damndest thing." Her gaze met his. "Such is the life of a vampire, right?"

He shook his head. "I don't know what you're talking about."

"I can hear you. In my head. Because we had sex."

"Sex doesn't forge that kind of connection. I've had sex with tons of women and none of them have been able to crawl inside my head. You're the first."

The only.

My one and only.

The truth hung between them for a long moment before he finally turned. "I guess I should get going. I've got a long drive."

Panic rushed through her as he walked away, the feeling growing with his every step. While she knew it was easier to let him leave now instead of later, suddenly she just wanted to seize this moment.

She went after him.

17

BRENT HAD JUST reached his car when he heard Abby's desperate voice.

"Wait."

Her plea crossed the distance to him and he turned.

She reached him a split-second later, her chest heaving, her eyes wild. As if she were about to lose the most important thing in the world to her and she was determined to hold on.

At least for a little while.

"I…" She caught her full bottom lip in her teeth and stared up at him. "Stay with me tonight. One more night. You can leave tomorrow," she added, dashing his hope that she wanted more with him.

A lifetime.

An eternity.

"Why?" If she didn't love him enough to give him forever, he wanted to hear it. He needed to hear it. To give him the strength to refuse her offer.

"Because I want to be with you." She swallowed, her voice small when she finally spoke. "I love you. I know that doesn't change anything, but I needed to say it. I need you to know it." Her hand touched his arm. "Stay with me tonight."

"And tomorrow?" He voiced his biggest fear.

She shrugged. "I don't know. I just know that I don't want you to go."

It wasn't the declaration he'd hoped for, but it was enough for now.

He swept her up and carried her back to the motel room. A sense of urgency rushed through him as he slammed and locked the door and set her on her feet.

Backing her up against the nearest wall, he grasped the hem of her T-shirt. He pulled it up and over her head and tossed it to the hardwood floor. His fingers went to the clasp of her bra and her breasts spilled free.

He dipped his head and drew one sensitive peak into his mouth, relishing the taste and knowing deep in his gut that he could never let her go after tonight.

He wouldn't.

He would fight for this. For her. For them both.

Abby closed her eyes against the wonderful pull of Brent's mouth on her bare breast. He sucked her so hard and so thoroughly, she sagged against him. Wetness flooded the sensitive flesh between her legs and drenched her panties. He drew on her harder, his jaw creating a powerful pull that she felt clear to her core. An echoing throb started in her belly, more intense with every rasp of his tongue, every nibble of his mouth.

The thought faded as she felt the razor-like sharpness against her sensitive flesh. Her body went stiff and he pulled away.

She opened her eyes and found herself staring up at him the way they'd been their last night together. A hot, wild, hungry *vampire*.

He stared down at her, into her, his eyes hot and vivid, his fangs fully visible. He didn't move. Rather, he waited, his body taut, his muscles stretched tight and she knew it took every bit of his strength and then some to hold himself in check.

But he did.

He held back for her, his body trembling with the effort.

She trailed her hand along his jaw, touched his bottom lip and smiled. And then she wrapped her arms around his neck and pulled him flush against her.

He licked at her pulse beat and nibbled as his hand slid into her sweats and between her legs. But he didn't bite her. Not yet.

No matter how much she wanted him to.

Heat flowed through her, pulsing along her nerve endings, heating her body until she felt as if she would explode. His fingers slid inside, plying her soft tissue and stirring the sweetest pressure.

He worked her until she moaned long and low and deep in her throat. Her body throbbed around him. Goosebumps chased up and down her arms. Her legs trembled. Her thighs clenched.

"Please," she murmured.

He plunged his fingers deeper and wetness gushed from her very center. She shivered and cried out.

He caught the sound with his mouth and she felt the sharpness of his fangs against her bottom lip. The sensation sent a ripple of excitement through her.

He pulled her close, his hands trailing down her bare back, stirring every nerve ending along the way. Fingers played at her waistband before slipping lower. His palms cupped her buttocks through the material of her sweats. He urged her up on her tiptoes until her pelvis cradled the massive erection beneath his zipper.

The feel of him sent a burst of longing through her and suddenly she couldn't get close enough, fast enough. She clawed at his T-shirt and wrapped her leg around his thigh. His erection rubbed against her sex and she moaned.

He tugged at the waistband of her sweats and pushed at the material until it slid over her hips, her thighs, to puddle around her ankles. His fingers snagged on the straps of her not-so-sexy panties and urged them down. Until she was completely naked.

He peeled off his shirt and unfastened his jeans. He shoved the denim down in one smooth motion and his erection sprang forward, huge and greedy and swollen. He pushed her onto the mattress, urged her legs apart and settled his erection flush against her.

He slowed down then, kissing her slowly, tenderly for a long moment. Sliding his hands beneath her bottom, he tilted her just so and with one powerful thrust, he slid deep inside.

Pleasure washed over her and forced her eyes closed. Her head fell back and she gave in to the delicious sensation of being filled to the brim with Brent Braddock.

"Open your eyes." His deep voice finally penetrated the desire beating at her temples and she complied.

Hunger blazed hot and intense in his gaze. He opened his mouth. His fangs glittered in the moonlight as he poised above her.

He was giving her one last chance to change her mind. She read the hesitation on his face, felt the hunger clenching his body. She arched her body and tilted her head, baring her neck, offering it to him. Proving beyond a doubt that she accepted him for what he was.

Who he was.

Not just a vampire, but a man.

A man she would never betray.

She wanted his trust. Even more, she wanted this connection with him. She wanted to take all that he offered and give everything back.

She wanted to love him. Completely and thoroughly.

If only for tonight.

He dipped his head. His mouth closed over the side of her neck where her pulse beat a frantic rhythm. He licked the spot, teasing and tasting, and then he opened his jaw wide. His fangs sank deep.

Oddly enough, it didn't hurt. She felt only a sharp prickle, followed by a rush of ecstasy so absolute and intense that it brought tears to her eyes.

But there was more.

He thrust into her, pushing deep with his body all

the while drawing on her with his mouth. The two sensations at the same time, sent her spiraling toward a place where she'd never been before. Higher and higher. The pressure sweeter and sweeter. Until she couldn't take any more. She cried out, splintering into a thousand pieces.

His entire body seemed to vibrate as she came apart. He trembled and buzzed, drinking in her power-infusing blood as he drank in the sexual energy that rushed from her lush body.

His mouth eased and he leaned back.

A fierce groan rumbled from his lips and he plunged deep and followed her over the edge. His body shook and bucked. A frantic heartbeat later, he collapsed atop her, his arms braced on either side of her head, his face buried in the crook of her neck.

His weight pressed her down, a sweet burden that made her chest hitch. She slid her arms around him and held for a few moments, until her heartbeat slowed and he rolled onto his back. He pulled her with him, cradling her close as if he never meant to let her go.

He would.

He was still leaving for New Mexico.

And she was walking away, as well. Rayne was coming home tomorrow and it would all be over. She would drag him back to South Carolina, away from Skull Creek and his new wife.

The thought had never bothered her before, until now.

Until Brent.

But Rayne had made his own bed. He'd run away when he could have easily stayed to face his situation. He could have done things right and returned to the woman he loved an honorable man.

He hadn't and so he had to face the consequences.

It was his fault. At the same time, a spiral of guilt went through her when she thought about breaking the news to his new bride, killing her newfound happiness.

But duty was more important.

Even if it didn't feel that way sometimes.

She ignored the depressing notion and focused on the warmth of Brent's arms. Snuggling deeper, she closed her eyes and tried not to think about tomorrow. Or about the all important fact that she would have to say goodbye.

18

THIS TIME IT WAS Abby who slid from the bed before the crack of dawn.

She tiptoed around the room and snatched up her clothes. Stuffing them into her suitcase, she pulled out the camouflage pants and T-shirt she'd buried her first day in town and dressed quickly. Quietly.

She'd just hoisted her duffel onto her shoulders and grabbed her boots when she spotted the red spandex dress laying on the floor where she'd tossed it all those nights ago. Her chest hitched and she had the insane urge to snatch it up and stuff it into her bag.

For what?

She would never wear it again. The dress had been a part of her fantasy and it was time to wake up now.

To leave.

She cast one last glance at the man sleeping on the bed.

He was sprawled completely naked on top of the covers, his arm flung above his head. Her gaze traveled the length of his body, pausing at all of her favorite spots before she worked her way up and drank in his face, his strong jaw and sensual lips. His lightly stubbled cheeks.

He looked like any other handsome, hunk of a man in the hazy gray that came just before dawn.

A man with needs and wants. Fears and insecurities.

And she was just a woman who felt those same things.

Once upon a time.

It was time to hide that woman away once again and get to work. Rayne was coming home today and while she had no clue when, she did have a hunch where he would go.

She intended to be ready and waiting when he arrived.

Unease niggled at her gut and she double-checked the weapon tucked away in a hidden pocket of her bag. Checking the chamber, she slid the gun into the back waistband of her pants and pulled her shirt down over it. Rayne wouldn't come quietly. Her gut told her that. And so she intended to be prepared for a fight.

She checked the blinds and secured the room against the bright light of day. Leaning over, she kissed Brent Braddock for the last time. She slipped from the motel room, locking the door behind her, and then headed for Rayne Montana's childhood home.

It was time to complete her mission and head back to South Carolina.

If only that thought was half as appealing as it used to be.

SHE WAS GONE.

Brent paced the floor of the motel room an hour later and ignored the exhaustion that tugged at his muscles. It was daylight and he needed to sleep. To rejuvenate.

She was gone. Friggin' gone.

He hadn't meant to fall asleep. But he'd been so tired and she'd been so warm and hell, that's what vampires did in the friggin' morning. They slept.

She'd packed up and hauled ass and he'd been none the wiser.

His gut clenched and awareness sizzled up and down his arms. A strange sensation that he knew all too well. He'd fought too many battles and chased too many outlaws not to recognize the current in the air.

Something bad was going to happen.

And he had no doubt it involved Abby, especially if she was headed to Rayne's old place.

She didn't have a clue what she was walking into. Neither did he, but he had a hunch. He'd tipped off Cody about Abby and he had no doubt that his brother had forewarned Rayne.

He'd hoped that the vampire would have the good sense to just run.

That's what Brent would have done, way back when.

No more. He was here. For better or worse.

He just wished his gut didn't keep telling him it was going to be 'worse'. He snatched up the phone and tried to call Cody, only his brother's voice mail picked up as expected. Cody was dead to the world.

And so was Abby if Brent didn't do something.

She might be able to hold her own in hand-to-hand combat, but Rayne was a vampire. And he wouldn't give up his new bride, his new life, without a fight. Of that Brent was certain.

If Abby had been his wife and they were building a life together, Brent would have fought until his last breath to preserve it and stay with her.

She wasn't. She'd made that painfully clear when she'd walked away this morning.

It was over.

She'd left.

And so they were right back to where they'd started despite what they'd shared last night. Blood and sex and a deeper connection that made him want to bust through the door and go to her.

His gaze went to the tell-tale stain on the pillow, proof that he'd bitten her. His nostrils flared and his mouth watered. He could still taste her. Even more, he could feel her. The determination that drove her. The fear of letting go and getting her heart broken and realizing she was as cold and emotionless as her father. The uncertainty of the future should she fail at the one thing she'd always been good at. The only thing.

They were linked now and as much as that should have bothered him, it didn't.

He loved her. He had from the first moment he'd spotted her at the Dairy Freeze. He'd just been too scared to admit it.

And she loved him.

But it didn't matter. Because she refused to take a chance on that love.

And she was about to walk right into the line of fire.

Rayne would fight. He would kill. Abby, no matter how strong, didn't stand a chance against a determined vampire. She would face off with him, but in the end, he would win.

The truth made Brent pace that much faster, praying for the time to pass quicker so that he could get to her before all hell broke loose.

If only he didn't have the sinking feeling that he was already too late.

SHE WAS WALKING into a trap. The truth struck as she stepped inside the ancient barn and noticed the footprint just in front of her. Just a smudge in the dust that no one else would have noticed except for Abby.

She came to a dead stop.

Her ears tuned to the sounds around her and then it struck her. There were no sounds. No early morning buzz of insects. No birds chirping in the distance. No sizzle of the early morning sun on the frost-covered ground. Nothing.

Just the stillness and the inexplicable feeling that someone was waiting for her.

The barn door slammed shut behind her, plunging the barn into near darkness, and Abby knew her hunch was right.

Someone was already here.

"I see you came back early," she called out, her gaze spanning left and right. "Who tipped you off?" She blinked, adjusting her eyes to the faint light. Only a spiral whispered through the cracks overhead and she wished she'd thought to grab her flashlight.

But then she'd been certain she would be one step ahead of him.

"It doesn't matter. All that matters is that you're here now and you're going back. Jimmy and Mac almost died because of you. Because you just took off and left them without any extra ammunition." She reminded him about their mission. They'd been doing recon, staking out a local militia. She'd taken half the team and circled back to an opposite vantage point. Rayne had followed so that he would know their location. He'd been expected to circle back around. To take extra weapons and join the two they'd left behind. To fight. "You left them there to die."

But they hadn't died.

They'd been captured.

They'd been spotted and attacked, and they'd run out of ammo in the first fifteen minutes trying to defend themselves. "You abandoned them."

"I didn't mean to." Rayne's voice carried from the dark rafters. "I couldn't help it. I couldn't get to them. I was attacked myself."

She had to keep him talking. Then she could

pinpoint his location and get the jump on him. "You were captured?"

"Changed." The voice came from the opposite side of the rafters this time and stopped her cold.

Wait a second.

She whirled, her gaze trained overhead, searching for a glimpsc. The hair on the back of her neck prickled and her hand went to the gun she'd stashed in the small of her back.

"I didn't have a choice. I had to leave the unit."

"For Lucy," she reminded him, eager to keep the conversation going. To find him in the darkness. Her interrogation certainly had nothing to do with the fact that she wanted to understand what had happened to him.

"There's no explanation for poor performance." Her father's voice echoed in her head. *"No room for mistakes or excuses."*

"Lucy came later. After what happened outside of Kabul."

"I don't understand."

"I don't expect you would. I'm AWOL and you're worried about covering your ass. It's that simple. You've always been a stickler for following procedure. I had no doubt you would show up here. I just didn't think it would be so quick. I figured you would follow my fake paper trail like the MPs."

"I'm smarter than they are and I know you better."

"Then you know that I'm not going back with you. If you're as smart as you think you are, you'll walk away and forget you ever found me."

"That's not a possibility."

"I don't think you understand." From the corner of her eye, she saw a flash of black and then just like that, he was standing in front of her. "You don't get to make the call on that, chief. I do."

"You *are* going back," she told him. With the flick of her wrist, she pulled the gun free and aimed it at him.

He smiled. "You really don't understand what happened to me, do you?"

She cocked the trigger and held steady. "Should I?"

"Considering you've been shacking up with a vampire for the past few days, I would expect that you might."

The comment sent her reeling, but she didn't so much as blink an eye. She held her hand steady. The gun ready.

Her gaze narrowed. "How do you know about Brent?"

"He's one of us."

His words echoed, followed by his earlier comments.

"Attacked."

"Changed."

"You're a vampire," she murmured as the pieces all fell together and started to fit. "You didn't leave the unit willingly. You were attacked."

"And killed. But then my attacker decided to really punish me by feeding me his blood, so here I am." His gaze met hers and she saw a flicker of the old Rayne. The man who'd fought beside her and had her back for so many years. "I had to leave. I couldn't endanger the team. I didn't understand what had happened to me. I just knew that something was wrong and that I couldn't control it. The hunger was overwhelming. It still is at times, but it's different now. I call the shots. I learned that from Cody."

"Brent's brother?"

Rayne nodded. "My wife is Miranda's sister." He held up his hands and stepped toward her. "I don't want to hurt you, Abby, but I will. I won't leave my wife to go back and face charges for something that wasn't my fault." He took a step forward, but she refused to be intimidated.

She held her ground. "You can explain what happened."

"And end up in a county hospital somewhere,

locked in a padded room? That's not going to happen."

"They won't think you're crazy when they find out there are others like you."

"No, they'll torch the entire town." Determination fired his expression. "I won't endanger my friends. And I won't let you jeopardize everything they've worked so hard to build. This is their home. My home."

"So what are you saying? That you're going to kill me?"

"That you're going to walk away from here and forget all about me." He stared deep into her eyes as if trying to impress his will.

Which was exactly what he wanted to do, she realized.

It didn't work for him any more than it had for Brent. He glared and stepped forward.

"Don't." She held the gun steady. "I'll pull the trigger if I have to."

"No, you won't."

"What makes you so sure?"

"Because I won't let you," came the soft, determined voice directly behind Abby. "I won't let you take my husband and punish him for something he didn't do."

A crack on the head punctuated the sentence.

Abby felt her knees wobble and the ground tremble. And then everything went black.

19

BRENT FELT THE BLOW to the back of his head and he staggered to his knees. The floor shook and for a long moment, his vision clouded.

He had the sudden image of Abby crumpled on the dirt floor and then it disappeared.

His nerves stopped prickling and dread settled in the pit of his stomach.

He forced himself to his feet and walked over to the window. A quick peek and his fingers started to smoke. Pain shot through him, but it was nothing compared to the ache in his chest because he could no longer feel Abby.

The connection had been broken.

She'd been broken.

The realization plagued him as he paced for the

next few hours, waiting and hoping he would feel her again.

Her feelings.

Her thoughts.

Something.

He felt nothing and finally the waiting was too much. His gaze scrambled around the room before focusing on the blanket. He snatched it up, draped it over his head and grabbed his keys.

And then he did the only thing he could think of.

He hauled open the door and went after her.

"I DIDN'T MEAN to hit her that hard." The woman's voice peeled back the layer of sleep that smothered Abby and pounded through her already pounding head.

"You did what you had to do. She had a gun."

"I know. But I don't think she would have used it," the woman insisted.

"You don't know Abby." It was Rayne's voice this time. "She does what she has to do to get the job done. It's reassuring when you're in the field. Not so much when you're holed up in a barn."

"I knew we shouldn't have come here."

"We didn't have a choice. She would have found us eventually. If not here, then somewhere else. It was better we faced her now. We're just lucky Cody was able to warn us."

Silence settled for a few moments before Abby felt a tentative touch at the back of her head. Soft fingers prodded, checking to see the damage that had been done.

"At least there's no bleeding."

"Stop worrying about it. The longer she's out, the bigger a headstart we'll get."

"She's tied up. Even if she comes to, she can't do anything. Speaking of which, maybe we should loosen the ropes a little. I don't want to cut off her circulation."

"You worry too much." Rayne's voice was softer this time and Abby watched through barely closed eyes as he touched his wife's face. "She'll be okay. We'll stash her over behind the hay bales and then we'll get out of here. By the time she wakes up, we'll be long gone."

"Where will we go?"

"I don't know yet, but we'll figure something out. I'm sorry about your school. I know how much Monday meant to you."

"Not half as much as you."

The woman touched her lips to his and for a split second, the world faded. They forgot all about Abby and the fact that her hand was slowly moving toward the knife that sat only a few inches away.

Abby's hand stalled as she watched Rayne hug the voluptuous blonde. Her own chest hitched and she thought about Brent and the fact that she'd walked out on him rather than risk her heart, her career, her life.

This woman had chosen to take the risk. To gamble everything for the man she loved. And here she was, losing everything, yet it didn't seem to matter.

He was all that mattered to her.

And she was all that mattered to him.

Regret knifed at her as she realized that she might never get the chance to take such a risk with Brent. And while that would have been okay a half hour ago, it wasn't now.

Not after seeing two people fight so hard to be together. To stay together.

Abby suddenly wanted to take the risk if it meant having even half of the happiness she saw in front of her.

She shifted her attention to the knife and inched forward. Her fingers had just clasped the handle when Rayne finally noticed.

He flew at her, snatching the knife from her hand and throwing her onto her back. A hiss sizzled in the air and his mouth opened. His fangs pulled back and she knew she'd pissed him off royally. This was it.

The end of the line.

She clamped her eyes shut and braced herself.

But he didn't rip her to shreds. Instead, the barn door crashed open.

In a flash, Rayne flew backwards and Brent leaned over her.

At least she thought it was Brent. Smoke surrounded him, his face red and charred, his hands nearly unrecognizable.

"You're okay," he murmured, his green eyes clouded with pain. But there was something else in them, as well. Relief glimmered, hot and bright, and she knew that he wasn't as destroyed as he looked. "I was so worried about you."

"I'm okay."

"You shouldn't have left—" he started, but the words ended in a fierce groan as Rayne grabbed him by the back of the neck and tossed him to the far side of the building.

Hay scattered and dust smoked. Brent stumbled, stunned for a long moment before he seemed to gather his wits.

With a furious cry, he retaliated and the two vampires went at each other for several moments before a gunshot exploded and cracked open a piece of ceiling.

A circle of sunlight spilled down into the room and both men jumped back out of the burning blaze.

"Stop!" Abby heard her own voice and realized her gun trembled between her bound hands. "Get away from him," she told Rayne who stood dangerously close to Brent.

She aimed the gun at Lucy, intent on making her point. Rayne's eyes flared for a quick second, but then he backed away.

Brent swayed for a few seconds, but then the floor seemed to give way beneath him. He toppled over in a heap of charred flesh and panic rushed through Abby.

"Untie me," she cried, motioning to Lucy. She held the gun at the woman's forehead, determined to do whatever she had to do to get to Brent. The blonde obeyed, working at the ropes for what seemed like an eternity. Finally, Abby was free.

She struggled to her feet, the gun still pointed at Lucy.

"I'll go back with you," Rayne said quietly. "Just don't hurt her."

"I'm not going to hurt her." She tamped down the

fear rushing through her and turned the gun upside down. She handed it over to the blonde, then turned away.

Her gaze riveted on Brent, she rushed toward him.

She dropped to her knees beside him and gathered his limp body in her arms.

"Don't leave me," she murmured, her gaze roaming his body. He was so badly burned that she couldn't imagine him climbing behind the wheel and making it all the way out here, much less surviving. "Please."

It had been the exact plea she'd whispered to Hockey Hunk all those years ago, but this was different. This wasn't the naïve love she'd felt way back when.

This was as real as it could get. She loved Brent. He was her life. Her love. Her man.

She was his woman.

And she wasn't letting him go.

Her eyes blurred then and she blinked, feeling the tears slipping down her cheeks and not caring one way or the other who saw her or whether they thought she was weak.

She was weak compared to Brent.

"I walked out on you. You had no obligation to me. You shouldn't have risked your own neck."

"Sometimes it's worth taking a risk. You're worth it." He gazed up at her, into her and this time she let him.

She didn't put up any fences. She didn't have to. She loved him. And while she'd been hesitant to believe that he really and truly loved her back, there was no doubt in her mind now. He'd braved the sunlight for her.

"I love you," she murmured.

"I know." He touched her face. "I've always known and now so do you." Then he closed his eyes one final time.

20

"DRINK UP."

The deep, familiar voice pushed into Brent's head and lured him back to reality.

He forced his eyes open. His head throbbed and the light hurt his eyes. Even more, his skin felt like he'd been set on fire. Pain gripped him like a vise, clamping tighter, building the pressure and urging him back toward the sweet peace of oblivion.

"Come on, bro. Stay with me long enough to get this down." A hand slid under Brent's aching head and the hard edge of a glass pressed against his cracked and swollen lips.

The first few drops of intoxicating heat touched his tongue and his gut twisted. His skin started to tingle. Then the hunger took control. Whereas he hadn't been able to move a muscle just a moment ago, an instinct as old as time took over and he reached out. His hands reached for the glass and he held on, his mouth open, eager for the sweet salvation drenching his taste buds.

"Easy. You'll make yourself sick drinking the bottled stuff so fast."

"More," Brent groaned when he finished the last drop of the life-renewing liquid.

His head dropped back to the pillow as he waited for Cody to slice open another bag of blood and refill his glass.

He closed his eyes, trying to ignore the pain that beat at his temples. He hadn't had nearly enough sustenance to heal. Rather, he'd consumed the minimal amount to clear the cobwebs fogging his brain.

His heart sped, beating a fast, furious rhythm as he started to think. To remember.

The images started back at the motel. He felt the hardwood floor beneath his feet, the anxiety ripping up and down his spine because Abby had walked away and he couldn't go after her—

"Holy shit." He bolted upright, only to be knocked back down by a rush of pain that gripped every nerve and had him gnashing his teeth.

"Take it easy. It's only been a few hours since Rayne brought you here. You need to heal."

"Where is he?"

"He went home with Lucy once the sun set. Until then, they were stuck in that barn with you. He's okay, but he got a little burned, thanks to the hole in the roof. Now stop talking and have another drink." Cody held up the glass. "This stuff works, but not as well as the real thing. Unfortunately, it's all we have at the moment."

He handed the glass over and Brent took it. He gulped the contents and handed the glass back.

"You need to get some sleep. You'll feel better tomorrow night." Cody went to kill the light, but Brent stopped him.

"I can't sleep." His body tensed and suddenly he needed to move. He forced himself upright, pushing his mangled back up against the wall. The movement felt like he'd taken a sharp knife right between his shoulder blades and he clenched his teeth. A hiss sizzled past his lips.

His gaze skittered around the basement and for the first time, he noted the big screen TV sitting against the far wall. A red bow sat center stage, along with several boxes of surround sound equipment.

"Where did that come from?" he groaned.

"It was a wedding gift from the guys last night. Garret, Dillon and Jake took me to see the bull riding preliminaries over in Travis County to celebrate my last night as a free man."

The party Brent had been responsible for. He'd missed it, just like he'd missed the past one hundred or so years with his little brother because he'd been too busy keeping his distance and staying on the move.

Afraid to get close. To connect.

For fear he'd lose it all over again.

That was the real reason he kept running. He'd had everything way back when and in the blink of an eye, it had been gone. The pain had nearly destroyed him.

So he'd pushed it all away and bricked himself up behind his hard-ass persona, pretending like he didn't care. He'd been at the point that he'd actually stopped caring altogether.

Because it was easier.

But there was nothing easy about the emptiness that sat in the middle of his chest as he stared up and saw the disappointment in Cody's eyes.

"The wedding is tonight." Brent noticed the dark blue slacks and the crisp white shirt his brother wore and he damned himself a thousand times over.

"Three hours and counting." He grinned, but the expression didn't quite touch his eyes. "I hate it that you won't be able to be there, but then, you're not really into weddings anyway."

No, he was into running and keeping his distance and being a bonafide shit.

That's how he felt at the moment. Not just outside, but inside, too.

"Rest up," Cody told him. He set the glass in his hand on the small nightstand and started to turn.

"She's gone, isn't she?" Brent voiced the one question he'd been wanting to ask since he'd first opened his eyes.

"Actually, she's right here." The soft voice crossed the distance to him and his heart lurched.

It couldn't be.

That's what he told himself, but there was no denying the sweet scent of strawberries that filled his head and the frantic heartbeat that echoed in his ears.

His chest hitched and every nerve in his body tensed. He turned. And sure enough, he found Abby standing in the doorway.

"I'll leave you in charge," Cody told Abby, handing her what was left of the bag of blood. "Miranda will kill me if I'm late." Cody ducked out and suddenly it was just the two of them.

"So this is where you've been sleeping when you're not at the motel." Abby swept a glance around the large room. There was very little furniture except for the media stuff sitting in the corner but she had a quick vision of what it would look like with a woman's touch. She couldn't help but smile. "Cody did a good job."

"Yeah," Brent groaned and her heart paused.

He still looked ravaged, but the healing process had already started. His skin still looked red and raw, but it wasn't as disfiguring as it had been before. His hair had started to grow back and she knew by the following day, he would be back to his old self.

Provided he fed, that is.

She reached for the hem of her T-shirt.

"What are you doing?"

"What does it look like I'm doing?" She pulled the cotton up and over her head. She wasn't wearing a bra tonight and the first whisper of air against her nipples brought them to throbbing awareness.

A rush of insecurity welled over her, but she was determined to do this. While she knew he loved her enough to risk everything, she'd yet to be completely open with him. She wanted him to know what he was getting into. And then if he still wanted her, well, they would cross that bridge when they came to it.

"I know I did a pretty risqué striptease the other night," she told him, "but that wasn't really me." She dropped the white cotton to the floor and bent to unlace her boots.

She caught her bottom lip and gathered her courage. "I'm not into fancy clothes or sexy lingerie."

A few frantic tugs of her fingers and she toed off the black monsters. "I've never really been comfortable with all that stuff." She hooked her fingers in the waistband of her camo pants and pushed them down to her ankles. Her panties followed until she was completely naked. "I usually go for fatigues and combat boots. And sometimes I even pick my teeth, but that's beside the point."

"Which is?"

"I'm willing to take a chance on you, on us, but only if you realize what you're getting into. I'm not the kind of woman who freaks out when she sees a spider or waits for a man to open the car door for her. I deal with my own spiders and open my own doors and while I can't say that dressing up was all that bad, for the most part I like to be comfortable. This is me. Take it or leave it."

Brent let his gaze rove over Abby and for the first time, he didn't feel the pain gripping his insides. Instead, he felt frustration. He'd nearly turned himself to dust to protect her and she *still* didn't get it.

Talk about stubborn.

He ground his teeth together and forced himself to his feet despite the flash of panic on her face. Stepping forward, he closed the distance between them until they stood only a few inches apart.

"You look pretty comfortable right now," he pointed out, her nipples rosy and tight.

She glanced down as if only now realizing she'd stripped bare and her cheeks flushed. "I wasn't sure which would help the most. Sex or blood."

"I'm thinking both," he murmured. And then he touched his lips to hers.

21

BOTH.

The word sparked her memory and pulled her back to the previous night. To his mouth feasting on her neck while his body plunged into hers.

"That's one way to do it." Brent's deep voice pushed into her thoughts and she realized he'd read her mind. Instinctively, she put the wall up, but he shook his head.

"Don't shut me out all the time. It's nice to know what you're thinking once in a while."

She relaxed and stared into his eyes. "So what am I thinking right now?"

"You're wondering if I'm going to bite your neck this time."

"Are you?"

"Maybe." He backed her up against the nearest wall and trailed a finger down her throat.

She swallowed.

"Or maybe I'll try it here." He touched the underside of one breast and traced her ripe nipple. "Then again, I might nibble here." A few tantalizing touches and he slid his palm down, over the soft skin of her abdomen, to the inside of one thigh. "Or here." Her breath caught as he dipped a finger between her legs.

"That would be good." The last word caught as he slipped another finger into her steamy heat and wiggled until a gasp bubbled from her full lips.

"Or maybe I'll try all of them." A hiss worked its way up his throat as he bared his fangs. His body trembled and he touched his mouth to her ripe throat.

She arched her neck, the movement pushing the soft flesh against his fangs and pricking her skin. Her gasp sizzled in the air as a sweet drop of blood bubbled and slid down the luscious curve of her neck.

Brent caught it, relishing the taste before he leaned down to lick the source. A few sweet drops spilled onto his tongue as he laved the prick point clean.

Need twisted inside of him and hunger seized control.

He leaned down and latched onto the ripe tip of her nipple. His fangs sank into the tender flesh of her areola and his groin tightened. Blood spurted into his mouth for a long, delicious moment before he managed to stop himself.

This wasn't just about drinking and healing. It was about branding her as his. Once and for all.

He dropped to his knees and slid his palms around to cup her ass. He gripped her leg and hooked it over his shoulder to tilt her more fully toward him. Then he licked her, tracing the seam of the slick flesh between her legs before he parted her.

She closed her eyes and flattened her palms against the wall, hesitant to touch him because she didn't want to cause him pain.

He knew that because he felt it. He felt her. The pleasure rushing through her and the maddening thought that she was going to die if he didn't take a bite out of her.

Now.

He drew her clit into his mouth and she jumped. He suckled her for a long moment before replacing his lips with his fingers. Shifting his mouth to the tender inside of one thigh, he licked the soft spot. The smell of sex filled his nostrils and fed the already ravenous appetite gripping him. A growl rumbled past his lips. He sank his fangs deep and drew on her.

Convulsions gripped her and her legs gave out, but Brent caught her.

He would always catch her. From this day forward.

A shudder ripped through him as he started to draw on her. Her essence filled his mouth and the tingling energy of her climax zapped him at every point of contact.

But it wasn't enough. He wanted to be inside of her. He needed to be inside of her.

Pulling back, he got to his feet and swept her up. He could feel his strength returning, his body recharging. And while the pain was still there, it faded in the rush of need that gripped him.

He urged her down onto the cot and followed. He skimmed her body, his fingertips brushing her neck, her collarbone, the slope of her breasts, the indentation of her ribs. She was his now and she knew it. And the realization made him all the more desperate for her.

He lowered his head and drew her nipple fully into the moist heat of his mouth.

He suckled her long and deep, until her lips parted and a gasp escaped.

Reaching down, he traced the soft folds between her legs before pushing inside just a fraction. She quivered and he lingered, suckling her breasts, first one then the other.

"I want you," he murmured. "I don't care what you wear or don't wear. I don't care if you get rid of your own spiders or open your own doors or wear a pair of high heels ever again. I want you." He pushed his finger deep to punctuate his statement. "Are we clear?"

"Yes." Abby stared up into his gaze and a rush of joy went through her, because she finally believed him. And she was going nuts thanks to his expert hands. She lifted her pelvis, focusing on the pleasure that gripped her as she worked her body around his decadent finger. She swayed from side to side, her movements frantic, desperate.

"I love you." The words pierced the humming in her ears and she went still. Her eyes opened to find him staring down at her. Waiting.

"I love you, too," she said.

His mouth swooped down and captured hers in a deep kiss that went way beyond anything she'd ever felt before. He coaxed her open and slid his tongue inside and drew on her as if he couldn't get enough. He plundered her mouth with his, exploring and savoring. The air stalled in her lungs and her heart sped faster. A few more seconds, and he tore his mouth from hers.

He slid down her body, now slick from the fever that raged inside of her, leaving a blazing path with the velvet tip of his tongue. With a gentle pressure, he parted her thighs and stroked the soft folds between her legs.

She was wet and throbbing and the discovery made him swear softly. Tremors seized her when she felt his warm breath blowing softly on the inside of her thigh. His tongue darted out, laving the tiny prick points where he'd drunk from her, and it was like being zapped by a live wire. Pleasure crackled through her and she gasped. She clutched at the sheets, desperate to keep her hands to herself since his body had yet to heal completely.

She wasn't sure what happened after that. She only knew that one minute he had his jeans on and the next, he was settling his naked body between her damp thighs.

With a swift thrust of his hips, he impaled her on his rigid length. Sensation overwhelmed her at first. The feel of him so hot and thick pulsing inside her nearly made her come then and there, but then he withdrew and the sensation eased just enough for her to catch her breath.

He slid back in a second time, his hard length rasping her insides and she caught her bottom lip. He kept moving, his body pumping into hers, pushing her higher with each delicious plunge. She lifted her hips, meeting him thrust for thrust, eager to give back as much as he was giving her.

She stared up at him, into the brilliant purple of his gaze and gave herself over to the convulsions that gripped her. He followed her over the edge, a moment later, in a rush of warmth.

They lay in each other's arms for several long moments afterwards, before she leaned up on one elbow and eyed him.

Sure enough, he looked a hundred times better than when she'd first walked into the room. The redness was fading. He was healing.

"Should we do it again?"

He turned his brilliant green gaze on her. "Darlin', we're going to do it so many times, you won't be able to see straight."

"Is that a promise?"

"One I fully intend to keep." He touched his lips to hers in a long, lingering kiss that filled her with such joy she felt her eyes sting. "You don't have to leave the military. I'll follow you anywhere, Abby. I can hire a private investigator to do the legwork and find Rose if I have to."

"You don't have to do that. I understand your need to get to the bottom of what happened."

"Not if it means losing you. I want you to be happy. And if going back makes you happy—"

"I wasn't happy," she cut in, pressing a finger to his lips to silence him. "I was hiding. I threw myself into my career so I wouldn't have to think about everything I was missing. A family. A home. I want both of them, Brent." She shook her head. "I'm not re-enlisting. I'll take the blame for Rayne's MIA and let them force me out with a dishonorable discharge. Then I'll come back here. Or I'll follow you to New Mexico. Or wherever you need to go. We're a team."

"It doesn't seem fair for you to take the blame for Rayne."

"What isn't fair is forcing him to take the blame for something that wasn't his fault. He doesn't deserve that. He deserves a little happiness. We all do." She grinned and eyed him. "What?"

"I never figured you for a hopeless romantic."

"You don't know everything."

"Is that so?"

"You need something to look forward to, otherwise forever is going to be a really long time."

"Not nearly long enough." He leaned down and

caught her in a deep, searing kiss that told her he was feeling much better. "Before we go for round two, there's something I need to do first."

22

AN HOUR LATER, Brent found Cody pacing the back hallway of the Sawyer Ranch as he waited his cue to join the guests and the justice of the peace behind the house where the ceremony was to be held.

Surprise gleamed on Cody's face when he spotted his older brother. "What are you doing here?"

"Being your best man." Brent shrugged on the jacket Miranda had thrust at him the moment he'd driven up with Abby. "If the job's still open, that is."

Cody gave him a questioning glance before his face split into a grin. "I thought you didn't do weddings?"

"This isn't just any wedding. My little brother is getting married for the first time." He caught his brother's gaze. "And the last time."

Cody's smile widened and a warmth spread through Brent.

He flexed his shoulders and, thanks to Abby, felt only a small stinging between his shoulder blades. Her blood flowed through his veins and her thoughts rooted in his head.

"Don't forget the tie."

He pulled the scrap of silk from his pocket and wound it around his neck just as Garret signaled them from the patio doorway.

"It's time."

Brent finished knotting the tie and turned toward his brother. "You ready?"

"I was born ready."

He clapped his brother on the back. "Then let's go get you married, hoss."

* * * * *

THE BRADDOCK BOYS: TRAVIS

BY
KIMBERLY RAYE

All the characters in this book have no existence outside the imagination of
the author, and have no relation whatsoever to anyone bearing the same name
or names. They are not even distantly inspired by any individual known or
unknown to the author, and all the incidents are pure invention.

First published in Great Britain 2011
by Mills & Boon, an imprint of Harlequin (UK) Limited,
Eton House, 18-24 Paradise Road, Richmond, Surrey TW9 1SR

© Kimberly Raye Groff 2011

ISBN: 978 0 263 88076 2

14-0911

Harlequin (UK) policy is to use papers that are natural, renewable and
recyclable products and made from wood grown in sustainable forests. The
logging and manufacturing processes conform to the legal environmental
regulations of the country of origin.

Printed and bound in Spain
by Blackprint CPI, Barcelona

Dear Reader,

They're baaaaaaack...

Travis Braddock is a wild and wicked cowboy with a ripped bod, a knack for horses and enough sex appeal to melt even the toughest woman's resolve. He's also a 150-year-old vampire dead set on revenge. His plans are derailed, however, when he meets wedding planner Holly Simms.

A three-time loser when it comes to men, Holly has given up on finding her own happily ever after. The last thing she wants is forever. Luckily, the sexy cowboy who arrives in Skull Creek to attend her latest wedding has *temporary* written all over him.

I hope you enjoy reading Travis and Holly's story as much as I enjoyed writing it! As a writer, the Blaze line has always been near and dear to my heart. I love intense, powerful stories that push limits and unearth the sensuality buried deep down inside all of us. For me, love and lust go hand in hand and it's been a dream come true exploring them both for the past ten years. Whether it's cowboys or vampires, I've been able to portray my characters with real passion and true emotion, and that means the world to me. My heartfelt thanks to Harlequin & Mills & Boon for allowing my stories to be a part of such a wonderful collection of books.

Kimberly Raye

This book is dedicated to the real
Holly and her hubby Tim.
Thanks for being such great friends!

1

THERE WERE WOMEN EVERYWHERE.

That was the first thought that struck as Travis Braddock pulled up at the front gate of the CB Ranch. The lawn in front of the sprawling two-story house had been set up for an outdoor ceremony, complete with a red carpet for the bride, huge flower arrangements and lots of free standing candelabras because it was an evening affair. He'd expected a small shindig, but there were at least a hundred people crowded into the rows of white chairs that flanked either side of the aisle. Mostly females

Hungry females.

A mix of perfume, lush sensuality and raw need wafted through the open window of the Land Rover and teased his nostrils. His groin tightened and he stiffened.

An overabundance of women was usually a good thing.

Particularly for a one hundred and fifty year old vampire who fed off sex as ravenously as he did blood. But Travis wasn't here because of the beast that lived and breathed inside of him.

Tonight was all about revenge.

He'd spent the last one hundred and fifty years blaming his three brothers for the massacre that had killed their family while they'd been off raiding for the Confederacy. He pointed the finger at his youngest brother Cody because he'd run off and joined the army in the first place, forcing the rest of the brothers to leave home just to keep an eye on him. He held Brent responsible because he'd refused to call it quits a week early when the war had been all but lost anyway. And he resented his oldest brother Colton because he'd forced them to detour to Austin to file an official report about their last raid before heading home to discover the carnage.

He'd blamed his brothers. But the real blame lay with his sister-in-law. Rose was the one responsible.

A traitor.

A *killer.*

He ignored that tiny niggle that told him he was jumping the gun. That maybe there was some crazy explanation for what had happened. That maybe, just *maybe,* Rose Braddock hadn't set fire to the Braddock spread and fed her own family to the wolves all those years ago.

His nephew had died in that tragic fire. So had his

mother. A half dozen ranch hands. And Rose herself, or so they'd all thought. The entire place had been a blazing inferno when Travis and his brothers had ridden in.

They'd been too late to save anyone that fateful night, even themselves. One minute they'd been trotting along, making plans for the future and the next, they'd found themselves smack dab in the middle of a fiery nightmare. Before they'd had a chance to figure out what was going on, much less rescue anyone, Travis and his three brothers had been attacked from behind and left for dead.

They'd died that night. But they'd also been reborn. Thanks to an ancient vampire who'd happened upon the scene and given the Braddock brothers a second chance.

He'd done the same for Rose.

That's the story Cody had recently uncovered when he'd tracked down their maker right here in Skull Creek, Texas. Rose hadn't died in the fire as originally thought. Rather, she'd fled the scene with a man. The pair had been attacked a few miles away by Indians. Garret Sawyer had arrived after the attack and done the only thing he could to help the innocent couple who'd been left for dead by a band of Commanches. He'd turned them, just as he'd turned the Braddocks.

Innocent?

Like hell. Rose wasn't the loving sister-in-law,

the caring mother, the perfect daughter-in-law they'd thought. She'd fooled the entire family. Every damned one of them.

But not for long.

Cody had sent a letter explaining the truth about Rose and the all-important fact that he now knew her whereabouts.

The news had chased Travis around a few weeks before finally catching up with him at the Bar T Ranch in Montana. He'd been hired on to break some horses for the owner and was smack dab in the middle of a midnight session when one of the hands had flagged him down with the frayed envelope.

Inside had been a brief description of the incriminating evidence Cody had on Rose, the news that he'd finally found her and—much to Travis's astonishment—a piece of engraved cardstock requesting his presence at tonight's event.

A bonafide wedding *invitation*. After all the bad blood between them.

He still couldn't believe Cody had invited him. Any more than he could believe his brother was fool enough to think he would ever be satisfied with just one woman. He needed sex as much as he needed the blood. It was a need that was fierce. Intense. All-consuming. The hunger didn't lend itself to monogamy, that was for damn sure. No matter what delusion Cody was operating under, he wasn't the marrying kind. None of them were.

Travis knew that firsthand. He'd tried to settle down with one woman. To pretend he hadn't changed that fateful night, that he didn't yearn for sex the way a man craved his next breath. He'd tried, all right. And he'd failed. And Amelia, his childhood sweetheart, had gone to her grave hating his guts because he'd cheated on her.

He wouldn't do that to another woman. He wouldn't make promises he couldn't keep.

But Travis wasn't here to warn his baby bro about the nature of the beast, and he sure as hell wasn't here as a guest. He was here for information.

For forgiveness.

The thought struck and he drop-kicked it right back out of his head.

Even if he did regret the fallout with his brothers—which he didn't—there were too many bad feelings between them to make amends now. He'd turned on them and they'd turned their back on him. That was that.

Travis stared through the windshield at the lavish spread. His hyper sensitive sight zoomed in on the rose archway where his youngest brother stood facing a petite blonde. To his left, stood his other brother Brent. That sucker-punched Travis right in the gut for a long moment. Brent was the last person

Travis expected to see standing next to Cody. Brent wasn't the stand-up type. He was wild. Free. Selfish.

Then.

But now?

There was no denying that he was here. Cody's best man. His friend. His *brother*.

Travis's chest hitched as he watched Brent hand over the ring. The gold band slid into place and Cody sealed the deal with a kiss. And just like that, the ceremony ended.

Which meant Travis was too late once again.

If he'd come to see the exchange of vows, that is, which he sure as hell hadn't. He was here for Rose. To find out her whereabouts.

Nothing else mattered.

He swallowed against the tightness in his throat and climbed out of the Land Rover. Walking through the gate, he crossed the massive lawn. It seemed his baby bro had done pretty well for himself riding bulls on the PBR circuit. Travis had kept tabs on him and knew Cody had won a few championships, but he hadn't realized the size of the payouts.

Obviously they had been big. Real big.

He closed the distance to the throng of guests and made his way toward the archway where the bride and groom stood amid a shower of camera flashes.

Just before he reached his target, a group of elderly women pushed in front of him to admire the bride's dress. He tried to slip through, but the women were intent on getting an eyeful.

"Doesn't she look lovely?" one woman said.

"That dress must have cost a small fortune."

"I heard her new beau took care of the tab AND bought her this place as a wedding present."

"Can we stop all this lollygagging and go find a seat? My bunions are killing me?"

"Excuse me," Travis said to one blue-haired woman as he tried to make his way past her.

She turned a pair of cataract-clouded gray eyes on him and smiled. "My, my but you're a strapping young man." *"You remind me of my dear, sweet, departed Walter before he kicked the bucket."*

The last thought echoed loud and clear in Travis's head as he made eye contact with the woman and his chest hitched.

Her name was Gladys Martin and she lived at the local senior's home where the bride worked as the activities coordinator. Miranda had personally invited all of the ladies at the home and had even taken them to Austin on a shopping trip so they could all buy something special to wear on her big day. She'd also promised to take a picture with each and every one of them, which was why Gladys was waiting in line.

Travis tipped his hat and grinned. "I hate to trouble you, ma'am, but I need to scoot by you and have a quick word with the groom if you don't mind."

She looked as if she wanted to protest, but then Travis stared deep into her eyes for a long moment and acceptance sparked. She smiled. "Of course, dear."

She started to move, but then an ancient little man with a bald head and a mean expression stepped in front of her and broke the temporary spell Travis had cast.

"Hold your britches there, sonny." Arbor Crabtree poked Travis in the chest with a bony finger. "We all want our picture taken with Miranda and we're not about to be sideswiped by some young buck who cain't wait his turn. You'll get back to the end of the line lickety-split if you know what's good for you."

While Travis's charm worked with the females, he was out of luck when it came to men. Particularly Arbor. He was a two-time decorated war veteran who'd carved up an enemy sniper with his witling knife in a one-on-one battle back in 1942. He still had the knife to this day, carrying it in his pocket for bragging rights.

He also had a hemorrhoid that was making him even crankier than the fact that he'd lost at checkers to Milton Decker earlier that afternoon.

The point? Arbor was not about to be crossed by man or vampire.

Travis held up his hands in surrender. "I'm not trying to put any one out, sir. I've just come a long way is all."

"So did I. Do you know how far away we had to park? Why, this place is busier than the Dairy Queen on senior citizen night."

"They give free ice cream to anyone over sixty-five," one of the women added.

"And whipped cream."

"That sounds real nice," Travis said. "But I just need to talk to my—"

"Is there a problem here?" The soft, feminine voice slid into his ear and cut him off mid-sentence. He turned toward the female who appeared on his left, her hands on her hips, her blue eyes drilling into him.

She was at least a head shorter than he was, with long, blond hair that had been swept up into a tight, no frills ponytail. She wore a knee-length black skirt and a plain white button up blouse. Sensible black pumps. *Boring.*

That's what he told himself. No legs up to here or breasts out to there.

At the same time, she had the most incredible eyes he'd ever seen. Pale blue with just a hint of green around the edges. Color so translucent that, for a split second, he saw only his own reflection in their sparkling depths.

No thoughts. None of her personal stats. Nothing. Not even her name.

Before Travis could delve deeper, she shifted her attention to the old man.

"What's going on, Mr. Crabtree?"

"This whippersnapper is trying to cut in line," the man declared. "But Miranda promised me I could have the first picture. I cain't stand for long without my arthritis acting up."

"Mine, too," a woman added. "I've got seconds."

"And I've got a corn on my big toe that's aching something fierce so I get to go third."

The pale blue eyes darkened just a hint, killing the reflection that had him so mesmerized and opening the door so that he could see straight into her thoughts.

Her name was Holly Simms. Mid-twenties. She was a wedding planner who loved dogs, Reeses' Peanut Butter cups and her job. Except when she had to deal with stubborn guests or a lying, cheating, line-cutting cowboy.

Ouch. "I wasn't trying to cut in front of anyone." He shrugged. "I'm just here to talk to the groom."

"And we're here to talk to the bride," Arbor added. "She promised us pictures and I'm not moving 'til I get my picture."

"Me either," a woman added.

"Neither am I."

"You'll all get your pictures. I promise." Holly turned on Travis. "Excuse me? What did you say your name was?"

"I didn't say, but it's Travis. Travis Braddock."

When her gaze sparked, he added, "I'm the groom's brother."

Her mind seemed to rifle for a memory before recognition dawned and she frowned. "The one who didn't RSVP?"

"My job keeps me really busy."

Too busy for your own brother's wedding?

The question rang loud and clear in her thoughts and guilt niggled at him.

"We're not very close." He wasn't sure why he told her. The words simply tumbled from his lips before he could stop them and he stiffened. "Listen, I don't want to cause any trouble. I just wanted to say a few words to my brother."

"He and Miranda are going to host a receiving line when they're finished with pictures. I'm sure you can wish him well then. In the meantime, you should move on to the reception area." *Otherwise these seniors are going to kick your firm, tight, totally amazing buns all over this ranch and I'm going to let them.*

Her thought echoed through his head and a strange sense of warmth stole through him. A grin tugged at his lips.

She motioned toward the massive tents set up just beyond the barn. "You can have something to drink and a bite to eat while you're waiting."

His groin tightened at the suggestion and his gaze

shifted to her creamy white throat. He could see the faint pulse beneath her skin and his fangs tingled.

"There's a full menu," she continued. "Swedish meatballs. Pigs-in-a-blanket. Mini chimichangas. Southwest egg rolls. I'm sure you can find some-thing you like."

"I already have," he said, staring deep into her eyes.

He expected to see passion flare in the blue depths, her lips to part, her body to lean toward his. Particularly since she thought his buns were firm and tight *and* totally amazing. That's the way it always was when he focused his complete attention on a woman. She couldn't help but fall under his spell.

Her eyes widened and then she blinked. Once. Twice. As if she couldn't quite believe she'd heard him correctly. "What did you just say?"

"I said I already found something I like." As anx-ious as he'd been to talk to Cody, he knew he wasn't getting anywhere near his baby brother for the time being. Which meant he might as well slow down and kill a few minutes.

On top of that, he really *was* hungry. And it wasn't a Swedish meatball or any of the other things she'd just rattled off he was craving. He'd been in such a hurry to get to Texas that he hadn't even stopped to feed. "I like you, sugar."

You.

Now he would see the flare of desire, the physical proof that she wanted him...

She stiffened and Travis knew in a glaring instant that she wasn't going to fall all over him the way other women did. She was stronger than most. Determined. *Different.*

And damned if he didn't like it.

2

WAIT A SECOND.

Wait just a cotton-pickin' *second.*

Holly Simms shook her head and tried to clear the cobwebs from her brain. No way had she heard this cowboy say that *he* wanted *her.*

A real, balls-to-the-bull *cowboy.*

Her brain snagged on that all-important fact as she noted the worn tips of his black boots, the soft, molded jeans holding tight to his thighs, the smell of leather and fresh air that clung to him. She knew cowboys. She'd almost married one. But then her very own Mr. Tall, Dark & Irresistible had stood her up in front of God, the Skull Creek Cattleman's Association and the entire Ladies Bingo club. The wedding had been called off and she'd been stuck with a six tier red velvet wedding cake to eat all by her lonesome.

She'd gained ten pounds thanks to her low-down

sneaky rat of an ex-fiancé and learned a valuable lesson. Namely, that she was more cut out to plan a wedding than actually participate in one.

She'd spent the past three years as Skull Creek's resident wedding planner. She'd orchestrated over one hundred ceremonies, overseeing everything from seating charts and bags of birdseed to sit down dinners and cages of live butterflies. She'd booked disc jockeys and ordered cakes and she'd even called in Marty and Serena, the 2010 Texas brisket cooking champions, to make an appearance at the Morgan reception last June. Marty and Serena had cooked all the food on-site over a live grill—much to the bride and groom's delight—and handed out bottles of homemade Serena Sauce as wedding favors. The event had been a huge success and she'd even got a mention in the *What's Up Y'all?* section of the *Skull Creek Gazette*. A huge coup that had doubled her business. Well, that and the fact that Eliza MacDonald, the eighty-eight-year-old owner of her only competition, From Courtin' to Cuddlin', had needed a double hip replacement and been forced into retirement.

Holly had been busy ever since, giving the couples of Skull Creek the happily-ever-after she, herself, would never have.

Her great-aunt Tootie had tried to warn her.

The old woman had always said there were only two types of women in the world. The kind who were doomed to settle down, get married and have babies and the lucky few who were actually meant to avoid all three and have some real fun. Tootie's definition of fun involved lots of wild parties, single cowboys and plenty of one-night stands.

The Simms women? They tended to fit into the second category. Aunt Tootie had avoided matrimony like the plague and spent her life sowing one wild oat after another. The few Simms women who tried to break with tradition and go the happily married route ended up divorced like Holly's own mother (five times as a matter of fact) and her three aunts. Not one of Holly's female relatives had ever had a long lasting relationship except Holly's Aunt Celia, but that was with a pet poodle named Sassafrass.

Bottom line, Holly simply wasn't the marrying kind. She had a pre-determined path. One that didn't involve his and her monogrammed towels.

She knew that now. She'd accepted it. She'd even joined an online group of women committed to overcoming their addiction to falling in love. As a full-fledged Love Buster, Holly had given up her childhood dreams of wedded bliss and decided to focus on living out her most wild and wicked fantasies.

But that was a little hard to do all by her lonesome.

She was a *wedding planner*. Translation? She scared the bejesus out of every bachelor in town.

They were convinced she only had marriage on her mind and so they all kept their distance. Since her moment of public humiliation at the altar, the only *fun* Holly had involved a case of batteries and a vibrator named Big Ben.

Which meant that no way had she heard this hunk of testosterone correctly.

She licked her lips and noticed the way his gaze followed the motion. Her stomach hollowed out and her heartbeat thundered in her ears.

"Would you, um, mind repeating what you just—" she started to ask, but Evan chose that moment to rattle over her headset.

"I hate to tell you this, but we've got a tiny little problemo with the PA system in the reception tent."

Evan Valentine was her twenty-six-year-old protégé and a die-hard romantic. He'd come to her last year after a hand full of various temp jobs and a six month online course on how to be a party planner. He was young, creative and hopelessly in love with his high school sweetheart, a once-upon-a-time quarterback named Bob.

"I like—" the hunk of testosterone said, but he was drowned out when Evan jumped in. "I told you not to hire that DJ. Seriously, what sort of lunatic plays the Chicken Dance at a PETA event?"

"Could you excuse me for just a sec," she held up a quick finger to Hot and Hunky before turning to blurt into her headset, "What are you talking about?"

"The disc jockey that yours truly *told* you not to hire is incompetent. His PA system doesn't work. It's completely dead and the natives are getting restless."

"And that's a *tiny* problem?"

"When you compare it to the fact that there are people starving in Third world countries, the ozone layer is slowly depleting and Bob's parents refuse to include me in the family Christmas card. Not that I'm crying over it, mind you. I know that if I just hang in there, they'll eventually see how hopelessly in love we are and welcome me into the family with open arms. Why, I bet they even ask me to pick the background for next year's card…"

Evan went on about red versus green while Holly tried to calm the sudden pounding of her heart. She stiffened, determined to ignore the fingers of heat dancing up and down her spine. She could feel Mr. Testosterone behind her, his gaze on her back.

Watching.

Waiting.

Wanting.

She ditched the last thought, gave her hormones a quick shake and tried to concentrate. "Where's the DJ now?"

"The last time I saw him he was running for the bathroom. He said he ate the enchilada special for lunch at the diner and now he's regretting it."

Her heart jumped into her throat and she swallowed it back down. Easy. Calm. She'd been down this path before. Unexpected situations were par for the course when it came to wedding planning. The key was to keep her head and think. "Get him an Alka Seltzer and meet me in the reception tent."

"You think that's going to help?"

"It can't hurt." She clicked the off button and turned back to face the megalicious cowboy standing behind her. She would talk to him, get everything straight and if he truly had said what she thought he'd said, then maybe...

The thought faded as she found herself staring at the empty spot where he'd been standing.

Her gaze swept the crowd, but he was nowhere to be seen. Proof beyond a doubt that her imagination had kicked into overdrive thanks to her deprived hormones.

I like you.

Yeah, sure.

She gave herself a great big mental shake, turned on her heel and went to find the MIA disc jockey.

"I'M SURPRISED YOU had the balls to show up," Brent said as he shoved Travis up against the backside of the barn.

Travis blinked and stared at his younger brother. One minute he'd been admiring the very attractive rear end of Cody's wedding planner, and the next, he'd been gripped by the collar and whisked away at preternatural speed by the vampire in front of him.

Green eyes so much like his own stared back at him. "Hello to you, too."

The green shifted and Brent's gaze fired a bright, vivid red. "If you're here to start trouble, you can forget it. I'm not letting you screw this up for Cody. No arguing tonight." The red flickered and anger sizzled in the air surrounding them. "I mean it."

"Easy." Travis held up his hands. "I'm not here to start anything. I just came to talk."

"You really expect me to believe that?"

He didn't. The last time he'd been face to face with his brothers, he'd blamed them for the massacre that had taken their family.

But he'd been wrong.

Travis eyed his brother. "Where's Rose?"

Silence stretched between them for a long moment before Brent relaxed his grip just a little. "Your guess is as good as mine."

"What's that supposed to mean?"

"That I don't know."

"You're lying."

"Believe what you want." He shrugged. "I don't know jack about her. That's Cody's bomb to drop and he'll drop it when he's good and ready. And I can promise you it's not right now. We're in the middle of pictures, for Christ's sake." Agitation washed over him as the photographer's voice echoed in the distance. His grip loosened. "Listen, if you want to talk, we'll talk. But later."

He wanted to argue, but then Brent disappeared as quickly as he'd first appeared, leaving Travis no choice but to bide his time until the photographer finished.

He straightened his shirt and started back around the barn. His attention shifted to the huge white tent that towered in the far distance before he chanced a glance at the spot where he'd last seen Holly Simms talking on her headset. She was nowhere in sight and damned if that didn't bother him. Not that he expected her to hang around, waiting for him. She undoubtedly thought he'd ditched her on purpose.

A damned fine idea.

That's what his head told him. There were too many women to choose from for him to set his sights on one who obviously didn't have the time to get up close and personal. She was the wedding planner after all, and busy as all get out. He needed a guest to kill some time with. Or a bridesmaid. Someone who wouldn't be missed for a few minutes.

Someone who would actually respond when he looked deep into her eyes and willed her to get naked.

The thought conjured a vision of long blond hair trailing down his bare chest. Feathering over his abs. Brushing his thighs. Swirling around his cock.

His stomach hollowed out and his mouth went dry. He picked up his stride, his boots kicking up dust as he headed for the tent and the bar that had been set up along one length. Sliding onto a bar stool, he ordered a beer and took a long swig. The golden liquid went down smooth, but it didn't quench the thirst that yawned in the pit of his stomach.

The tent filled up quickly. The sound of laughter echoed around him. Glasses clinked as the bartenders shifted into action. The scent of vanilla candles wafted through the air, blending with the sugary-sweet smell of the stacked wedding cake that sat center stage on a nearby table.

Travis tried to focus on the women surrounding him. A tall brunette with a purple dress. A shapely redhead wearing a pink suit. A blonde in a hot, tight, red number with lips to match. There were plenty. All his for the taking.

All except for Holly Simms.

The thought struck and he signaled for another beer. She was just one woman, he reminded himself. A damned infuriating one at that since she didn't seem susceptible to his vamp charisma. No falling into his arms or rubbing her soft curves up against him. Nothing. Just that crazy disbelief.

As if his thoughts had conjured her, she rushed around the bandstand toward the pale looking man who'd just taken his place behind a large mixing board. Static cracked open the steady chatter of guests and in a split-second, a slow, twangy Jason Aldean song spilled from the speakers.

Jason sang about big green tractors and taking a

ride, and relief seeped into Holly's expression. She actually smiled and his chest hitched. It was the damndest thing, considering his response was always centered below the belt when it came to women.

He took a swig of his drink and watched as she touched her headset and informed the person on the other end that the music was on and the dancing could commence. Disaster averted. Or so she thought until she got the news that the champagne was missing. Her smile faded in the blink of an eye and he had the sudden insane urge to cross the distance between them, haul her into his arms and do any and everything to bring the smile back to her beautiful face.

Her tight skirt pushed and pulled, hugging her shapely ass as she made a bee-line for the house. His groin tightened, throbbing to the point that a growl worked its way up his throat.

She was different, all right.

But not *that* different.

While he hadn't wowed her with his vampness, he'd still read every thought that had flashed through her pretty blond head. He knew she was sexually frustrated and that she had a thing for cowboys, that she'd been hurt by one. She'd sworn off love and relationships, and had resigned herself to brief, meaningless, one-night stands.

Exactly what he needed at the moment.

Not an entire night, mind you. In the deprived

state he was in, a good fifteen minutes would do him just fine. He was already *this* close to the edge. Pain twisted at his gut. His hands trembled. His throat tightened. His fangs tingled.

Travis downed the last of his drink, set the glass on the bar and went after Holly Simms.

"I CAN'T BELIEVE they misplaced the Cristal," she murmured into her headset as she entered the house through the back kitchen door and glanced frantically around the large room. Platters of food covered every available granite countertop. Boxes sat stacked against the walls and in front of the custom cherry cabinets, but not one had the familiar name she was looking for. "How do you lose ten cases of ultra expensive champagne?"

"I love Cristal," Evan declared. "Bob ordered it on our first date. After dinner, we went up to Lucky's Point and watched the sun set. Say, maybe someone snuck off with the champagne because he wants to propose to his girlfriend. Why, they could be sitting on the tailgate of a pickup truck as we speak, bottles in hand, watching the stars dance across the sky."

"Are you on medication?"

"It's called love, dearest. In case you've forgotten."

If only.

But she remembered all too clearly the pounding

heart, the rush of excitement and the pie-in-the-sky notions—

"The bartender said all ten cases were supposed to be delivered to the bar," Evan cut in, effectively killing her spiral down memory lane. Thankfully. "I called the delivery service and they said someone in the kitchen signed for it."

"Which means it has to be here somewhere." Holly moved out into the massive hallway and headed for the walk-in pantry a few yards down.

The Braddock spread was one of the newest and biggest ranches in the area. The house itself was over nine thousand square feet with tons of closets and way too many places to stash several cases of the bride's favorite beverage.

"Maybe it's in the barn," Evan offered.

"Who would move it all the way from the kitchen to the barn?"

"A loony tune who needed more room to craft her masterpieces." Evan referred to Millicent Dupree, the one and only gourmet chef in Skull Creek, Texas. Millicent was temperamental, stubborn and very focused when it came to her work. "I asked her, but she told me she couldn't listen because she was in her pigs-in-the-blanket zone. She also said if I bothered her again, she would come after me with a pair of cooking shears."

"You check the barn," Holly told him, "and I'll look in the house." She pushed open the door to the walk-in pantry area which rivaled the size of the small bedroom she'd grown up in. A ray of light pushed back the shadows and illuminated stacks of catering boxes, crates of fresh fruit and vegetables, and the empty white boxes that had carried all the petit fours and cheesecakes over from the bakery. Shadows hid the rest and she reached for the light switch.

She was just about to flip it on when she felt the presence directly behind her.

"I've been looking for you." The deep, familiar voice slid into her ears and stirred every nerve in her body. And then a hard wall of muscle urged her forward, the door shut and she found herself standing in the darkness with Travis Braddock.

3

HE'D PROBABLY GOTTEN lost on the way to the men's room.

No way was he in this closet with her on purpose. Because he wanted her and she wanted him and it was meant to be. Definitely a great, big, fat *no*.

That's what she told herself but then he turned her around, his mouth descended on hers and just like that, he was kissing her, his lips covering hers, his tongue thrusting deep. *Yes*.

He tasted like cold beer and hot, decadent thoughts and the air stalled in her lungs.

Stop!

That's what her head said.

Wrong time.

Wrong place.

Wrong man.

If only he hadn't felt so *right*. Like a cold drink of water on a blistering hot summer day. She couldn't help herself. She kissed him back and kept kissing him. Longer. Deeper. His hands were everywhere, trailing down her back, tugging up her skirt.

It was the best thing that had ever happened to Holly.

And the worst.

Not because it was exciting. Heaven knew she needed a little *oomph* in her life. A little wild, mindless sex with no second thoughts. But it was the *worst* because she was smack dab in the middle of a wedding reception for two hundred guests. And the champagne was missing. And Evan kept repeating as much over the headset every few seconds, in between humming the tune from "Unchained Melody." And she was wearing a pair of heavy duty Spanx to keep her tummy flat and her thighs shapely. *And* it was just too friggin' dark.

"Please tell me you found it," Evan declared.

She managed to tear her lips away. "Not yet, she gasped, her lungs struggling for air, "but I'm getting warm." Boy, was she ever.

A slow, chuckle rumbled over her lips and goose bumps chased up and down her arms.

Evan's voice, along with the sound of music and laughter, faded into the sudden pounding of her heart as she became acutely aware of the man standing in front of her, surrounding her. His fingertips seemed to melt through her skirt and the dreaded Lycra smoothing her thighs.

Okay, so dark was good considering the last thing she wanted was for him to see her struggle out of her modern day version of a girdle. But the thing was, *she* couldn't see *him*.

And despite all the extra baggage on her hips, she really wanted to see him. The broad shoulders and muscular arms rippling beneath her touch. The long, hard thighs braced on either side of her own. The prominent erection pressing just below her belly button.

She reached out a hand to her left to feel for the light switch, but he caught her wrist and pinned her arm above her head. He went stiff in the next instant and if she hadn't known better, she might have thought he was purposely trying to keep her in the dark. But just when his grip grew a little too tight, he eased his hold and drew the palm of her hand to his lips.

His lips pressed against her palm. The kiss was soft, tender, *loving* and for a split-second, she actually forgot this was meaningless sex.

"Exactly how warm are you?" Evan's voice pushed past the frantic staccato of her heart and yanked her back to reality and the fact that she was getting naked in a storage closet with a man she'd met less than five minutes ago.

Romeo and Juliet it wasn't.

"I think it's here somewhere—" she offered, but

then strong hands plucked off the headset. A heartbeat later, it clattered to the floor.

"But I'm working—" Strong, sensual lips silenced the rest of her protest in a fierce, determined kiss that scrambled her common sense and drew her full and complete attention.

He tugged the blouse from her skirt. Long, determined fingers worked at the buttons until the silk parted. A flick and her bra clasp opened. The cups fell away. Thumbs rasped her nipples and her breath caught.

Before she had a chance to drag some much needed air into her lungs, he dipped his head and drew the aching tip deep into his mouth. He sucked her so hard that she felt the tug between her legs.

She shuddered as he slid his hot, wet mouth to her other nipple. He caught it with his teeth and flicked her with his tongue, over and over, making her squirm until he opened his lips and suckled her again.

Heat spiraled through her body and pleasure gripped her for several sweet, intoxicating moments before she felt the sharp prickling sensation on her sensitive skin. His teeth, she knew. But it felt different. Sharper.

Just as the thought struck, he pulled away. His mouth closed over hers, drawing her tongue deep. She thought she felt the same sharp sensation against her bottom lip, but then he plunged his own tongue deep and the floor seemed to tremble.

Desire welled up inside her and suddenly she couldn't help herself. Since she couldn't see him, she needed to feel him.

Now.

Frantic fingers grappled at his shirt, pulling and tugging until she found her way underneath. Soft, silky hair met her hands and she trembled. Muscles rippled beneath her palms as she trailed them over his chest and down to the waistband of his jeans.

She unbuttoned him with several fierce, frantic tugs. He sprang hot and huge into her hands and she stroked his length. Her fingers slid back and forth, tracing the bulging head, the hard, smooth shaft. She cupped his testicles and massaged them, and his arousal pulsated against her.

He reached for her skirt then, tugging it up and hooking her underwear. He pushed them down her legs until the lycra sagged around her ankles and she stepped free. He reached down, dragging a finger over her sex in a smooth, sweet rhythm that made her moan.

For a fierce moment, she thought she saw a flash of blue in the darkness, like twin laser beams aimed directly at her.

Eyes. His eyes. Staring back at her.

A red alert went off in her brain. His eyes were green. She'd seen them herself.

She blinked and the bursts of color faded into the nothingness that surrounded them.

Still, something wasn't right.

She reached for the light again, but then he caught her hand and guided it around his neck. "We're not finished yet, sugar. Hold on tight," he murmured, his voice deep and raspy. And then he was inside of her and her thoughts scrambled as exquisite heat flooded her body.

He moved in and out in a fierce rhythm. Pleasure needled her brain with each thrust until she couldn't take any more. She closed her eyes as her orgasm crashed over and consumed her entire body. Tremors racked her and her knees buckled. She went limp, but Travis was there, his strong arms around her, holding her as he plunged deep one last time.

He followed her over the edge, his body rigid. A growl rumbled in her ears and she saw the pinpoints of blue light again. Brighter this time. Fierce.

Gone.

She blinked, but there was nothing there. Just the consuming darkness and the tiniest sliver of light underneath the door that illuminated her discarded Spanx and the forgotten headset.

She became keenly aware of the noise and Evan's frantic voice buzzing in the earpiece.

"I have to find the champagne," she said, but Travis had already stepped back to give her some space.

Cool air washed over her and a strange sense of loneliness crept through her. It was an absurd reaction. She should be feeling anything but lonely. Relieved. Satisfied. Smug.

The sex was over. It was time to get back to work and forget all about this yummy cowboy.

No strings.

The thought stirred an expected rush of disappointment and she stiffened. Not that she wanted the past fifteen minutes to mean something. No sirree.

She'd been there, done that. Not once, but three times as a matter of fact. Each time she'd inched a little closer to wedded bliss. Allen had been her first serious boyfriend. They'd dated exclusively for six months, but he'd bailed before popping the question. Ben had been number two. They'd dated a year and a half and he'd gone so far as to give her an engagement ring. But then he'd asked for it back the next day so he could run off with a waitress from some truck stop. Chad had been number three. They'd dated for two years before he'd asked her to marry him. She'd spent the following year planning her dream wedding.

Third time's a charm.

That's what everyone had said, but in Holly's case, the third had been the last and final piece of evidence that she just wasn't the marrying kind. Chad had literally left her standing at the altar.

Which was why she'd joined Love Busters and decided to fall into lust instead of the big L.

Sex was easy. Fun. Satisfying.

Over.

Still… It had been awhile.

A long, *long* while.

No wonder her fingers tightened around the doorknob and she paused. Meaningless sex was hard to come by for Holly. It stood to reason that she wouldn't want to turn her back on her sudden good fortune.

"We could try for round two if you're game," Travis's stirring voice slid into her ears as if he'd read her thoughts. "But I think we might be doing it in front of an audience."

She became aware of the distinct footsteps that grew louder with each moment that passed. A steady click of leather on tile that told her Evan and his new Feragamos had given up on the barn.

She bent down and snatched up the headset. "Meet me on the back patio," she blurted. "Now."

"Where have you been? I've been calling you *forever!*"

"I was busy going through all the boxes the caterer left on the back patio. Stop with the twenty questions and give me a hand."

"But we found the champagne already. It's being served up now. That's what I was coming to tell you. I figured you had a malfunction on the head-set and—"

"We have extra on the back patio," she blurted. "Lots of extra. I'm practically drowning in the stuff. Help!" The footsteps turned abruptly and then a fading clatter signaled that Evan had bought the distraction and was heading to the opposite end of the house.

"Does that mean you're staying?" Travis asked when the footsteps finally disappeared and Holly could actually breathe again.

"He'll be looking for me again when he realizes I'm not on the patio." She turned the knob.

"Wait." Before she could pull open the door, he stepped up behind her and pressed her up against the wood.

She could hear his voice distinctly, his lips feathering over her ear. But there was no warm rush of breath against her temple. No heartbeat pounding against her shoulder blade.

He was there, yet he wasn't there.

Just as the strange thought struck, he murmured "Thanks." The knob seemed to turn beneath her fingers and suddenly the door was open and she was free.

She resisted the urge to turn and catch a glimpse of him standing in the shaft of light from the hallway. His hair mussed. His shirt hanging open. His pants still undone. His eyes still gleaming with passion—

She stiffened and ignored the image whispering through her head. Sure, it was a purely sexual image. But that was beside the point. If she turned around now, they would have sex again. And possibly again. And then before she knew it, she would be hopelessly in love. A repeat offender.

These boots were made for walking.

She squared her shoulders, stepped forward and went to intercept Evan.

4

TRAVIS MANEUVERED HIS way through the crowd gathered on the front lawn just in time to see Cody follow his bride into the back of a black stretch limousine. It was barely nine-thirty, but there was no mistaking the birdseed in the air and the shouts of congratulations. The crowd waved goodbye and panic suckerpunched him smack dab in his gut.

"They had to cut the reception short to catch an early plane," Brent's deep voice sounded next to him just as the limo door closed, "otherwise they won't make it to Colorado before sunrise. They're going to Aspen for the honeymoon."

Travis glanced at his brother. "You're kidding me, right?" When Brent shook his head, he ran a hand over his face and damned himself a thousand times for following Holly Simms into that storage closet and wasting precious time. What the hell had he been thinking?

But then that was the point—he hadn't been able to think. Not with the lust raging through his veins, the hunger gnawing at his gut. He should have stopped to feed before he left Wyoming, but he'd been in a hurry to catch his plane. He'd figured on holding out until after he talked to Cody.

But then he'd seen Holly—her soft lips and lush body and those sparkling, surprised eyes—and all his *figuring* had gone to hell in a hand basket. Now it was too late to talk to Cody. To find out the truth.

Like hell.

He shoved a hand into his pocket to retrieve his keys. "Which airport?"

"They're flying out of San Antonio."

"If I leave now, I can catch him before he boards the plane—" The words died as a vice grip tightened on his arm. His gaze swiveled to his brother and he saw the steely determination in his eyes.

"You're not going after him," Brent told him. "It's his honeymoon, for Christ's sake."

"I just need five minutes. He'll tell me what I need to know and that'll be that."

"No." The grip tightened and Travis knew he wasn't budging a step without a fight. "He's not talking until Colton gets here and that won't be until Saturday. Cody will be back Saturday night and we can all have a sit down."

"That's a week from tomorrow."

"That's the way it is. Rose was Colton's wife. He should be the first to know."

"We all have a right to know."

"Damn straight we do, but not until Colton gets here and we're all together."

Which meant he was stuck here for the next seven days.

The truth sank in as he stood there, staring at the crowd that walked past him. People laughed and smiled as they headed back to the reception. While Cody and Miranda had cut the evening short, their guests weren't inclined to do the same. The DJ had kicked up the music and the promise of a great party hung in the air.

Brent clapped him on the shoulder. "Seeing as how you've got a little time to kill, why don't you come on back inside and have a drink."

Travis shook his head, his mind still trying to wrap itself around the fact that he would be forced to hang out in Skull Creek if he wanted to find out Rose's whereabouts.

And he *was* going to find her. He owed her and he intended to see that she got what was coming to her for destroying his family.

"It's just seven days," Brent added. "Think of it as a vacation."

"I don't take vacations."

"Think of it as work then. I could use some help out at my place." When Travis arched an eyebrow, he added, "Skull Creek's not a bad place. The people are nice and there are even a few vampires to keep things interesting." At Travis's surprised look, Brent added, "Garrett Sawyer and his buddies own Skull Creek Choppers. They live just up the road from me."

"Since when did you become the settling down type?"

The last Travis had heard, Brent had been making his fortune as one of the most sought-after guns-for-hire. He went from job to job, guarding the rich and famous and doing his damnedest to not get too attached to any one person or place.

"I'm tired of living out of a suitcase." He gave Travis a pointed stare. "Aren't you?"

"I like moving on. It keeps things much more interesting."

"I can't imagine anything more interesting than Abby, that's for damned sure."

"Abby?"

Brent glanced at a petite brunette who stood talking to a nearby group of women. As if she felt him, her head snapped up and their gazes locked. She smiled and a strange expression lit his brother's eyes. "I bought a hundred acres just down the road from here. I'm going to try my hand at ranching."

"How much does she know about you?"

"How much doesn't she know? Abby is ex Special Forces. Nothing gets by her." His attention shifted back to Travis. "Take you for instance. She knew you were a vampire the moment she saw you. She also knew you were my brother. She said we have the same eyes."

"And the same fangs."

Brent grinned. "There are some people who aren't bothered by what we are. Abby's one of them. So is Cody's wife Miranda. Garrett's business partners are both married to humans, too, though Garrett himself is with another vampire."

"He's smart. Meanwhile, you're playing with fire."

"Maybe, but I like the heat." A wistful look twisted his features. "That's the one thing I miss the most about being human. Being warm from the inside out. When I'm with Abby, I feel it again, bro. Deep inside my bones." He must have noticed Travis's *get real* expression because he added, "Don't knock it until you've tried it. You don't sit still long enough to meet anyone, let alone warm up to them."

"I like moving."

"That or you're just so used to it you don't know how to stop."

"You buy a spread and suddenly you're a shrink."

Brent shook his head. "Just a rancher. Speaking of which, I've got three mustangs that might make damn fine cutting horses if I could ever get close enough to them."

"And?"

"And since you're sticking around for the next seven days, I thought you might help me out."

"Horses don't like vampires."

"They like you," Brent argued. When Travis cut him a glance, he added, "Ranchers talk. You've become a hot commodity." When Travis shrugged, Brent added, "I could really use the help."

But the less time Travis spent with Brent, the better. Already, he felt the strange pull he'd once felt with his brother. The camaraderie. The sense of *family.*

But his was gone. Rose had seen to that.

She'd destroyed them all and there was no rebuilding what was permanently damaged. They'd turned on each other and gone their separate ways, and that was okay.

It was better than okay.

Out of sight, out of mind.

That had been his motto all these years. He'd done his damnedest to forget his brothers and his life before. And he'd managed to do just that. Hell, it had been easy. The farther away he stayed, the less he thought about them. No doubts. No regret. No remorse.

Just the hunger.

Until Cody's invitation.

His little brother had stirred it all up, reminding him of the man he'd been, of the injustice he'd dealt out and the fact that the real culprit had yet to be punished.

Travis knew now that he couldn't forget again.

Not unless he spent the anger inside of him and dealt it out to the real murderer. Then he could move on again. He *would* move on. And forget.

His gaze shifted to the woman standing several feet away, herding people back to the reception tent. Her cheeks were pink, her eyes bright. A few tendrils of hair had come loose from her ponytail. His fingertips tingled and he had the crazy urge to cross the lawn, tug her hair loose and run his fingers through the long, blond silk.

He stiffened. He wasn't here for sex, despite the past half hour. He was here for information.

For vengeance.

Just as soon as Cody returned and Colton arrived and the Braddock boys were back together once again.

"So what about it? You gonna help me out?"

Travis shook his head. "I can't."

"Can't or won't?"

"Does it matter?"

Brent looked as if he wanted to say something, but then thought better of it. "If you change your mind, my place is just a few miles north of here. I could use you." And then he turned and headed toward the petite brunette.

She smiled and Brent smiled and for a split second, Travis had the crazy thought that his brother had found the real deal. One man. One woman. *Love.*

If there'd been such a thing.

But Travis knew better. There was no such thing for their kind. Sooner or later, the hunger would get the best of Brent and he'd grab the first woman that crossed his path.

That's what had happened to Travis tonight. He'd gotten hungry. Holly had been handy. And bam, he'd satisfied that hunger in the storage closet.

He watched her gather up a group of seniors and steer them toward the dessert table, and the familiar pang hit him hard and fast. Hunger. Because he'd only partially fed.

He'd drank in her sweet energy, but for Travis it wasn't enough. He'd grown accustomed to taking sex *and* blood. While most vamps leaned more toward one or the other, Travis was a fan of both. It made him feel more alive. More in control. More in touch with his senses. For a vamp who made his living by being in tune with each of the five senses, a double whammy was essential.

But he hadn't bitten her.

He wasn't sure why. He'd wanted to more badly than anything else. At the same time, he'd felt a moment's hesitation, as if drinking her in would make it impossible to get rid of her. She'd be under his skin. In his head. His heart.

Crazy.

While drinking and having sex with the same woman often created a bond for most vampires, that wasn't the case for Travis. He was too much of a hard-ass. That, and he kept moving. The distance weakened the connection until, eventually, it snapped altogether and there was nothing. He'd learned that early on with Amelia. She'd been his girl before he'd gone off to war and she'd been more than eager to rekindle the fire in the weeks after his return.

But the night of his return had changed him. He'd been hardened by the war and devastation at the ranch. Insatiable thanks to the beast that lived and breathed inside of him. The hunger had been all-consuming and he'd quickly learned that he could never go back to being just a man.

And one woman would never be nearly enough.

The hunger had driven him into the arms of another and Amelia had been devastated. Thanks to the sex and blood they'd shared, he'd been completely in tune to her feelings. He'd hurt the way she'd hurt. But then he'd left town and the farther he'd gotten from her, the less he'd felt her sorrow and angst. No hitch in his chest. No knife twisting his gut. No piercing white hot pain when she'd finally ended it all and pulled the trigger. Rather, the news of her death had caught up to him months later in the form of a letter from her parents.

We just thought you should know...

But he hadn't known. Not even a clue. Because he hadn't felt a thing. He was a vampire now and incapable of feeling anything other than lust.

He knew that. He'd accepted it.

Which is why he should have bitten Holly and gotten it over with. The attraction would have ended, and he wouldn't be standing here at the entrance to the tent, as hot and horny as a cowpoke about to crawl into bed with his first saloon girl.

That was the only reason.

Damn straight it was.

And if he downed enough Jack Daniels over the next few hours, Travis might actually start to believe it.

IF TRAVIS BRADDOCK looked at her one more time, Holly was going to dunk her head under the nearest champagne fountain.

She forced her gaze from the man standing at the bar and busied herself replenishing the dessert table for the remaining guests. The newlyweds had departed, but the party was still in high gear. The band cranked out a lively Kenny Chesney tune and a sea of Stetsons bobbed across the dance floor. Waiters moved here and there, passing out glasses of the newly discovered champagne. The sweet smell of cake infused the air.

"Methinketh this is one more fabulous set of event pics for our Facebook page." Evan's voice sounded behind her. "I think the worst is over."

She turned to see her assistant balancing a platter of chocolate covered cheesecakes. "Don't count your chickens yet. The DJ doesn't wrap up until midnight."

"By then people will be too drunk to even notice if something goes wrong. As long as the champagne is flowing, everyone's happy. You can lose the worried look."

"I don't look worried."

"You look flushed, which means you're in panic mode, which means you're worried and headed straight for a Prozac prescription if you don't lighten up. Girlfriend, you need to slow down and enjoy the moment. Don't sweat the small stuff. *Carpe diem* and all that."

If he only knew.

But he didn't and she wasn't about to broadcast to the world that she'd spent the last fifteen minutes seizing not only the day, but one ultra hot cowboy. Not that she cared if everyone knew that Holly Simms had had her first of many one-night stands. She would welcome a little notoriety. Maybe then available bachelors would stop treating her like she had some deadly disease.

At the same time, she was on the clock, and more than an active sex life, she valued a good work reputation.

"Take a load off and enjoy." Evan handed her a plate of chocolate ganache cheesecake and a fork. "I'll make sure the rest of the desserts get put out." He handed her another piece of cake.

"What? One for each hip?"

He wiggled his eyebrows and stared past her. "That one's for the hot cowboy checking you out at three o'clock."

She chanced a glance at Travis. Her gaze met his and heat rippled through her body, from the soles of her feet, to the top of her head. Time pulled her back and suddenly she felt his strong arms around her, his hands on her back, his body pushing into hers.

The urge to grab his hand and haul him back into the storage closet hit her hard and fast. Her nipples tingled and her hands trembled and she stiffened.

Hello?

She had a mortgage to pay and a gluttonous St. Bernard to feed, and that meant controlling her impulses.

For now.

"I think he likes you. Why don't you walk over and offer him a dessert. You'll sit down and the two of you will stare longingly into each other's eyes over bites of decadent cheesecake. One thing will lead to another and bam, I'm planning the event of the century and you're playing the difficult bride."

"You've been watching too much Oxygen."

"Actually, it's the Soap Opera Channel. Mitchell just proposed to Loren on *The Sands of Time*." He let out a deep sigh. "He gave her a ring on top of a piece of cheesecake. Do you think Bob might do that?"

"I think you need to ditch the cable TV."

"Don't be such a hater."

But she wasn't a hater. She was an official Love Buster and she had the t-shirt and screen saver to prove it. Holly was through setting herself up for heartache. From here on out, it was all about busting the myth and having fun.

But not with Travis Braddock.

The entire point of what had happened was that it wasn't supposed to happen again. That's why they called it a one-night stand, even if they hadn't technically had a full night together. It was the principle of the thing.

She didn't want more.

Okay, so she wanted more, but she wasn't giving in to it.

She forced her attention back to the buffet table and the all important fact that the clock was ticking. Two hours to go and she would be home free.

Travis free.

She set aside the duo of cheesecakes in her hands and reached for Evan's platter. "Maybe you could worry about refilling the coffee urn while I finish setting out the desserts?"

"Fine." Evan turned to stomp off. "But don't blame yours truly if you never get the opportunity to register for his and her tray tables."

5

THERE WASN'T MUCH that surprised Travis Braddock. He was a vampire, after all, with super charged senses. He could feel the moisture in the air before the first raindrop fell. He could smell the lightning when it struck clear into the next county. And he could hear a clap of thunder from fifty miles away.

Honestly, though, he had to admit he was damned surprised when Holly Simms walked into the Iron Horseshoe bar later that night after the wedding.

After several hours of watching her rush around and worry over everything from desserts to punch to a guest who'd misplaced her purse, he'd called it a night and headed for the most crowded bar he could find and some real sustenance. A warm woman, a quick bite and he could quench his thirst and forget a certain wedding planner with silky blond hair and big blue eyes.

At least that had been the plan.

But here she was, screwing things up and surprising the hell out of him.

Despite her lush body and long legs and full lips, she wasn't the last call type. She was the sort of woman who headed home after a hard day's work, to a hot bath, a steaming cup of tea and a good man.

But Holly Simms didn't want a good man. She wanted a good time.

At least that's what she was telling herself.

Mission accomplished and now it was over. She didn't do seconds any more than he did.

And truthfully, he wouldn't have considered a round two if he'd finished what he'd started in the first place. But he'd only had sex with her. No sinking his teeth into her sweet neck and drinking in her delicious heat. No feeling the rush of energy and the swell of satisfaction.

He'd missed his shot, but here she was, ready to give him another opportunity.

Obviously she wasn't as immune to him as he'd first thought.

To think he'd actually entertained the notion that she was different from all the other women he'd met over the years. She was one and the same. She'd gotten a taste of the beast and she couldn't help herself. She wanted more.

He saw it the moment her gaze locked with his. Heat swept through her, firebombing several key targets along the way—the backs of her knees, the insides of her thighs, her nipples. Her breath caught. Her heartbeat revved several frantic beats. Desire flooded between her legs and filled the air with a sharp, sweet, succulent scent that stirred his hunger even more.

A vision rushed through her head—of him dragging her into the nearest restroom, lifting her up onto the counter and plunging into her over and over while his fangs sank so deliciously deep.

Bring it on, baby.

He sent out the thought and expected the usual. Her eyes to glaze. Her lips to part. Her chest to heave.

She stiffened and he heard the words echo in her head.

Love's a bitch.
I'm not falling for this guy,
I'm keeping my head and avoiding the lie.

Love's a bitch.
I'm not falling for this guy.
I'm keeping my head and—

"Hey there, cowboy." The voice pulled him out of Holly's thoughts and back to the neon lights, the crowded bar and the Lady Antebellum song playing on the juke box. "Can I get you anything else?"

Travis turned his attention to the waitress who set a beer on the table in front of him. She looked like all the other women packed into Skull Creek's only hotspot. Big hair. Big boobs. Too much eye make-up. Too little clothes.

Her tongue swept her bottom lip and her heavily-rimmed eyes flashed suggestively. "Some salt? A lime?" *Me?*

Okay, now this made sense.

Women wanted him. All women. He had mucho sex appeal. A by-product for any vampire. Add a dose of Texas charm and semi-decent looks and the females were powerless to resist.

A grin crooked his lips as he held up the beer he'd been nursing. "I'm good right now."

"You sure? It's no trouble. I'm here to serve." He shook his head and disappointment chased across her expression. She shrugged. "The name's Amy. Holler if you need anything." She smiled and lust shimmered in her eyes. "Anything at all."

"I'll keep that in mind." He tipped his hat and she reluctantly turned away. He turned back toward the door and caught Holly staring at him as if she were about to jump into the deep end of a swimming pool and all she could do was dog paddle.

He winked and she stiffened, and he knew then, beyond a doubt, that she hadn't come begging for seconds. She seemed to gather her courage as her gaze went past him, to the adjoining room over-flowing with people and pool tables. The clack of balls split the air. Holly squared her shoulders and started forward as if she were power walking her way through a marathon.

He didn't mean to reach out. If she could bolt past him as if he hadn't just loved her within an inch of her life, he could certainly do the same. Hell, that's what he did best. Move on. To the next town. The next woman.

He didn't do the territorial thing.

At the same time, Travis Braddock didn't do half-ass either. He never left things unfinished, and he sure as hell didn't sleep with a woman without biting her.

He reached out and caught her warm hand in his.

"WHERE'S THE FIRE, sugar?" came the deep, familiar voice.

Right here.

The notion struck before Holly had a chance to think. She was too deep in sensory overload with Travis Braddock so close. His strong fingers held hers. The intoxicating aroma of leather and fresh air and a touch of wildness filled her nostrils. Her gaze collided with his. Eyes the color of lush green grass stared back at her and her breath caught.

For a split-second, she was mesmerized before the thump of a cue ball hitting its pocket jarred her from the sudden daze. "No fire," she finally managed to stammer, determined to keep her perspective. "I'm meeting someone."

"It's a little late for a date."

But not for a booty call.

That's what she should have told him. Make him think the worst. That's what she wanted in the first place, wasn't it? For everyone and their Chihuahua to believe that Holly Simms had gone from being the proverbial good girl to becoming Skull Creek's biggest good time girl?

And how.

But Travis wasn't everyone. He was a total stranger from out of town and so it didn't really matter if he considered her the latter. That and there was just something about the sudden flash of jealousy in his gaze that warmed her heart and made her open her mouth and tell him the truth. "I'm meeting my aunt."

A grin tugged the corner of his mouth, but it didn't quite touch his eyes. "And here I thought you might be following me."

"Oh, I would never do something like that," she blurted. She'd followed Chad home from work one night with a picnic basket stocked with all his favorite foods. Meat loaf. Mashed potatoes. Fried pickles. Sweet potato pie. The goal had been a romantic picnic under the stars in his backyard. But Chad hadn't gone home that night. He'd driven to the next county to meet with one of his ex girlfriends.

Nothing.

That's what the rendezvous had meant, or so he'd

told Holly when she'd confronted him in the parking lot. He'd had a long relationship with his ex and he'd wanted to break the news to her that he was getting married before she heard it through the grapevine. End of story.

Obviously, though, instead of letting his old girlfriend down, he'd decided to patch things up. A week later he'd left Holly at the altar and taken off with the ex.

Holly had learned her lesson then and there. No following a man home. No cooking him dinner. No putting herself out there. No falling in love.

Never again.

The minute the thought struck, Travis's gaze flickered and his lips thinned even more. If she hadn't known better she would have sworn he was disappointed.

But she knew better. Boy, did she ever. Her own wishful thinking had turned her into a three-time loser in the first place, a die-hard romantic that kept reading more into each and every situation, firing her hope, urging her to fall for men who didn't fall back.

She stiffened and the clack of pool balls echoed in her head. Her gaze shifted to the next room and through the crowd she caught a glimpse of a snow white beehive, bright pink lipstick and silver blue eye shadow. Another clack of pool balls, a familiar shriek of "Hot damn," and Holly knew there was a room full of truck drivers getting their butts kicked at that moment. "My great Aunt Tootie plays pool here every Friday night and I'm her designated driver."

"Too many Cosmos?"

"Too many fender benders." When he arched an eyebrow, she added, "She's had ten in the past six months and is now sitting at the top of the DMV's Most Wanted list. The doctor gave her a prescription for glasses, but she says they make her look old, so she refuses to wear them."

"Contacts?"

"Her vision is so bad she can't see well enough to put them in."

"That's nice of you to help her out."

"I owe her." She wasn't sure why she told him. She shouldn't have. But when he stared at her so intently—as if he actually cared about what she had to say—the words seemed to come on their own. "My mom was always MIA with whichever cowboy paid her the most attention and so I spent a lot of time with Aunt Tootie. She was more of a mother to me than my own mom, though she'll be the first to deny it." She shook off the sudden sadness that niggled at her and forced a smile. "She likes to think of herself as the older, wiser, hotter sister."

"She'll have to settle for two out of three." A grin crooked the corner of his sensuous mouth and her stomach hollowed out.

"So what about you?" she asked, eager to distract herself from her body's traitorous reaction. "Shouldn't you be on your way back to wherever it is that you came from?"

"Cody and I have some unfinished business, which means I'm in town until he gets back from his honeymoon." He toed the chair next to him. "Sit down."

She entertained the idea all of five seconds before the reality of what was happening hit her and her chest tightened. "Listen, you don't have to do this."

"Do what?"

"Be nice to me."

"You want me to be mean to you then?"

"Yes. No." She shook her head. "I mean, I don't want you to feel obligated to be nice to me just because of what happened between us. I had a really great time in that closet, but I have no intention of making more out of it than what it was."

"And what was it?"

"A little harmless fun. The last thing I'm looking for is a serious relationship." When he gave a pointed stare at the pink button that read *I Love Happily-Ever-Afters* pinned on her collar, she added, "It's my job. Personally, I plan on staying single for a really, *really* long time."

"Sugar, I'm offering you a drink and a little conversation, not a marriage proposal."

The deep timber of his voice echoed in her head and coasted along her nerve endings, bringing them to full, tingling awareness. She had the sudden image of the two of them sprawled in bed together on a bright, sunny morning, arms and legs intertwined, his lips moving against her ear as he whispered sweet nothings.

"You feel obligated after what we did," she rushed on, determined not to let herself get caught up in the fantasy. That's all it was. Her own crazy imagination blowing things out of proportion, trying to turn a physical connection into something more. Something real. "You shouldn't. I don't have any misconceptions about what happened. I don't need you to be nice to me or try to get to know me. I know I look like that kind of girl, but I'm not."

Not anymore, she reminded herself. Even if she did have the urge to slide into the seat next to him and ask him how he'd gotten that scar on the back of his hand. Her gaze lingered on the tiny strip of white that ran from his thumb to his wrist. Her finger itched to trace the path and feel the rough skin beneath her own.

She stiffened and pulled her hand from his grasp. "I really need to go. It was nice seeing you again."

And then like any devout Love Buster committed to non-committal sex, she gathered her courage, turned and walked away.

6

"NICE DOING BUSINESS with you boys," Aunt Tootie told the two red-faced men holding pool sticks. Years ago, Tootie had been one of the most beautiful women in town. At eighty-one, the looks had long since faded, but not her personality. She was still as big and bold and outlandish as ever.

She tucked a twenty dollar bill between the overflowing cleavage visible above her low-cut pink knit blouse. Grabbing Holly's hand, she yanked her front and center. "Say, have you boys met my niece?"

"We went to kindergarten together," Holly told her great aunt. "And middle school. And high school."

"Really?" Melvin Meyers exchanged glances with his twin brother Cecil. "Were you in one of our English classes? 'Cause we sat front row so we never really got to see who else was in there. Mrs. Jenkins watched us like a hawk."

"It was Mr. Wolinski's biology class. I was lab

partners with you and your brother. For three years in a row."

"Oh, yeah." Recognition seemed to dawn. "You were the one who brought the bridal magazines to class every day."

"That was back then," Aunt Tootie said. "But she's totally given up that nonsense, haven't you, dear?" Before Holly could respond, she rushed on, "She's my running partner now. We're happy to be single and ready to mingle, ain't that right, sugar?"

Before Holly could utter an enthusiastic *yes!*, Melvin asked, "Didn't you plan my older brother Jim Bob's wedding last year?"

She had half a mind to deny it, but as the only wedding planner in town, she didn't exactly blend into the woodwork. "I might have made a few arrangements—"

"She's a beauty, ain't she?" Tootie cut in, effectively killing the walk down memory lane. "It's all the good genes that run in our family, ya know." She winked. "All the women are lookers."

"I'm married, Miss Tootie," Melvin offered.

"Me, too," Cecil added.

"That don't make no never mind. You can still admire a woman's attributes, cain't you?"

The twins exchanged glances. "If we say she's a looker, will you stay a little longer so we can win back our Justins?"

"If I stay here another hour, the both of you will

likely end up naked and broke." She picked up the two pairs of cowboy boots sitting on the ledge of the pool table. "While I've got nothing against getting naked, I won't be the cause of either of you starving to death. Think of your families, boys." She hooked an arm through Holly's free one. Excitement twinkled in her eyes as she turned to her niece. "Now then, why don't you tell me who that cowboy is that you were just talking to?"

"What cowboy?" Holly followed Tootie toward a nearby table where her purse sat, careful not to glance in Travis's direction. She could feel his gaze brushing up and down her skin. Awareness skittered along her spine and her nipples throbbed.

"The one sitting over at that table." Tootie waved a hand and Holly stiffened. "Watching us."

"I doubt he's looking at us."

"Why, I'll be first in line for a colonoscopy if he ain't." Tootie pulled out a tube of pink lipstick and touched up her already bright lips. "I'm telling you, honey, his eyes are practically eating us alive." She glanced into her compact mirror and rubbed her lips together. "Then again, I cain't really blame him. When there's this much eye candy, even the strongest man turns to mush." She smoothed her hot-pink blouse over her black and white zebra striped pants. "It's that there Darwin's theory, ya know. Strong, virile, handsome men cain't help themselves. They're just pre-wired to gravitate toward the most attractive females on account of good looks scream fertility."

Holly had half a mind to remind Tootie that at eighty-one, the only thing she screamed was *Where's the Metamucil?* But her aunt looked so excited that she heard herself say, "You *were* the Cherry Junction Dance Hall Queen six years in a row. A man can't help but look when you walk by. Speaking of walking, I really think we should go." Holly helped Tootie gather up her things. "It's Saturday tomorrow. My busiest day of the week."

Awareness rippled over Holly as she navigated toward the door. A few seconds later, she stepped outside into the sultry night air and sent up a silent *thank you*.

"I've always been the charitable sort, honey. Maybe I should waltz back in and give that boy a little thrill." Tootie stalled just a few feet shy of the exit and glanced over her shoulder. "I bet that would sure-as-shootin' make his day—"

"No," Holly cut in. "I mean, you wouldn't want to get his hopes up, now would you? It's not like you're actually going to hook up with him or anything like that." When Tootie frowned, Holly added, "Not that you couldn't hook up with him if you wanted to. You're a mature, vivacious, intelligent woman. You could have any man that you want."

"You forgot sexy."

"That, too. But while you've obviously still got

it," Holly went on, "you really shouldn't be using it, what with the dangers associated with high blood pressure."

"High blood pressure?" Tootie stiffened. "Why, I'll have you know that my pressure's just fine, thank-you-very-much. That was a bad reading. I told the nurse she ought to get a new one of them doohickeys. Hers was obviously broken."

"Not *your* high blood pressure," Holly rushed to smooth Tootie's ruffled feathers. "His. That cowboy could be a walking cauldron of boiling cholesterol for all we know. You wouldn't want to be the fire that sends him rushing over the edge of the pot, now would you?"

"He did look a little red in the cheeks," Tootie finally agreed, letting Holly steer her back around. "Men are more inclined to have high blood pressure than women. I saw that on Discovery Health when I was flipping channels, looking for the latest *Jersey Shore* episode. At the same time," she added, digging her silver glitter heels into the gravel parking lot and stalling again, "he might be perfectly healthy and eager for some company." She patted Holly's arm and cut her a glance. "I know he had his sights set on me, but if there's one thing I've learned about men over the years, it's this—they ain't picky. Especially when it's close to last call and they haven't a prospect in hell."

"Please don't tell me you're thinking what I think you're thinking."

Her pale blue eyes twinkled. "You should mosey back in there right now and be his rebound woman."

"Don't most rebound women generally end up miserable and alone?"

"That's 'cause they're wanting a happily-ever-after. But if the only thing you're interested in is a little rub-a-dub-dub, you're sure to be one hundred percent satisfied. Why, when I was your age, I used to waltz right up to whichever man caught my fancy and drag him into the nearest broom closet. That's exactly what you ought to do."

"And have him run the other way?" The comment came from one of the waitresses who pushed through the door behind them. "A man that hot isn't the least bit interested in a woman like Holly." Amy Harold was only twenty-three, but she'd been around the block so many times that she looked a good ten years older. Add a pack-a-day habit and she could be the poster child for *Just Say No*.

Tootie's gaze narrowed. "Are you sayin' my niece is a loser when it comes to men?"

"I'm saying she's the marrying kind when it comes to men. And there isn't a man out there who doesn't know it."

"I am not."

"Girl, everything about you screams *take me to*

the altar from those cover-everything-up-clothes, to your minivan." Amy's gaze shifted to the white Honda parked a few feet away, *Here Comes the Bridal Consultant* in blazing pink letters on the side.

"It's my profession."

"It's the total package, which is why I chased you out here. See, my cousin Jeanine is thinking about getting hitched next month. I'm the maid of honor so I told her I'd take care of stuff for her, but I don't have a clue. I know I'm supposed to do the bachelorette party, which I've totally got covered, but I've never planned a shower and I don't know shit about flowers or cakes or..." Amy went on about being nuptually challenged while Holly's brain launched into major denial.

Maybe once upon a time she'd been the marrying kind, but those days were long gone. She was a wild woman now. The sort of woman who had sex with strangers in storage closets on the spur of the moment.

Not that anyone knew that little tidbit of information, which presented her problem in a nutshell. Every available man in town saw her as wife material and they always would.

Unless she could prove them wrong.

"So can you help me?" Amy asked.

"Stop by the shop on Monday. Wait here," she told her aunt. "I think I forgot something."

"Atta girl," Tootie called after her as she headed back inside the bar. "See?" she said to Amy. "I told you she was a chip off the old block."

Which is exactly what Holly intended to show everyone in Skull Creek. She was a Simms through and through. Sexy. Fun-loving. Uncomplicated. And ready for action.

If Travis Braddock agreed to cooperate, that is.

Drawing a deep breath, she gathered her courage and started toward his table.

"LET ME MAKE sure I'm hearing this right." Travis leveled a stare at Holly who sat across from him, an anxious look on her beautiful face. His brain was still reeling, along with his other senses. She was too close. Too beautiful. Too damned sexy. "You want to *date* me?"

"I don't want to *date* date you. I just want the single men of this town to see me hanging out with you. Here. The local honky tonk. The Dairy Freeze. The rodeo arena. Cherry Blossom Junction, the local honky tonk, is even gearing up for their annual indoor rodeo next Saturday night. It would be the perfect place for us to hang out and have a few drinks."

"That sounds like a date."

"Not if you factor in that I don't want a relationship and I have absolutely no intention of falling for you."

Been there.

Done that.

No, thank you.

He read the thoughts loud and clear and his chest tightened.

Not that he wanted a relationship with Holly. Hell, no. It was the principle of the thing. All women wanted him and Holly Simms should have been no exception.

She was, and damned if it didn't bug the living hell out of him.

"See, here's the thing," she continued. "You're not the type of guy a serious, marriage-minded girl would go for."

"Is that so?"

She nodded. "You're the type of guy who goes out with lots of different women and likes to have a good time, like what happened between us earlier tonight. On top of that, you're only in town for a little while, which means you won't be sticking around. That makes you all the more perfect for this."

When he didn't say anything, she added, "No marriage-minded woman would go after a guy like you. You're temporary. And a temporary man only hooks up with a temporary woman, which I most definitely am. Unfortunately, I also coordinate happily-ever-afters and so I might as well have *Marry Me* tattooed on my forehead." Determination charged her gaze. "I want to kill that image once and for all and let everyone in this town know that Holly Simms is single and ready for action."

"As in sex?"

"Non-committal sex. Being seen with a guy like you will send a loud and clear message that I don't want to open a joint checking account. I just want to have a good time."

"And what do I get in return?"

"What do you want?"

To finish what they'd started.

The thought conjured a vivid image of Holly's soft throat tilted toward him, her fragrant skin drawing him closer, her lush curves pressed flush against him, her sweet blood flowing into his mouth.

Christ, he wanted it so bad that it was all he could do not to bolt out of the seat, back her up against the nearest wall, and taste her right here and now in front of the entire crowd packed into the tiny bar. He'd never been much for an audience, but it seemed like a damned fine idea right about now.

"Well?" She arched an eyebrow at him. "A big screen TV? An Amazon gift card? Cash?"

"Sex," he murmured.

As much as he wanted to bite Holly, that wasn't an option. She didn't fall under his spell the way other women did and so he had to consider the possibility that she might remember every detail of the time they spent together. He couldn't bite her and risk all hell breaking loose should she discover his true identity.

But he could drink in enough of her sexual energy over the next five days to curb his appetite enough so that he wouldn't crave her blood. Rather, he'd be full and sated and primed for a confrontation when Cody returned and revealed Rose's whereabouts. Then he could go after his sister-in-law at full speed and deal out the punishment that she so desperately deserved.

"I don't think that would be such a good idea," Holly said after a long moment. "But I'd be more than happy to pay you for your time. Maybe an hourly rate."

"I don't need your money." But he did need sustenance, so it seemed like the perfect way to the pass the time. To him, that is.

Holly, on the other hand, didn't look the least bit happy about the situation and damned if that didn't make him all the more determined to get her to agree to his terms.

"You could always find someone else to help you out."

But that was the thing. She couldn't.

He saw the truth in her gaze and watched the push-pull of emotion. A full-fledged throw-down between excitement and *uh-oh* that had him wondering which one would actually win.

As much as she wanted him, she'd sworn off seconds, and as he'd already discovered, Holly wasn't a woman easily swayed once she'd made up her mind.

After what seemed like forever, she finally nodded. "Okay then. Let's do it."

7

Travis stood in the shadows and watched Holly unlock the door of the two-story Colonial house that sat in the heart of Skull Creek, directly across from the small city park. A white picket fence outlined a picture-perfect yard lined with flowers and shrubs. A swing hung from the porch rafters and a large Welcome Mat sat in front of the door.

The place had *family* written all over it, despite Holly's claim that she intended to stay single for a really, *really* long time.

Lights flicked on inside and spilled through the windows. He watched as she set her stuff on the dining room table and headed back outside.

The front door opened. A steady *click-clack* echoed as she crossed the hardwood porch and headed down the steps. She punched a button on her key fob. The trunk made a soft *popppp* and opened wide.

She slid her keys into her pocket and leaned into

the opening to gather up a cardboard box overflowing with wedding leftovers. Her skirt stretched tight over her sweet ass and hunger hit him hard and fast and sharp.

His mouth watered and his fangs tingled and he wondered how in the hell he was going to hold off until tomorrow night.

That's when the charade would start. Nine o'clock sharp at Cherry Blossom Dance Hall, in front of a packed house. The honky tonk was holding the preliminaries for their weeklong indoor rodeo and practically every available cowboy in the county would be there. It was the perfect opportunity to debut the new and improved and totally non-committal Holly, or so she thought.

His chest tightened and tension zipped up his spine. The urge to push her up against the edge of the car, sink his fangs deep and give her the best orgasm of her life nearly overwhelmed him. A few seconds and she would be screaming in ecstasy, totally ruined for any other man. She would give up her stupid quest for mindless sex and spend the next twenty years dreaming about him every night.

If she'd been any other woman.

But this was Holly. They'd already had earth-shattering sex, yet she wasn't the least bit anxious for seconds. Instead, she was scared. And determined.

While she'd agreed to their arrangement, she wasn't the least bit happy about it. Not because she didn't *want* to have sex with him again. She did. But she didn't want to want to have sex with him, and damned if that didn't bother the hell out of him.

Which explained why he'd followed her home. He hadn't been able to help himself. She puzzled the hell out of him and damned if that didn't make him want her all the more.

She pulled the box free and set it at her feet. As she bent down, her luscious breasts heaved against her silky blouse. The top button strained, threatening to pop open. A second later, she straightened and the material relaxed.

Disappointment ricocheted through his body, bulls-eyeing him straight in the crotch. The scent of her—so warm and moist and rich—crossed the distance to him and shattered his already tumultuous control. His blood rushed and his cock throbbed.

He focused, zeroing in on the button and just like that, it slid free of its own accord.

Startled, she glanced down and made quick work fastening it back up. She was about to lean back into the car after the next box when the button popped open again, setting off a chain reaction that didn't stop until the edges of her blouse parted.

He pursed his lips and blew into the still night air. The material fluttered open as if brushed by a faint breeze. He glimpsed the dark shadow of her nipple beneath the lacey cup of her bra and his stomach hollowed out. Another whisper of air and the hem of her skirt lifted, sliding up to reveal one round ass cheek barely concealed by a pair of skimpy bikini panties. A surprised gasp bubbled in the air and a split-second later, a desperate hand smoothed the skirt back down. Trembling fingers caught the edges of her blouse and tugged them closed, killing his view altogether.

Aw, hell.

Just as the thought struck, her head jerked up and he had the crazy notion that she'd actually heard him.

Crazy because he knew good and goddamned well that such a thing just wasn't possible. Vampires forged connections with blood. She would have to drink from him and he would have to drink from her for them to be that closely linked.

No, she hadn't heard him and she never would. The last thing Travis intended was to drink from Holly Simms or have her drink from him.

This wasn't about blood. It was about sex. Sweet, succulent, satisfying sex.

Starting tomorrow night.

In the meantime...

He gave himself a great big mental kick in the ass, turned and headed for the nearest motel. And straight into an ice cold shower.

HOLLY PULLED HER blouse closed and peered into the surrounding darkness. Awareness skittered up her spine and goose bumps danced the length of her arms. The hair on the back of her neck prickled and she had the distinct feeling that someone was watching her.

It was a feeling she knew all too well.

Every day, as a matter of fact, since this past Christmas when her neighbors, the Dunbars, had bought a bird-watching set for their fourteen-year-old son.

Mitchie Dunbar was a video game addict whose parents were desperate to get him off the couch and outside. Instead of the new Xbox 360 he'd been begging for, Santa had brought him a bird-watching set, complete with binoculars, a book on the various species and an online membership to Bird Watchers International where wannabe ornithologists the world over could post about their latest sightings.

Thanks to his adolescent hormones and the desperate need to impress his equally horny friends, the only thing Mitchie had been posting was how many times Holly bent over while watering the grass.

She summoned her most intimidating glare and turned toward his window to scare the bejeesus out of him. She would tell him off, report him to his mother, and then he'd be the one watering her lawn for the next two weeks.

"I see you, Mitchie—" she started to yell, the words stalling as soon as her gaze fixed on the closed window.

The glass was down, the drapes pulled tight, the

house dark. She kept staring, looking for the slightest movement that would give him away.

Nothing. Not even the glow of a computer monitor.

His covert skills were definitely improving.

That, or someone else had joined the party.

She turned back around, her gaze sweeping the lawn before pinpointing a huge tree that sat at the far edge of her property. A strange tingling awareness worked its way through her body before settling in the pit of her stomach. It was the same feeling she'd had back at the bar when she'd made eye contact with Travis Braddock.

Moonlight spilled down through the trees, illuminating the empty spot and proving beyond a doubt that her own imagination was running away with her thanks to the deal they'd made just a half hour before.

Sex.

She still couldn't believe she'd agreed to it. She'd vowed off seconds when she'd taken her Love Busters pledge and gotten her free t-shirt. Not that she didn't *want* to have sex with him again. She did. More than anything. That was the reason she'd sworn not to. Seconds led to thirds and thirds led to fourths and fourths to a bona fide relationship that would inevitably end in major heartache. She didn't want to get hooked on Travis Braddock and end up binge eating another wedding cake.

Not this time.

She'd changed over the past two years. She was stronger now. Wiser. She'd learned her lesson the hard way and it wasn't one she intended to repeat. She had different expectations when it came to the opposite sex—namely, she wasn't looking for love with any one man. She was looking for lust. Hot, raw, uncomplicated lust.

She ignored the *yeah, right* that niggled at her and turned back to the trunk.

"Little perv," she muttered as she re-fastened her blouse and tried to ignore the sudden realization that there wasn't even the slightest breeze in the air. That, and she didn't feel the same aggravation she normally felt when she caught Mitchie playing Peeping Tom.

Because it wasn't Mitchie, a voice whispered.

It was *him*. His tall, powerful body standing in the shadows. His attention fixated on her. His eyes devouring her from head to toe.

The notion didn't disturb her half as much as it made her anxious.

Excited.

"It's about damned time, sugar."

Tootie's voice replayed in her head and she remembered the gleam in her aunt's eyes when Holly had waltzed out of the bar and announced that she and Travis were going to get together the following night.

It *was* about damned time.

Holly had wasted enough of her life falling in love with the wrong men. It was time to have a little fun with the right man.

Right as in perfect for her specific situation, that is. Not *right* as in Mr. Right. Travis was wild and uncomplicated and sexy and temporary.

Mr. Right Now.

Or he would be, once tomorrow evening rolled around and their little arrangement officially began.

She swallowed against her suddenly dry throat. Her tummy quivered and her knees trembled and anticipation rippled through her. Her nipples pressed against the lace of her bra and heat spiraled through her. Drawing a deep, steadying breath, she slammed the trunk and picked up her boxes.

And then she started for the house, and what she knew was going to be *the* longest night of her life.

8

HOLLY HAD LEARNED a long time ago that there were only two certainties in the life of a wedding planner. The first? Despite the pessimistic divorce rate, people still believed in marriage. Regardless of the season, there was never a shortage of couples ready to dish out an incredible amount of cash for a groom's cake shaped like a monster truck or an ice sculpture that looked like Elvis. The second? Out of all those marriage-minded individuals, there was at least one bridezilla at any given moment.

And at this moment, the monster in question was a petite redhead sitting on the pink settee directly across from Holly.

"I've been thinking about the whole floral motif." Darla Lancaster flicked an invisible piece of lint from the lapel of her cherry-colored blouse. "I think we need to forget the tea roses and go with something else. Maybe lilies or peonies."

"I love lilies," Evan offered from the far corner where he sat at his desk, a book of material swatches open in front of him. "They're so romantic."

Holly ignored his vote and focused on the woman sitting across from her. "But the roses are being flown in from Italy as we speak." She'd tracked the order just that morning. "They're in Chicago about to wing their way here for a Monday delivery."

"The roses are fine," chimed in the woman sitting next to Darla. Shelley was the sister-of-the-bride and the first female in the history of nearby Travis County to serve as deputy sheriff. She wore a beige uniform and had her dark brown hair pulled back and pinned at the nape of her neck. "Flowers are flowers." She shrugged. "What difference does it make?"

Darla shook her head. "I just don't think tea roses represent the real me. I want everything at this wedding to scream *Darla*."

"But the cost of changing at such short notice would be astronomical," Holly informed her bride.

"You can't put a price on love." She glared at Shelly before shifting her attention back to Holly. "Tea roses don't scream. They whisper. Lilies, on the other hand, definitely make a louder statement." Blue eyes stared pointedly at Holly. "Don't you think?"

What?

Holly tamped down on her frustration and tried to keep a calm demeanor in front of her biggest client.

Not only was Darla the most high maintenance

of all Holly's brides, she was also the most high profile. In exactly one week, she was marrying Sam McGregor, the son of a Texas congressman and one of the most powerful lawyers in the state. Sam was wealthy. Educated. Successful. On top of that, he looked like a Ken doll with his blond hair, great tan and Crest-worthy smile. Once upon a time, his dad had been the mayor of Skull Creek. He'd grown up just two streets over on the most affluent block in town.

Darla herself had grown up in the Happy Trails trailer park just on the other side of the railroad tracks that circled the town. She'd never been to the governor's mansion or hobnobbed with Dallas' richest oil men. She was Cinderella and Sam was her Prince Charming, and it only made sense that she would be a little freaked.

At least that's what Holly told herself every time she got a visit or phone call changing yet another detail of the over-the-top event.

First the food. Then the champagne. The band. Even the dress. They'd gone back and forth between princess and mermaid styles before Darla had finally decided to buy one of each. One for the ceremony and the other for the reception. Now if she could only decide which one to wear to which event.

Holly forced herself to take a deep, calming breath. "I really do think the tea roses are perfect for a formal daytime event, which is what we've planned."

"About that…" Darla frowned. "I was thinking that we might actually bump up the time a little. Make it later, after sunset, so that I can have candles. Lots of candles."

"I love candles," Evan offered again. "They make everything look so dreamy."

Holly cut him a warning glance before smiling at Darla. "I thought you wanted sunlight streaming through the stained glass windows of the church?"

"She doesn't know what she wants," Shelly chimed in.

"I most certainly do." Darla shot a glare at her sister before shifting her attention back to Holly. "Sunlight and stained glass were fine when I was going for a more sedate, classy look." Darla waved a hand and her three carat diamond engagement ring flashed in the early morning sunlight. "But Sam and I really want this to reflect our personalities. I think I'm a little more dramatic than afternoon chic. I'd rather go for something that suits my sophisticated side. Maybe a black tie event with lots of ball gowns. Sort of like *Phantom of the Opera*." She smiled. "I totally loved that movie."

"I loved it, too—" Evan started, only to clamp his mouth shut when Holly shot him another sideways glance. He shrugged. "I mean, it's okay if you buy into the whole dark, dangerous, wounded hero thing, which I don't. Although I absolutely *loved* the costumes. And that mask… Girl, that's definitely the stuff of fantasies."

"That's what I was thinking, too," Darla exclaimed before launching into a quick discussion about possibly handing out masks as party favors at the reception.

"Shoot me," Shelley whispered to Holly.

"I was thinking the exact same thing."

"So it's settled then," Darla smiled. "*Phantom of the Opera* it is."

"But the wedding is in seven days. The classy, afternoon, sunlight-streaming-through-the-windows wedding, complete with a cage full of rare butterflies to release immediately following the nuptials."

Darla waved a hand. "Plenty of time for you to do away with all that nonsense and give me what I really want."

"But the invitations have already gone out specifying the time and the details."

"I'm sure we can send new invitations via overnight mail. Or a text message." Brilliance seemed to strike and she beamed. "Or an email. I'll forward you my contact list as soon as I get home."

"But most of your guests have already made travel arrangements based on the information in the original invitation?" She knew she sounded like a broken record with the *buts, but* months of planning were spiraling down the drain and she couldn't help herself.

Darla stiffened and her gaze narrowed. "It's my wedding and I want *Phantom of the Opera*. If that doesn't work for you, then I'm sure I can find another planner who shares my vision and understands what it's like to marry someone like Sam. You haven't actually been married yourself, have you?"

"No," Evan offered. "She came really close—and I mean *really* close—but didn't quite hit the bulls-eye."

Not that Darla didn't already know that. Skull Creek was a map dot where everybody knew everybody and gossip traveled faster than the speed of light.

Darla shook her head. "No wonder you can't understand."

Holly's chest tightened. Not that she wanted to be a bride. She'd given up on that fantasy a long time ago. It was the thought of losing an entire shipment of tea roses. She loved tea roses. And it seemed such a shame for them to go to waste.

"I love *Phantom of the Opera*," Holly finally declared. "I'll call the florist first thing and make the changes."

"Okay, now you've both gone off the deep end," Shelley added. "I knew it was just a matter of time."

Darla ignored her sister. "Make sure to tell the florist I don't want small lilies. I want large ones, and have them done up in some really elaborate arrangements. Something that says bold. Aggressive. Something that screams *Darla*."

Or royal bitch.

Holly tamped down the unkind thought and reminded herself that the young woman was just under a lot of stress. She was out of her element and so it made sense that she would be a little on edge. And bitchy. Holly would have done the same had she been in Darla's shoes.

She summoned her most reassuring smile. "I'll take care of everything."

True to her word, she spent the next two hours on the phone tracking down shipments and negotiating prices before she finally managed to pull off Darla's latest request. After that, she tackled the multitude of changes that had to be made.

"You're fired," she told Evan when she finally hung up after an exhausting phone call to the caterer. She'd barely made a dent in all the work that needed to be done, which meant she would have to come in on Sunday.

"For what? Helping you plan the wedding of the century?"

"Killing my one day off. Do you know how much work this is going to be? Or how much it's going to cost?" She stared at the endless list of figures that the various vendors were going to charge for the last minute changes.

"First off, I'm happy to help with the extra work.

Bob plays tackle football with his straight buddies on Sunday and I'm not invited because I busted out crying the last time he got tackled. As for the extra cost, what do you care? It's not your money. If the girl wants lilies, give her lilies."

"She doesn't know what she wants. That's the problem. Tomorrow it could be daisies."

"I love daisies," Evan offered, only to clamp his mouth shut when Holly shot him a withering glare.

"You love everything."

He shrugged. "Love makes the world go 'round."

Amen.

She squelched the thought and spent the rest of the day making changes and going through the list of email contacts Darla had sent her. She had to notify as many guests as possible, as fast as possible.

Forgive me, Martha Stewart.

She sent up the silent plea as she typed in the last address and hit send.

"Closing time," Evan's voice drew her attention and Holly glanced at the clock for the first time since Darla had dropped the bomb on her.

Five o'clock? Seriously?

"I'm meeting Bob for drinks." Evan packed up his desk. "Want to come with?"

"I'm busy tonight."

"Oh, honey, your toes can wait until tomorrow."

"I'm not giving myself a pedicure." She finished making the last of her notes in Darla's file and reached for her purse.

"Manicure?"

"No."

"Facial?"

She gave him a pointed stare. "I'm going out."

Evan arched an eyebrow. "I thought you swore off dating."

"It's not a date. We're just going to hang out."

"Since when do you just hang out?"

She leveled a stare at her assistant. "Since now." And then she headed out the door. It was time to show the entire world that Holly Simms wasn't the woman everyone thought she was.

9

Travis dropped to his knees, shoved his hands into the icy stream and splashed the cool liquid onto his face. Water ran in rivulets down his neck, drenching the collar of his shirt and cleansing the grime of the past few days on the trail. But it wasn't enough to wash away the tickle in his gut. It stayed with him, following him back to the other men sleeping by the fire.

He stretched out on his bedroll and closed his eyes. The seconds ticked off in his head. The uneasiness rolled through his gut. It was stronger tonight than it had been before. Stronger, but not strong enough.

The enemy wasn't close enough yet to alarm the others. The best thing to do would be to keep quiet and push on southward, the way they'd planned, heading straight for the Union supply train on its way to Vicksburg. If they stopped now and waited *for the group of men following them, they would miss the rendezvous point and months of work would go to hell in a hand basket. They had to reach Vicksburg first, and that meant no slowing down.*

His gaze shifted to his oldest brother on the bedroll a few feet away. If Colton knew the damned feelings niggling at Travis, he would vote to stay and take care of the most immediate threat. To play it safe. Colton wanted to get home in one piece.

Hell, they all did. Brent had a steady girl he'd left behind. For Cody, it was a damned saloon full of them. And for Colton? A wife and a son.

Travis was the only one who didn't have anything to go back to. It would suit him just fine if they never made it back to Texas.

Laura Mae Sooner had dumped him the minute he'd told her they were riding out after Cody. She'd forced him to choose and he'd chosen his brothers. They'd always stuck together. They'd had to when their pa had taken off chasing yet another woman. He hadn't come back that last time and Travis and his brothers had been looking out for one another ever since.

When Cody had left for the war, they'd all gone after him. And they'd been busting their asses for the Confederacy ever since.

They'd raided more gun and supply shipments than Travis could count and there had been plenty of times when they'd had somebody tailing them.

But this felt different.

He tamped down on the crazy thought and rolled onto his side. Wadding up the blanket, he shoved it tighter under his head and watched the flames lick at the surrounding darkness.

He was antsy. That was all. Colton had gotten captured a few weeks ago and they'd had a helluva time getting him back.

But they had, he reminded himself. They'd snatched him out of those carpetbaggers' hands just in the nick of time and everything had turned out okay. They'd even had a decent meal that night, thanks to the extra supplies his kidnappers had been stashing. The entire situation had been a close call, but the Braddock Boys had come out on top.

It was all about moving and staying one step ahead.

Travis held tight to the thought and forced his eyes closed. He concentrated on the sounds around him. The crackle of the fire. The buzz of insects. The crunch of footsteps just behind—

The thought slammed to a halt as a bullet cracked open the night sky. A burning sensation ripped through his right shoulder. And then all hell broke loose.

TRAVIS BOLTED UPRIGHT, his body shaking, his shoulder tingling. He could still feel the cold steel of the bullet followed by the hot rush of blood. The smell of gunpowder burned his nostrils. The shouts echoed in his ears.

He touched the jagged scar and fought the nagging voice.

You knew it. You felt it.

Bullshit.

He'd been on edge like everyone else. They'd been ambushed before and so when they'd caught wind that someone was tailing them, he'd feared the worst. Expected it.

He sure as hell hadn't *known*.

But that's not what his granny had told him. She'd died of a heart attack when he was seven, but before then she'd lived with them at the ranch. He and Colton were the only ones old enough to really remember her.

"You've got the sight, boy."

She'd said it all the time when he was a child. Like when he'd shown up for supper before his mother rang the dinner bell. Or when he'd taken off fishing just when his ma was about to make him shovel the barn. Or when he'd side-stepped a rattler that no one else had seen coming at a church picnic.

But Travis had never listened to her. She'd been old and barely playing with a full deck. His mother had said she'd gone a little crazy when his grandfather had died. And while he'd always respected his grandmother, he'd never really paid much attention to anything she said. No one had.

But she'd been right.

He drop-kicked the thought and threw his legs over the side of the bed. The sun had already set and the light from the bare bulb hanging outside his door pushed around the blinds, fighting to get inside the small room. He eyeballed the clock. He'd meant to sleep an extra hour or so, but he knew that wasn't going to happen. A few seconds later, he stepped into a hot shower. The water flowed over him, washing away the memories and the pain.

For a little while anyway.

Without enough rejuvenating sleep, his muscles still ached. Emptiness gnawed at the pit of his stomach and his gut tightened. He desperately needed another round with Holly. Another sweet, succulent orgasm to satisfy the craving deep inside.

But there was something else, as well. An anticipation that had nothing to do with feeding and everything to do with the desperate need to see her. Touch her. Talk to her.

And his granny had been the crazy one?

He gave himself a great big mental kick in the ass. This was all about sex. Sustenance. He needed to kill some time and regain his strength and she needed to sully her glowing reputation. End of story.

With his mind set, he stepped out of the shower, grabbed a towel and went about getting ready for his first official sex date with luscious Holly Simms.

"HOW DOES THIS look?" Holly asked as she walked into the living room where Tootie had planted herself on the couch a half hour ago after marching in and handing Holly her coveted bag of tricks—a tube of red lipstick, some blue eye shadow, a box of safety pins, a pack of pasties, a tube of denture cream and a five dollar bill. "Too skimpy?"

"Way too skimpy," Aunt Tootie said, giving Holly the once over, from the red button down shirt tied just under her breasts, to the cut off blue jean shorts that barely covered her butt cheeks, to a pair of three inch come-and-get-me red stiletto heels. Tootie smiled and her face erupted in a mass of wrinkles that a hundred dollar a month moisturizer habit hadn't been able to touch. "It's perfect." She patted her snow white beehive. "'Course, you could have saved your money and borrowed a few things from me. I've got a pair of shorts just like that, you know."

Holly ignored the sudden image of "Tootie the sexpot" that popped into her head and smiled. "I'll be sure to remember that next time." *Not.*

"Where'd you find that get-up anyhow? One of them adult specialty shops over in Austin?"

"Not exactly."

Her eyes sparkled. "A sex party?"

"Uh-uh."

"The internet?"

"The Piggly Wiggly."

Tootie's excitement turned to bewilderment. "Are you pulling my leg?"

"I got tied up at work today and it was the only place that was still open by the time I got off."

"Since when does the Piggly Wiggly have a clothing section?"

"They were clearing out last year's Halloween costumes. It was either Daisy Duke from the *Dukes of Hazzard* or Tinkerbell from *Peter Pan*. Since I doubt I could pull off a pair of fairy wings, I thought this would be the most realistic." A wave of insecurity rolled through her. "Then again, maybe it's too much of a stretch—"

"It'll do just fine," Tootie interrupted. "Just don't you worry about it."

"I borrowed the shoes from Evan," Holly added. "He and Bob like to play dress up."

"I knew there was something I liked about that boy." Tootie gave her another once over and winked. "Why, they'll be talking nonstop about you at church tomorrow. I just know it."

A girl could only hope.

Holly tamped down the butterflies in her stomach and summoned a smile. There was no way the men in town would fail to take her seriously now. Not when she two-stepped across the floor in this get-up with Mr. Tall, Dark and Delicious himself.

Not that she could actually two-step.

She'd spent so many years dreaming of happily-ever-afters, having fun had sort of fallen by the wayside. Sure, she could waltz. That was a couples thing. She'd taken a few lessons when she and Chad had gotten engaged so their first dance as man and wife would be magical. But waltzing didn't really up the sex appeal value like the salsa or the rumba or the lambada.

You're not cut out for this, a voice whispered.

It was that same familiar little voice that had kept her waiting on Mr. Right all through high school and college instead of sowing her wild oats. But no, she'd listened. And held out for The One. First Allen. And then Ben. And then Chad.

She was breaking the cycle once and for all.

Besides, it's not like they *had* to dance. The point was to naughty up her image by being seen with *the* naughtiest man in town. Not land a spot on *So You Think You Can Dance.*

Drawing a deep breath, she reached for her purse. "Do you want me to drop you off at Bingo on my way?"

Tootie shook her head. "You just run along and have fun. I'll pull out my little black book and have someone here in no time. Maybe Ronald Dupree. He's a handsome one. With his new dental implants, I swear the man doesn't look a day over forty."

"Didn't he have cataract surgery and have to give up his driver's license?"

She stopped to think. "You might be right. Then I'll just call Wade Harlington. He was a Texas Ranger once upon a time and can still fit into the same pair of jeans he wore on his first case. Or maybe I'll give Jim Miles a ring. Or Bob Callahan." She shook her head. "It makes no never mind. I'll find somebody." Her mouth pulled into a thin line. "And I can guaran-damn-tee that I won't be calling Buck Gentry. That man is as old as dirt and just as irritating."

"You went to high school with him, didn't you?"

Tootie stiffened. "I most certainly did not. He was a good two years older than me. Maybe even three. 'Course, he always wanted me, but I never gave him the time of day. He's a great big horse's ass."

He was also the only man in town who hadn't been wowed by Tootie's pink hot pants and massive cleavage. She'd carried a grudge ever since.

"Why, I saw him at the diner last week and he had the nerve to tell me I should stop wearing such bright colors. Said I needed to dress my age. You know what I told him? You're only as old as you feel and I feel twenty-five. So he can just mind his own damned business. I had to take an extra blood pressure pill after that little encounter." When Holly gave her a concerned look, she waved a hot-pink manicured hand. "Stop worrying about me and get on out of here."

Holly forced aside her nerves and gave Tootie a

kiss on the cheek. She swiped on an extra layer of Wild & Wicked Red lipstick, and headed for the door.

If she was going through with this—and she was—it was now or never.

10

THIS WAS *NOT* a date.

Holly reminded herself of that all-important fact when she pulled into the parking lot of the honky tonk and spotted Travis waiting outside for her.

He looked as sinfully sexy as ever in jeans and a plain black T-shirt. The soft cotton molded to his broad shoulders, the sleeves falling just shy of a pair of intricate slave band tattoos that wound around each bulging bicep. A woven leather strap clung to his strong neck and a Stetson sat low on his forehead. He leaned on an old hitching post, arms crossed, booted feet hooked at the ankles.

When she climbed from the car, he straightened and tipped his hat back. The shadow lifted from his handsome face and her stomach hollowed out. Green eyes gleamed with an intensity that kicked her pulse into high gear. His sensuous mouth hitched in a wicked grin.

"You look…different," he said when she walked up to him. His gaze slid down her body and back up, lingering at her breasts for several seconds.

If she hadn't known better, she would have sworn she felt a distinct pressure on her nipple. Like the soft flick of a finger against the ripe tip, teasing, taunting. *Crazy.*

She drew a shaky breath and tried to ignore the frantic pounding of her heart. "That's the idea. I want people to see me differently."

"They'll definitely see you. A lot of you." A thread of jealousy filtered through the words and his brows drew together into a frown. "Don't you think you're going a little overboard?"

Hearing him voice the doubts that had haunted her since she'd first pulled on the skimpy outfit made them seem that much more real. She blurted, "Do I look that bad?" before she could remind herself that it didn't matter what he thought. *He* didn't matter.

But at that moment, he did.

Her gaze searched his and oddly enough, his expression softened.

The frown eased. "Sugar, you look incredible. It's just that I signed up to keep you company, not fight off every man in the place."

The words whispered through her head and sent a rush of warmth through her. The scent of him, so raw and masculine, teased her senses. For an insane moment, she had the urge to lean closer and simply breathe. Fully. Deeply. To draw him in and lose herself.

The way she'd done with every other man in her past.

The realization hit and she stiffened. "I should be so lucky." She reached for the door before he had a chance to open it for her and hurried inside.

Neon beer signs plastered the walls and cigarette smoke fogged the air. A sea of Stetsons bobbed across the massive dance floor, keeping time to the Billy Currington song that vibrated through the building. The smell of beer and sawdust tickled her nose.

"Where to?" Travis's deep voice rumbled in her ear as he came up behind her and awareness skittered through her.

She tried to ignore the sensations and swept a gaze around the room. Small round tables edged the dance floor and a large bar ran the full length of one wall. A crowd filled the far corner, surrounding the pile of mattresses that flanked a mechanical bull that was in high swing. She contemplated crawling onto the monster right here and now, but she was busting at the seams in her outfit as it was. Sharp turns and serious bouncing she didn't need. She was shedding her good girl image, not her clothes.

Then again—

"Don't even think it," Travis murmured in her ear. Before she could give a second thought to the fact that he'd just read her mind, he added, "The bar is more visible." He pressed the hand into the small of her back and steered her forward.

"What now?" she asked when they reached their destination.

"Now, we order a drink." He signaled the bartender and a few seconds later, two shot glasses full of sparkling gold liquid sat in front of them.

She took a huge gulp of the Jack Daniels and nearly spewed the stuff back out. She'd never been a big drinker and when she did indulge, she stuck to the occasional glass of wine. "It's good." *Not*.

A sinful grin tugged at the corner of his mouth. "You can order something a little softer if you want."

She glanced down the length of the bar, her gaze zeroing in on Susie Cantrell, Skull Creek's reigning bad girl. Susie was tall and sexy and always the life of the party, not to mention the sole subject of at least half the prayer meetings over at the church. Forget the daiquiris and the cosmos. She stood amid a group of cowboys, laughing and tossing down tequila shots.

"I'm fine with this." Holly stole another glance at Susie. "It just comes so naturally for her. My Aunt Tootie is the same way. She just gives off this vibe that says *Hey, I'm a party and a half*."

"And what's your vibe?"

"Run for your single life?"

He grinned. "That's not such a bad thing."

"Not if you want to settle down. But if you don't, it's the kiss of death."

"So you've sworn off settling down completely?"

"It's not that I wouldn't like to. Someday. I just don't think it's in the cards for me." She watched as Susie cast her a surprised glance and then whispered to one of the males next to her. The man looked at Holly, a startled expression on his face that quickly turned to *wow*. "Aunt Tootie says I should revel in being single but I've never really liked it that much."

"Maybe you've never taken the time to enjoy it."

"Have you ever been married?"

He shook his head. "Never have, never will. It's definitely not in the cards for me either."

"Family curse like me?"

His mouth hinted at a grin. "Something like that."

"Looks like Cody broke it."

"For now."

"You don't think it will last?"

"I don't see how it can."

"And I thought I was cynical."

"It's not about being cynical. It's called being practical. Some men aren't cut out for marriage."

"That's what my Aunt Tootie says. Except she says it about women. About us."

"But you don't actually believe her." It was more of a statement than a question, as if he knew she'd yet to toss out the stack of Bridal magazines collecting dust in the back of her closet.

"I'm here, aren't I?" She downed the last of her drink and signaled the bartender, suddenly eager to shift her attention to a different subject. "Hit me again." She was just about to take another gulp when Travis plucked the glass from her hand.

"We'd better do this now while you can still stand up."

"Do what?" she asked as he pulled her from her seat.

"Dance."

"I don't know if that's such a good idea." She dug in her heels as he tried to tug her onto the large saw-dust covered dance floor.

"Too drunk?"

"Too clueless." When his gaze caught and held hers, she added, "I don't really do this kind of dancing."

"What kind do you do?"

"The boring kind." Her gaze slid to a man currently spinning his partner and her stomach lurched. "I'm liable to fall on my face."

"I'll catch you first," he promised. As much as she wanted to turn and walk the other way, she knew she couldn't back down now. Everyone in the place was watching her, including Suzie Cantrell and her group of admirers.

She fought down her fear and let him lead her out onto the dance floor.

"Now what?" she asked as he turned to face her.

"Now you relax." He slid an arm around her waist and took her hand. "Dancing is all about letting loose and having fun. If you're worried about what you're doing, you'll screw it up for sure."

"Let loose," she murmured to herself, rolling her head from side to side and shaking out her shoulders. "I can do that."

"And have fun."

"I don't know if I can do that." And that was her problem in a nutshell. She'd been so busy searching for Mr. Right, she'd never taken the time to slow down. Relax. *Enjoy.* And she wasn't sure she even knew how.

A knowing gleam lit his eyes as he stared down at her. "Just follow my lead."

He started slow at first, his foot sliding forward, pushing against her leg and urging her backward. And then the move started all over again with the opposite foot.

They moved around the dance floor slowly, tentatively at first. But soon she fell into step with him and she didn't have to think so much. Her body followed his, leaning this way, sliding that way until she stopped worrying about looking like a hussy. Instead, she started to feel like one with each sultry sway and twist.

"You might be right after all." His deep voice slid into her ears and drew her from the hypnotic rhythm of their movements.

"About what?"

He winked. "You might have a little hussy in you."

His words startled her and she stiffened. "How did you know—? Whoa!"

Before Holly knew what was happening, he twirled her in the opposite direction. She was dead certain she was about to eat some hardwood, but then his fingers tightened around hers. Just as she teetered to the side, he pulled her back to him, turned her under his arm and the roller-coaster ride started all over again.

By the time the song faded to a close, Holly could hardly breathe. Her heart hammered and her pulse raced and she experienced a rush of excitement unlike anything she'd ever felt before.

Okay, so she'd felt it before. The burst of light headedness. The surge of *wow*. The *I can't believe this is happening*.

She'd felt it last night in the closet with Travis. When he'd felt her up and kissed her senseless and plunged so deep that she'd forgotten everything except the lust pulsing through her body.

A slow, sweet George Strait song poured from the speakers and Travis pulled her close. He felt so strong and smelled so good. She actually stopped thinking about what she should do—namely strut her stuff back to the bar now that she'd gotten everyone's attention and toss down a few more drinks to give them something to really talk about.

At the same time, the two drinks she'd already had had obviously gone to her head because instead of *should,* she did what she wanted to do. What felt right.

She moved closer to Travis.

He was so strong and powerful and suddenly she couldn't help herself. She leaned into him, molding herself to his hard frame and closing her eyes.

And for the next few moments, the world slipped away.

TRAVIS HAD NEVER been much for dancing. Sure, it provided a nice little warm up for getting up close and personal, but he'd stopped with the pretenses the night he'd lost his humanity. He much preferred ditching the formalities and getting right to the good stuff.

But when Holly slid her arms around his neck and leaned into him, he had the crazy thought that there might be something to this. It had been a helluva long time since he'd just held a woman.

Since he'd wanted to hold one.

He cursed the crazy notion just as soon as it moseyed into his brain. He didn't *want* to hold Holly Simms. He wanted to push her up against the wall and sink his cock into her lush body and his fangs into her sweet neck.

Sustenance.

That's all he wanted from her.

He tried to focus on the way her pelvis cradled his crotch. He moved against her, setting the pace with a subtle side-to-side motion that made his hard-on pulse and his fangs tingle. He needed to forget about her soft, warm breaths against his neck and the feel of her silky hair tickling the underside of his jaw. He wanted to forget, but then her warmth seeped inside him, chasing away the cold that gripped his bones. His nerves started to buzz.

He held her so easily, as if he'd been doing it his entire life.

He hadn't. He knew that. But there was just something about the steady *thump thump thump* of her heart against his chest.

It felt right.

She felt right.

And Travis held her tighter.

HOLLY FELT HIS arms tighten and a burst of happiness went through her, followed by a whisper of contentment that scared the bejeesus out of her. Because this wasn't about happiness or contentment or happily-ever-after.

Reality bolted through her and every muscle in her body went tight. "I think I need some air." She pulled away, suddenly desperate for a deep breath that didn't smell like Travis Braddock.

A few seconds later, she pushed through the rear door of the honky tonk and out into the back parking lot. A few cars dotted the area and two Dumpsters sat to her right. Laughter and music filtered from inside, mingling with the buzz of crickets. She drank in a huge lungful of oxygen and tried to calm the explosive pounding in her chest.

Happy? Content? *Seriously?*

What kind of Love Buster was she? She could *not* fall for this guy. No matter how strong his arms had felt sliding around her. Or how his eyes glittered so hot and bright. Or how he smelled like leather and fresh air and something so incredibly alluring that she couldn't seem to think straight when he was close.

It was only physical, she reminded herself. Those things were only the result of the intense chemistry that sizzled between them. The lust. It wasn't like they had an actual emotional connection. She hardly knew this guy and he hardly knew her. No way was he meant to hold her like that again and again, 'til death do us part.

"Holly?" His deep voice rumbled in her ears and she became acutely aware of the man standing behind her.

She hadn't even heard the door open and close. No footsteps. Nothing. Yet here he was.

The facts whirled in her head, hinting at something that she didn't have time to think about because *here he was*.

Get it together, girl. Remember your objective.

This is a business arrangement. He gives you something. You give him something.

And that was the problem itself.

She knew the deal she'd made with him, what she'd promised, and what waited at the end of the night—the best sex of her life. And it was that all-important fact that played with her sanity. Sex had always been part of a relationship, the culmination of time spent together and feelings shared. So it only made sense that she would think crazy thoughts her first time out of the gate. Like how no man had ever held her quite so firmly, so purposefully, so perfectly. How no man ever would.

She shook away the ridiculous sentiment. This had nothing to do with a relationship and everything to do with a business deal. Sex was just sex. It was all a matter of keeping her perspective.

She knew she didn't have a chance in hell of doing that inside. It felt too much like a date at this point, the anticipation building with each smoldering glance, each lingering touch.

She needed to get out of here, head for the nearest motel, chuck all the niceties and just get to it. Down and dirty. Cheap and tawdry. No strings.

She drew another deep breath and forced her feet to turn. "Okay." She nodded and did her best to control the sudden fluttering in her stomach. "I'm ready."

A frown creased his brow. "Ready for what?"

"You know." She braced herself. "The rest of our deal." She rolled her shoulders as if about to climb into a wrestling ring. "Let's do it."

The words were like a direct bolt of heat to Travis's already throbbing erection. His undead heart pounded. Adrenaline surged through his body and his nerves came alive.

But while it was exactly the invitation he'd been waiting to hear from her luscious mouth, there was just something about the way she said the words— as if she were agreeing to take a spoonful of Castor oil—that jabbed at his ego and tightened his already tight muscles.

"You want to leave now?"

She nodded. "I got what I wanted—everyone saw us. So it's only fair that you get what you want."

And the sooner we get this over with, the better.

Her desperate thought punctuated the statement and kept Travis from throwing her across his shoulder and heading back to his room to collect payment for services rendered.

But suddenly, he didn't want her to have sex with him half as much as he wanted her to *want* to have sex with him.

Plain and simple, he wanted her to want him, the way he wanted her. The need was so fierce and raw that it compelled him to reach out when every ounce of common sense told him to run the other way.

Though she was turned on and anxious, pulling

her into his bed wouldn't be enough. She was still thinking. Still worrying. Still fortifying her guard.

He wanted her to stop. To feel. To *want*. So much that *she* reached for *him*.

"If that's the way you want it." He stepped toward her. "Then let's do it. Right now."

She arched an eyebrow. "Here?"

"Why not?"

11

"I DON'T KNOW if this is such a good idea—" Holly started to say. But then he kissed her, his lips wet and hungry, his tongue greedy.

The humid night air closed around them, upping her body temperature and making it hard to breathe. Or maybe that was him. He surrounded her. His scent filled her head.

"Shouldn't we go somewhere," she breathed when he finally pulled away. "Somebody might see us."

"Isn't that the point, darlin'?"

It was. At the same time, there was just something about the way he held her—so firm and possessive—that sent a wave of *uh-oh* through her.

"You want to convince the entire town that you're a bad girl?" His gaze smoldered. "Then play the part and give them something to talk about."

Amen.

That's what her brain said. She'd waited for this

moment forever. The chance to prove to everyone that she was through being good.

At the same time, she and Travis were in a back parking lot. Their only audience was a crate of old liquor boxes, a Ford Prius that belonged to one of the waitresses and a beat-up GTO.

At least that's what she told herself.

She certainly didn't hesitate because this felt like something more. Her heart pounded at the thought of kissing him, touching him, regardless of their surroundings. There was just something about the way he stared so deeply into her eyes that made her want to slide her arms around his neck and never let go.

She balled her fingers, determined to resist as he dipped his head and caught her lips in another scorching kiss.

His tongue plunged deep, stroking and stirring the inside of her mouth and her heart pounded faster. He tasted of whiskey and dark desire and her knees trembled. Before she knew it, her fingers flexed and tangled in the soft cotton of his sleeves and she held tight. The kiss was thorough, consuming, mind-blowing.

And then it was over.

Thankfully.

That's what she told herself, but there was no mistaking the disappointment that spiraled through her as he pulled away, quickly followed by a rush of anticipation when he reached for the button on her shorts. Strong fingers worked at the opening. The zipper slid and the denim sagged. The frayed ends tickled her legs as he urged the shorts down over her thighs, her knees, until they pooled around her ankles.

He slid his hands around her bottom. His fingertips burned through the lace of her panties as he drew her legs up on either side of his hips and lifted her. A few seconds later, he set her down onto the hood of the old GTO.

He wedged himself between her parted thighs and urged her backward until her back met the cool metal hood. He unbuttoned her shirt and unhooked the front clasp of her bra. The cool night air washed over her bare skin and pebbled her nipples.

"These look good enough to eat," he murmured, touching one ripe tip. He circled the sensitive bud, tracing the areola until it throbbed and her skin flushed hot.

His gaze drilled into hers for a heart-stopping moment before he lowered his dark head. The first leisurely rasp of his tongue against her throbbing nipple wrung a cry from her throat.

Her fingers threaded through his hair as he drew the quivering tip deep into his hot, hungry mouth. He suckled her long and hard and she barely caught the moan that rippled up her throat. Her skin grew itchy and tight. Pressure started between her legs, heightened by the way he leaned into her, the hard ridge of his erection prominent beneath his jeans.

She spread her legs wider and he settled more deeply between them. Grasping her hips, he rocked her. Rubbed her. Up and down and side to side and—

"Where did you say you parked the truck?"

The question barely penetrated the haze of pleasure that gripped her senses. Her eyes snapped open and her ears tuned in to the footsteps in the far distance.

"It's right over here," a man's voice said. "Just relax."

The reality of what she was doing right here, right now, sent a burst of panic through her.

"Wait." She grasped his muscled biceps, but Travis didn't miss a beat. "Someone's coming." She tried to stare past him, but the Dumpster blocked her view.

"Easy," he murmured against her skin. He sucked her long and deep for a heart-stopping moment before leaning back. "If we can't see them, then they can't see us." His fingertip traced the edge of her panties where elastic met the tender inside of her thigh. "Stop worrying," he whispered, dipping a finger inside and testing her moist heat.

One rasping touch of his callused fingertip against her swollen flesh caused her to arch off the hood. She caught her bottom lip and stifled a cry.

With a growl, he spread her wide with his thumb

and forefinger and touched and rubbed as he dipped his head and drew on her nipple.

It was too much. And yet not enough. She clamped her lips shut and forced her eyes open. But he was there, filling her line of vision, his fierce gaze drilling into hers. Searching and stirring and begging her to fall…no!

Her hands trembled and she fought against the pleasure beating at her senses. She stiffened, her hands diving between them to stop the delicious stroke of his fingers.

As if he sensed her sudden resistance, his movements stilled. His chest heaved and his hair tickled her palms. Damp fingertips trailed over her cheek in a tender gesture that warmed her heart almost as much as her body.

"You're going the wrong way. This is the back of the building." The voice pushed through the haze of pleasure beating at her senses. "Let's head around the side." Gravel crunched and the footsteps faded into the pounding of her own heart.

"Do you want more?" His gaze was hot and bright and feverish as he stared down at her, into her. But there was something else, as well. A desperation that reached down deep and touched something inside of her.

She eased back down onto the hood. She spread her legs wider and he slid down her body. At the first rasp of his tongue, she almost jumped out of her skin.

He licked her up and down, side to side and...*there.* Right...*there!*

Her lips parted and she screamed at the blinding force of the climax. Her voice echoed, blending into the sound of music coming from inside. Travis gripped her and held her firmly to his mouth, tasting and laving as she exploded into a million pieces.

Once she could breathe again, she reached down and tugged at the button of his jeans, hungry for more, pulling his zipper down, she freed his hard length. She squeezed him, stroking him from root to tip once, twice, and then she let go, determined to let him take the lead.

To take what he wanted.

He growled, the sound so low and deep that it sent a tremble up her spine. The head of his penis pushed just a fraction of an inch inside her. He swore under his breath, the sound sizzling across her nerve endings and set them ablaze. A split-second later, however, the fire died as a cool wind whispered over her.

"Next time," he murmured.

Her eyes snapped and—

He was gone!

She struggled upright, her gaze searching for him, but the parking lot was empty.

"Next time."

His words echoed in her head and disappointment rushed through her. She'd wanted it tonight. Now.

Just to keep her on track, of course. Sex was a reality check. A reminder that this wasn't a real date.

But damned if she didn't feel as if he'd walked her to the front door and left her with a chaste kiss on the forehead.

TRAVIS LEANED ON the fencepost of Brent's new spread and stared at the cluster of horses grazing just up on the ridge. To the average eye, they looked calm and peaceful. But Travis didn't miss the flare of nostrils or the way one of them—a jet black female with white spots—danced just a little too much when the other horses got too close.

The animal was as wild as the day was long. It was a damned shame. She had the makings of a good cutting horse. A quick gait. An alert eye.

Easy, girl.

The thought whispered through Travis's mind and the animal's head snapped up. Her gaze cut through the distance separating them and her ears perked.

I'm not going to hurt you.

The animal obviously wasn't so sure and she danced backwards after a few moments. Travis debated hopping the fence and seeing how close he could get, but he wasn't here to train horses. Even if Brent had asked for his help.

He'd just driven out to take a look because it seemed like the easiest way to forget Holly and her screaming orgasm.

His fingertips still tingled where he'd drank in her delicious energy for those few precious moments. But it hadn't been nearly enough. He'd wanted to sink inside of her and stir another climax. And another. Until she finally admitted that she really and truly wanted him. To him. And herself.

It would take a while. He already knew that. He'd had no illusions that she would give in tonight. Sure, he'd hoped. But then that was part of what attracted him so strongly to her. Because she was strong. Different. Stubborn.

And he was too damned worked up to head back to his motel room.

He hopped the fence and the herd of horses scattered. All except for the black. She eyeballed Travis, sizing him up as if he was the enemy and they were standing on opposite sides of a battlefield.

As far as she was concerned, they were.

Travis took another step. Slow. Steady. Then another. The animal reared and he stopped.

They stared each other down for several minutes before the black finally turned and bolted after the others.

"She likes you. Otherwise she would have been long gone before you got so close." Brent's deep voice sounded behind him and Travis turned to see his brother standing on the other side of the fencepost.

"How long have you been here?" Travis asked as

he hopped back over the fence to stand beside his brother.

"I heard your truck from the house." Travis arched an eyebrow and Brent added, "and saw you, thanks to the surveillance camera posted at the road."

"A vampire's got to look out for himself, right?"

"You can't be too careful. It's pretty safe here, but we have had some crazy vampire hunters before. I rigged up the system myself. I've got two wireless cams posted at the turn-off. They communicate directly to my laptop. If anyone heads for my place, I know it. So what are you doing out here?"

"Just killing time. You've got a nice spread here." He glanced around at the rich, green pastureland.

"Thanks. I'm pretty proud of it."

Travis nodded toward the herd barely visible in the far distance. "She's good stock."

Brent shrugged. "She's not worth much if I can't get close to her."

Travis drank in a huge draft of air, desperate to kill the scent of Holly that lingered in his head. If he intended to make it through more nights like tonight without giving in to his own hunger, he needed a distraction.

"I'll see what I can do."

12

"You're late," Evan declared when Holly walked into her office at noon the next day.

"We're not open on Sundays. So I'm early for Monday." She sat her purse on a nearby table and sank into her desk chair. "How long have you been here?"

"Long enough to have your coffee ready and waiting." He handed her a steaming cup. "Two sugars. No cream. Just the way you like it."

"Thanks."

"Oh, and I picked these up on the way." He handed her a plate with a fresh cinnamon bagel slathered with cream cheese. "Your favorite." And then he dropped into the chair opposite her. He watched her take a bite, an expectant look on his face. "So?"

"It's good," she said around a mouthful.

"Not the bagel." His eyes twinkled. "The date. Did you wear the shoes?"

Holly took a sip of coffee. "Yes and I already told you, it wasn't a date. We just hung out."

"Bob's best friend's sister said you were dancing." She nodded and he added, "Bob's best friend's sister also said it was one of those slow, sexy numbers where you wrap your arms around each other and hold on for dear life." He wiggled his eyebrows. "Did your cowboy whisper sweet nothings in your ear?"

"It wasn't like that."

"Did he kiss you good-night?"

He kissed me all over.

The words were there, but for some reason she couldn't quite push them past her lips. Crazy, right? The whole point for her to build a reputation as a good time girl. Lewd and lascivious behavior definitely qualified as a good time. At the same time, this was Evan. Her employee. Her friend. And *the* most die-hard romantic she'd ever met.

He stared so intently at her, a dreamy look in his eyes, that she suddenly didn't have the heart to bust his romantic bubble by going into the tawdry details.

"We had a nice time," she heard herself say.

Evan jumped from his seat and gave a loud squeal. A split-second later, he threw his arms around her neck. "I'm so happy for you. I knew you would find someone."

"He's only in town for a few days."

"Love will find a way. It always does. Just don't

give up hope. And promise me I'll get to be the mister of honor when you tie the knot."

"It's not that serious." *Yet.* The traitorous thought punctuated her words and she shook it away. "I'm just helping him out while he's in town." When Evan looked at her as if she'd just kicked his brand new puppy, she added, "But if the time ever comes, I promise the title will be yours." Not that it ever would. And certainly not with Travis Braddock.

He wasn't the marrying kind any more than she was, which made them perfect for each other.

Right now, that is.

"I knew it." Evan continued. "I don't care what Bob's best friend's sister said. You *do* like this guy."

"I don't *like* him. He's only in town for a little while and I'm showing him around. That's all. Sort of like a good Samaritan. So," She eyed her assistant. "What exactly did Bob's best friend's sister say? Besides the play-by-play action?"

"She said you've climbed aboard the crazy train and you're headed straight to Harlotsville. But don't you worry, I know better." Excitement crept into his expression. "Are you going out with him again?"

"Not tonight. I've got too much going." She stared at the pile of work sitting on her desk. A stack of swatches sat to one side. She had to pick new linens for Darla Lancaster's reception, new place settings, new cardstock for the place cards, new color schemes for the new venue. And, of course, she needed a new venue itself. But it was Sunday, which meant these details would have to wait until tomorrow morning when everyone opened up and she could do a few walk-throughs. In the meantime, she was making decisions and getting as much ordered online as possible. "Plus it's all-you-can-eat wing night at the Iron Horseshoe. Aunt Tootie and I never miss it," she reminded Evan. She'd even gone so far as to leave a message at Travis's motel telling him as much. Tonight was definitely out of the question.

As for tomorrow...

She tried to force the thought from her head. While she was completely committed to changing her image, she wasn't eager for a change of profession. She'd worry about tomorrow night when that came. In the meantime...

She reached for a book of swatches.

"WHAT DO YOU mean you can't make it tonight? It's two-for-one on the fry-the-hair-off-your-ass habanera wings. I've been overdosing on Maalox all day to get ready," Tootie whined.

"I'm sorry," Holly said. "But I'm neck-deep in satin birdseed roses. I tried to get Darla to go for bubbles with the late notice, but she wanted the satin roses. The ones we initially ordered were pink, but Evan found a few hundred red ones leftover from the Valentine's dance we catered at the senior center last year. We filled those with conversation hearts, but they'll hold birdseed, too. Since my week is going to be hellacious as it is, I have to knock out as much as possible, as quickly as possible."

"If I ever get married, I'm having bubbles. Everything else is just too damned much trouble. Not that I am," Tootie added as if she'd just realized what had come out of her mouth. "Marriage is too damned much trouble."

"Do you want me to give you a ride to the bar?"

"You just finish up your work. I can manage. I've got men standing in line, you know."

"I know. See you later."

Instead of sitting at her desk, Holly boxed up her supplies and headed next door to her house.

She changed into a spaghetti-strap tank top and shorts and grabbed a diet soda. Flipping on the TV, she settled cross-legged on the floor—a Jersey Shore marathon blazing on one of the cable channels—and went to work.

The next few hours passed painfully slow as she filled rosebud after rosebud with birdseed. By the time she reached the halfway mark (two hundred and fifty down, two-fifty to go), her neck was stiff, her arms felt *this* close to falling off, and she'd more than earned the carton of Cookies & Cream ice cream sitting in her freezer.

She'd just collapsed onto her couch, fixed her gaze on yet another fight between Ronnie and Sam (the Jersey Shore couple most likely to strangle each other), and shoveled a spoonful into her mouth when the doorbell rang.

A few heartbeats later, she found Travis Braddock standing on her doorstep in faded jeans and a red T-shirt that read *Save a Horse, Ride a Cowboy,* his black Resistol sitting on top of his head. The porch light outlined his broad frame and made him seem big and intimidating. Or maybe it was his frown doing that.

"I went by the Horseshoe and you weren't there." His gaze swept the length of her, from her bare toes covered with pale pink nail polish, up over bare legs, her shorts and tank, to her face. "I thought it was wing night."

"It is. But I was too busy to make it."

"Doing what?"

"Difficult bride." She stepped back and opened the door so he could see the living room and the pile of satin roses stacked high. "She changed her colors and her theme, and everything else, which means the pink roses that were already done won't work. I need red ones." She drew a deep breath and tried to ignore the delicious aroma of hot, sexy male that filled her nostrils.

Some un-nameable emotion flashed in his eyes. Pleasure? Relief? As if he'd been worried she was out with some other guy. As if he cared.

As if.

He rubbed his hands together. "Then I guess we'd better get to work."

"I really don't think that's a good idea." She didn't need Travis sitting in her living room, distracting her, no matter how appealing the idea of a helping hand was.

"Afraid you won't be able to resist my charm?"

"I know I still owe you for last night, but I don't have time for sex. I really need to finish this."

"I'm not here to collect on last night. I was worried about you."

He looked so sincere that she almost believed him. Almost.

But that would mean that he actually liked her. And *that* would really throw a crimp into her plan because she was having a hard enough time not liking him. If he liked her, then she would start liking him, and that would make it impossible to spend time with him and not feel like she was on a date.

At the same time, she was only halfway done. Her hands hurt and she could really use some help. "Okay, but you have to swear to be careful. The satin pulls away from the stem very easily."

"Careful's my middle name," he said. She stepped back, but he didn't make a move forward.

"What?"

"Are you going to invite me in?"

"Didn't I just do that?"

"You said I could help. You didn't say I was welcome inside."

His words struck something inside of her, tugging and pulling at a few memories, but she shook the strange thoughts away. "Please come in and help me."

A grin creased his handsome face. "I thought you'd never ask." He moved past her, his arm brushing the tip of her breast through the soft cotton of her shirt. Heat bubbled inside her and she caught a gasp just before it slid past her lips.

Not tonight. Tonight she had to finish the mountain of roses.

And after they finished?

The question rattled her nerves as she closed the door and turned to follow Travis Braddock into her living room.

13

TRAVIS SURVEYED THE mountain of roses. "Show me how to do this."

"First you take one of these empty ones and open the top…" Her words trailed off and he knew she felt his gaze, stroking up her bare legs.

Heat sizzled along her nerve endings and he read the startling truth in her gaze. The sensation had nothing to do with the way he was looking at her and everything to do with the fact that he was standing in her living room, offering to help her fill birdseed roses, of all things. And she liked the situation far more than any freedom-loving, no-strings-attached good time girl should have.

"You're looking at me."

"So?"

"So don't look at me."

"It's just looking. I'm not doing anything."

"You want sex," she said, accusing.

"Every man wants sex, sugar." His grin stopped her heart for a long moment. "It's genetic." His gaze collided with hers. "But if you want to know the real truth, I think it's you who wants sex. You're the one interpreting my looks. Which means it's *you* who's got sex on the brain. I'm just appreciating the view."

And what a view.

Where she'd looked drop-dead gorgeous last night, it was nothing compared to the woman he saw standing before him now.

She was barefoot, her legs smooth and tanned, with hardly a hint of makeup on her face. A tiny spaghetti strap inched down the curve of her shoulder and his fingers itched to reach forward and push the strap back up again.

But he wasn't here to give in to his own impulses. This was about stirring hers. About turning her on and making her want him until she let go of her inhibitions and reached for him the way she desperately wanted to.

And that meant he wasn't touching her. No pushing the strap back up or pulling it all the way down. Or stripping her bare and laying her down on the living room rug and spreading her long, tanned legs and—

"Travis?"

"Yeah?" He shook away the lustful images and ignored the tightening in his gut.

"Did you hear what I said?"

"Open rose, pour birdseed inside. Gotcha." Just to resist his own damned lust and bolster his defenses, he sat down on the opposite side of the pile. With a few feet between them, he was sure to keep his head and resist the beast growling inside of him.

He tried to tell himself that for the next few hours, but it was damned hard to believe it with her sweet scent filling his head and her soft breaths echoing in his ears. Despite the distance, he'd never felt quite so close to a woman. Or so at home.

The thought struck and he gave himself a mental shake. He'd lost his home. Rose was responsible and he was going to make her pay just as soon as Cody came back and spilled the beans on her whereabouts.

Until then, he was stuck here.

Stuck, he reminded himself.

If only he wasn't starting to feel as if this was the one place he was always meant to be. Here. With her.

"Why not just fill up a bucket and have everybody grab a handful?" he blurted, eager to distract himself from the dangerous thoughts. "It would save a helluva lot of time."

"It's not about convenience. It's about creating a moment that's memorable."

"How is this memorable?"

"It's one of the small touches that come together to make one big memorable event. It's not always birdseed roses, either. Some people like bubbles. Some shoot off fireworks while the bride and groom run for the car. I even had one couple that wanted the guests to blow whistles." At his questioning look, she added, "They were the girls and boys basketball coaches from the local high school. When they tied the knot, they wanted to feel like they were about to start the championship game. Hence the whistles."

"Sounds ridiculous."

"Maybe to you, because you're not a basketball coach. Speaking of which, what do you do?"

"I train horses."

"More of a hay tossing guy."

"I don't want people tossing hay at my wedding."

"You say that now, but once the wedding bug bites, you'd be surprised what you start asking for. First it's a little hay at the reception, maybe a rawhide neck tie to go with the tuxedo. The next thing you know, you want an ice sculpture that looks like Mr. Ed."

"You're a regular comedian."

She grinned and worked on a few more roses. "So how did you get into working with horses?" she asked after a long, silent moment.

"My family used to own a ranch in West Texas. I trained all of our cutting horses." He paused. "We lost it all in a fire. So now I go from ranch to ranch, working other people's horses."

"I hope no one was hurt."

"My brothers and I were the only ones to make

it out. My mother and my nephew both died. Not to mention our foreman and some of the workers."

"I'm really sorry."

He'd heard the same sentiment time and time again. From all of the people in town. From everyone who'd ever known about his past. But the words had never really eased the ache in his chest. Until now.

"I like fireworks."

"Excuse me?"

"Bubbles seem kind of lame and birdseed isn't very exciting. I think fireworks would be cool."

She smiled. "Me, too." Excitement leapt into her eyes. "The fourth of July has always been one of my favorite holidays. Aunt Tootie used to take me to the park and we'd stretch out on a blanket and watch the fireworks."

He had a quick vision of a small, blond-haired girl in pigtails, lying flat on her back on a gingham blanket, her eyes reflecting the spray of fireworks. His chest hitched.

"It sounds nice." So much that the vision quickly shifted and he saw the two of them, hands intertwined, staring up at the brilliantly lit sky.

They fell into a comfortable silence for the next few moments until he asked, "Is that what you had planned when you were engaged? A spray of fireworks?"

Her head snapped up as if he'd tapped some deep,

dark secret, but then her expression eased. "I guess it was just a matter of time until you heard the gossip. Hazards of a small town, right?" She shrugged. "Don't I wish. But Chad—my fiancé at the time— hated fireworks. He had a roman candle backfire when he was a kid and he never got over it."

"So what did he want?"

"I don't really know." She shook her head. "He didn't help in any part of the wedding planning. He said it was a girl thing and to just do what I wanted— with the exception of the fireworks, of course. But it was his wedding, too. I wanted to do what he wanted." She laughed, but there was a sadness in the sound that made his chest tighten. "Turns out, he wanted not to be married." She shrugged. "At least I figured it out before we actually said 'I Do.'"

"Did you love him?"

"He was a great guy. Nice-looking. Good job. Liked animals."

"But did you love him?" Travis persisted.

"I agreed to marry him, didn't I?"

"That still doesn't answer my question."

"It's a dumb question. If you agree to marry some-one, of course you love them."

"That or you love the idea of being in love."

The minute he said the words, she wanted to refute them but nothing came to her lips.

Because he was right.

The realization hit her as she sat there stuffing

birdseed roses, Travis sitting so close, his gaze so intent that she felt as if he could see all the things inside of her that even she couldn't see.

But Travis could. He saw inside her thoughts, to her deepest darkest feelings. How she'd wanted so badly to be the one in her family to break the cycle. To fall in love and live happily ever after like the proverbial fairy tale.

It was a silly notion. Travis didn't believe in fairy tales and he sure as hell didn't believe in the whole one man/one woman. Particularly since he was only a shell of a man now. But sitting there, staring into her soft eyes, feeling the contentment seeping through him, damned if he wasn't starting to think that maybe, just *maybe,* Cody and Brent were a damned sight smarter than he was giving them credit for.

"So where's this guy now?" he asked, eager to kill the sudden silence. His brothers were playing with fire by thinking for even a second that they could be happy. It was just a matter of time until the whole thing went down in a smoldering mess.

"Married to someone else." She laughed, but there was a sadness in the sound that made his chest tighten. "It turns out he didn't have an aversion to getting married. Just an aversion to getting married to me." She stiffened. "But all's well that ends well. I've got a great career and now all I have to do is move my personal life in the right direction. So what about you? Have you ever been engaged?"

"Once. A long, *long* time ago. But it didn't work out. We were too different."

"At least you both realized it before it was too late."

"I did, but she wasn't so lucky."

"What's that supposed to mean?"

"After the breakup, she committed suicide." Travis wasn't sure why he told her. He shouldn't have, but the softness in her gaze compelled him and damned if he could help himself. "She killed herself because of me." He'd thought those words many times, but he'd never said them out loud to anyone. He'd never wanted to. Until now.

Until Holly.

He waited for her to turn horrified eyes on him, to order him out of her house because he was such a despicable person. Instead, she shook her head and stared at him, her gaze sympathetic. "People don't commit suicide because of someone else. They commit suicide because they're weak. I should know. I've spent enough time watching my mother destroy herself, quote—over someone else—end quote, when it's really not their fault, but hers. While my Aunt Tootie refuses to ever get married, my mom refuses to give up on it. She thinks if she finds someone who loves her, it will make her love herself. But it doesn't work, because at the end of the day, she's still the same person. Needy. Dependent. Insecure. She gets so wrapped up in a man, so determined to ignore all her shortcomings, that the breakup is a devastating eye-opener and she can't deal with it. After number one, she started drinking. Number two sent her into a bottle of Prozac and lots of therapy. Three and four pushed her into prescription pain meds and five sent her on a six month sabbatical with a religious zealot who worships a ceramic turtle. She's about to marry a guy she met at one of the revivals. She'll probably end up on an episode of *Cult Intervention* after this one."

"Or the sixth time could be a charm and actually work out."

Her tense expression eased into a grin. "If I didn't know better, I'd say there was a romantic streak buried deep down inside of all that sex appeal."

"It's called practical. She's already been through the worst. The odds are in her favor for a good outcome." His gaze met hers. "And there you go, making a pass at me when I'm on my best behavior."

"I'm not making a pass at you."

"You said I had sex appeal."

"That's not a pass." She shrugged. "It's a fact." They fell into silence for a few moments and he knew she struggled with the push-pull of emotion rising inside her. Right versus wrong. Crazy versus common sense. Lust versus love. "A pass would be if I touched you or kissed you. I haven't done either one of those things." *And I won't.*

Determination gleamed hot and bright in her

gaze and he knew the emotional battle was over. Common sense had won and disappointment ricocheted through him. Still, Travis wasn't about to be put off.

"But you want to," he persisted.

"All I want is for you to pretend to be my boy toy when we're out in public. You're the one who wants sex."

"And you don't want it at all? Not even a little bit?"

He watched her struggle a bit more before she found her courage.

"What I really want is to finish these birdseed roses before midnight." She shifted her attention to the task at hand, as if she weren't this close to launching herself at him and kissing him senseless.

She was.

He saw the truth in the trembling of her hands and the quivering of her bottom lip. Felt it in the heat radiating from her luscious body.

She wanted it, but she didn't *want* to want it.

It wasn't enough. Not yet.

"What are you doing?" she blurted when he reached across and stroked the smooth inside of her leg.

"Making a pass." He caught her lips in a desperate kiss, his tongue plunging deep, stroking and tasting until she moaned into his mouth. His gut twisted and the beast stirred and it was all he could do to tear his mouth from hers.

And then he got the hell out of there before he gave in to the hunger that urged him to forget his pride and simply feed.

That day was coming, he knew. He could only hope that Holly made her move first and ended the deprivation. Otherwise, Travis was going to find himself well past the breaking point. And he feared that once he reached for her, he wouldn't be able to stop until he'd tasted her completely.

Her body and her blood.

14

IT WAS ALMOST nine o'clock when Holly finally opened her eyes the next morning. She took one look at the clock and panic bolted through her. She raced for the bathroom and had just stepped into a hot shower when she heard Aunt Tootie's voice over the answering machine.

"Rise and shine. It's a beautiful morning."

Wait a second.

She wiped at the soap dripping into her eyes and peeked past the shower curtains at the clock hanging on the wall.

Eight fifty-two. In the *morning*.

At the best of times, Aunt Tootie didn't roll out of bed until noon. Especially after tying one on with a platter of hot wings and several beers to wash them down. Even when she wasn't out the night before, she liked to sleep in.

"You don't stay looking as hot as me all these years without getting plenty of shut-eye."

Holly snatched up a towel, her hair still dripping with soap, and rushed for the phone.

"What's wrong? Are you okay? You're not hurt, are you?"

"Good morning to you, too," Tootie said. "And I'm as right as rain."

"You do know what time it is, don't you?"

"'Course I do. I been up since seven. Listen, I need a lift to Bingo tonight."

"Isn't Bingo for blue-haired ladies who have nothing better to do?"

"Bingo is a game for all ages. Besides, if you win three pots in a row, you go into a drawing for a singles cruise. That's what Buck said."

"Buck? *The* Buck Gentry? I thought you hated his guts."

"I do, but it's not like I could throw a wing in his face just for telling me about bingo. Besides, he was there alone and I was there alone and it seemed pretty damned silly for us to eat at separate tables. Do you know he likes the chile lime wings, too? Not without a Maalox chaser, of course. He's as old as dirt, after all. Did you know they have discos on those cruise ships?" Tootie went on a few more minutes about the dancing and the fun night life before Holly finally managed to hang up and head back to the shower to rinse the soap out of her hair.

Ten minutes later, she grabbed her birdseed roses and headed to the office.

"No way," Evan declared when she walked in, her arms overflowing. "You must have been up all night."

"A wedding planner's gotta do what a wedding planner's gotta do." Holly sat the roses aside and collapsed at her desk while Evan went on and on about how dedicated she was. She stifled a pang of guilt and kept her mouth shut about the extra pair of hands she'd had on the task. She knew what would happen. Evan would blow the whole thing out of proportion and before Holly knew it, she'd be picking out a china pattern and changing her relationship status on Facebook.

And really, they hadn't even fooled around.

They'd talked. Gotten to know each other. Shared. *Like a date.*

She shook away the notion and reached for the steaming cup of coffee sitting on her desk. She'd been honest about the sleepless night, but not because she'd been working on the roses. Thanks to Travis, she'd been almost done when he'd cut and run, and so she'd finished up before midnight.

No, she'd stayed up all night tossing and turning. Thinking. Wanting.

Sex.

Her sleepless night certainly had nothing to do with the fact that she liked Travis and that she couldn't forget the strange camaraderie she'd felt as they'd worked side by side. Or the connection between them when he'd told her about his past and she'd shared hers.

It didn't mean anything. He was only here until the end of the week. And she'd sworn off relationships. So nothing could come of it.

To drive the point further home, she powered on her computer. The familiar Love Buster logo blazed across her screen. The chorus of Love Stinks by the J. Giles Band blared from the computer speakers.

"Here," Evan said, handing her an energy drink.

"I've got coffee. I'm fine."

"I think you should drink it."

"Why?"

"Because you've got a long day ahead."

"Actually, it isn't so long because I made a dent in things last night with the roses. I do need to look at venues. I was thinking we might actually go with the old theater downtown. With the right décor, it could hold the number of people attending and it would really suit the new theme."

"I've already booked it. We've got bigger fish to fry."

"Meaning?"

"Darla called a few minutes ago. She wants another dress."

"She's already got two."

"She's thinking a ball gown might be nice to change into for the reception. She also wants to look at bridesmaids dresses."

"We already have bridesmaids dresses."

"Tea-length dresses. She wants floor-length."

"For twenty-two bridesmaids?"

"Twenty-three. She added her cousin's wife."

"By Saturday?"

"Exactly."

"*This* Saturday?"

"That's the one."

"That's impossible," Holly blurted, panic bolting through her. "Did you tell her that's impossible?"

"Of course." He averted his gaze and Holly knew in an instant that something was up. "What else would I say?"

"Maybe that the idea of a floor-length ball gown and elbow gloves sounds positively dreamy?"

"Actually, I used the word stunning, but it's practically the same thing." Excitement leapt into his eyes. "Doesn't it sound totally awesome? And she's going to have all the girls carry these super fab little opera glasses I found online." He shoved a printout in front of her. "Aren't they divine? If we order today, we can get them over-nighted for only an extra hundred dollars."

Holly shook her head. "I think I feel sick."

"I promise to hold your hair if you start puking. Now drink up." He indicated the energy drink. "We're meeting Darla and her girls at the dress shop."

"When?"

"In five minutes."

"THE SLEEVES ARE just too puffy," Darla declared later that afternoon, vetoing dress number twenty the moment the salesperson held it up.

Holly resisted the urge to pop another Tylenol and settled for downing the rest of her Diet Coke. "Hit me again," she told Meg Sweeney, the owner of It's About You, the one and only exclusive dress boutique in Skull Creek.

Meg and Holly had grown up together. She'd married her high school sweetheart, once-upon-a-time-geek Dillon Cash, and they were now living happily-ever-after at a nearby ranch. Meg specialized in special occasion wear, from wedding to prom dresses to evening wear. She'd pulled out her entire stock the minute Darla had walked in, but after eight hours of Darla trying to make up her mind on not only her own dress, but the one for her bridesmaids, the choices were dwindling. They'd narrowed things down, but Darla still hadn't quite made up her mind.

Holly took the soda Meg handed her and glanced at the short black cocktail dress that hung on a nearby peg. Meg had brought it out a few hours ago out of desperation when Darla had quickly done a thumbs down on nearly every dress Meg put in front of her. The dress had looked great on, but Darla still wasn't sure it was what she wanted. Nor was she sure the silver number hanging nearby, floor-length and full, was what she wanted either.

And so they were all still here after five o'clock on a Monday afternoon.

"Don't you even want to try it on?" Darla's sister Shelly sprawled in a nearby chair, an anxious look on her face. She was decked out in her deputy sheriff attire, complete with a walkie talkie on her hip that buzzed every few minutes with an update on what was happening at the local sheriff's office.

"I can see how puffy the sleeves are without trying it on," Darla told her sister.

"Maybe your arms will fill up enough space to eliminate the puffiness," Shelly offered before pressing the button pinned to her lapel and informing the dispatcher that she still wasn't done. "Just try it and let's get this over with."

"I need to think," Darla declared. "Why don't you try on a few more dresses?"

"Because I already tried on twenty-three and you said we could go with number sixteen. Which means it's done. I'm finished. End of story." Shelly pushed to her feet. "I've got to get back. They're transferring a prisoner this afternoon from Austin and I have to be there to process him."

"You can't go now," Darla insisted. "I still haven't picked anything."

"If you don't like number sixteen, pick something else. Go long." She indicated the rack of floor-length gowns that they'd spent the whole day looking at.

"Go short." She indicated the one short black cocktail dress that Meg had scrounged up out of desperation when Darla had vetoed her entire stock. "They're all fine. I don't care."

"Me neither," offered another of the bridesmaids. "I've got a dinner I can't miss."

"Me, too," another bridesmaid offered.

"I've got a yoga class."

"Zumba," another added.

In a matter of seconds, the dressing room had cleared out with the exception of Darla, Meg and Holly. Even Evan had made a run for it, claiming a dinner date with Bob's parents who already hated his guts and would totally despise him if he showed up late.

Holly gathered her courage, preparing herself for the fit Darla was about to throw. But instead of frowning, a sad expression touched her face. Her eyes widened and grew bright. "I guess I'm doing this by myself," Darla's words faded into a sniffle and her chest caught.

So much for bridezilla.

Holly felt her own eyes burn and she blinked. "Meg, why don't you clear some of these dresses out of here while I talk to Darla for just a second?" Meg nodded and left the room, the curtains swishing closed behind her.

"I'm sorry," Darla blurted. "I know I shouldn't get

upset over something so small. Sam keeps telling me that. But it's just that he's so perfect and I want this wedding to be perfect."

"It will be. As long as the two of you are there, that's all that really matters. You just need to re-member why you're doing all of this in the first place. Because you love him." A strange expres-sion crept over Darla's face, as if Holly had struck a nerve. She knew then and there that something wasn't right with her bride-to-be. "You do love him, don't you?"

"Of course, I do." Darla forced a laugh, as if Hol-ly's question was the most ridiculous thing she'd ever heard. "Are you kidding? I'd be crazy not to love him. He's everything I've ever wanted in a man." She wiped at her eyes and gathered her com-posure.

Just like that, her cool, confident, everything-better-be-my-way-or-else mask slid back into place. "I'll go with the silver gown." She pointed to number six that hung nearby. "And the girls can wear that one." She pointed to a floor length taffeta number with red and silver trim. "I really need to get going. Sam and I are having dinner with his parents. Make sure they put a rush on the dresses," she added when Meg walked into the dressing room. And then she was gone.

"You think you can pull this off?" Holly asked the boutique owner.

"I've got a store in Austin that I work with. They've got more of the bridesmaids dresses. We'll have to have them altered, but we can pull it off. The bride's dress is custom, but she's close to the sample size so we can alter that one. All in all, I think we can make it happen." She let out a long breath, then turned to Holly. "What about you? You've been eyeing that little black number all day. Are you going to try it on or what?"

"I can't imagine where I would wear something like that," Holly said, before she caught herself. If she wanted people to start seeing her differently, she needed to start acting differently. "Okay, I'll try it."

Meg smiled, grabbed a handful of dresses to return to stock and disappeared from the dressing room. The curtain swished closed behind her.

Holly glanced outside—it was starting to get dark. Still, she had time. She unbuttoned her white blouse and shimmied out of her black pencil skirt. She reached for the little black number and was about to step into it when she heard the deep, familiar voice.

"I like it."

Her head snapped up and she found Travis Braddock lounging in the doorway behind her, a sinful grin on his face and a wicked light in his eyes.

And where he'd been dead set on helping her out with the roses last night and keeping his hands to himself, she knew the moment their gazes locked that he had something much different on his mind tonight.

Sex.

A girl could only hope.

15

I LIKE YOU.

The words whispered through her head and sent a prickle of heat to every erogenous zone—from her earlobes to her nipples, the backs of her knees to the arch of each foot and a zillion spots in between.

Her hands stalled and she became keenly aware of a few all-important facts. Number one, she was almost naked. Number two, she was almost naked in front of Travis Braddock who lounged in the dressing room doorway. Number three, she was almost naked in front of Travis Braddock, and it made her very nervous because she couldn't help but wonder what he was thinking.

Crazy.

It didn't matter what he thought. Or what she thought. Their relationship was strictly physical. There were no games. No guessing. No wondering when the other would call or show up or what food they liked to eat or what they liked to drink.

Never again.

She concentrated on the buttons rather than the handsome picture he made standing there wearing jeans and a button down black shirt, the sleeves rolled up to the elbows, his hat tipped low on his handsome face.

"That's definitely my favorite outfit in the store."

"I'm still wearing my underwear." She indicated the dress in her hands. "I haven't actually put anything on yet."

A fierce green gaze swept the length of her in a leisurely motion that made her nipples pebble and press against the cups of her favorite lace bra. "That's the point, sugar." He grinned and stepped inside the room. The curtain swished shut behind him.

She put her back to him, as if that could shut him out. The room, set up like a giant octagon, had mirrors on all sides and she couldn't escape his reflection. "What are you doing here? We're not supposed to meet for another couple of hours."

His gaze captured hers in one of the mirrors. "I thought we could get started early. You need all the help you can get." He grinned and an echoing shiver went through her body.

She tried to undo the buttons on the dress, but before she could take her next breath, his arms came around her and his hands closed over hers. "Let me help," he murmured as his long, lean fingers helped her work the buttons through the openings.

She tried for a calm voice. "I think I can manage on my own."

"Two's a charm."

"I thought three was the charm."

"Not in this case." His deep, compelling voice vibrated against the shell of her ear.

"This isn't part of our deal," she heard herself protest.

His hands fell away and he let her slide the last button free, but he didn't step back. He simply stood there, behind her, close but not touching. "What are you talking about?"

"The flirting. You're flirting with me and I didn't agree to flirting."

"Darlin', flirting implies playing and I'm doing no such thing. I'm serious." His fingertip prowled along the slope of her bare shoulder and goose bumps danced down her arms. Her fingers went limp and the dress slithered to the carpeted floor.

She managed to swallow. "Then let's do it."

"To get it over with?"

"Something like that."

"Something like that or that?" He stared at her. "You either want to or you don't."

"I want to." Her voice softened as the sleepless night spent thinking about him finally overwhelmed her. "I really want to."

He closed the heartbeat of space between them, his denim-covered thighs pressing against the backs of her legs, his groin nestled against her bottom so she could feel just how serious he truly was. His cotton shirt cushioned her shoulder blades. The material brushed against the sensitive backs of her arms as he slid his hands around her waist. Strong, work-roughened fingertips skimmed her rib cage, stopping just shy of her lace-covered breasts.

It was highly erotic watching him in the mirror, his dark hands on her skin, his powerful body framing hers. It was like tuning in to one of those HBO after hour shows, but even better. Because it was real and she could actually see what he was doing to her, as well as feel it.

The heated flush creeping up her neck, the goose bumps chasing up and down her arms, the part to her lips, the catch of her breath.

"So pretty," he murmured huskily as his large hands cupped her breasts.

"It's Belgian lace."

"Not the bra, sugar. I was talking about this." He fingered the tip of one dark nipple peeking through the scalloped pattern. "And this." He touched the other throbbing crest, rolled it between his thumb and forefinger. "Definitely the prettiest thing I've seen in a long time."

Lightning zapped her and she barely caught the moan that slid up her throat.

His hand moved down, stroking over her abdomen until he reached her panties. He caught the edges, tugging them down her hips, her thighs, until they pooled on top of the dress at her feet.

He slid his fingers between her legs and touched her. He slicked his thumb over her clitoris in a delicious touch that made her close her eyes and clamp down on her bottom lip.

She wanted to melt, but he was there to keep her from sliding to the floor, his strong arms anchoring her to the hard length of his body.

"Open up, sugar. I want to see you when you go wild." He rubbed her a few more breathless moments before sliding a finger deep inside. She trembled and he drew her closer, holding her with one hand while he drove her crazy with the other. He moved his fingers, plunging and stroking. The pleasure was intense, but it was nothing compared to the brightness of his gaze as he held hers in the mirror. The green of his eyes was so intense that it seemed to shift, brighten, glow into an amazing purple—

She blinked and the color faded. He moved his fingers again and sensation bolted through her. A delicious orgasm gripped her body. She caught her lip, fighting back the cry that worked its way up her throat, the same way she fought back the sudden fear coiling inside of her, a feeling intensified by the way he stared so deeply into her eyes.

As if there was something much more intense going on here than a little quickie.

His shoulders shuddered and she had the incredible thought that he was feeling the same sweet orgasm that crested inside of her. His muscles tightened and the tendons in his neck stood out in stark relief. Ecstasy glittered in his gaze and a growl rumbled up his throat.

At the same time, there was no mistaking the hardness throbbing against her buttocks. Proof that he hadn't come close to a climax.

She somehow knew that he didn't need to. This was more than just sex between them. The connection was deeper. Stronger. *No!*

"I—I need to get out of here," she said, grappling for her panties.

For a split-second, she didn't think he would let her go, but then they heard the swish of drapes.

Holly grabbed the dress pooled at her feet and yanked it up a heartbeat before Meg's familiar voice echoed around them.

"I found a couple more dresses you might like to try—" The words stumbled to a halt as the boutique owner came up short in the doorway. Her gaze darted between Travis and Holly, and a knowing gleam lit her eyes. "I'm sorry, I didn't mean to interrupt. I didn't know anyone was back here—"

"I'll take this one," Holly blurted, yanking up the

straps on the dress at the speed of light. "Can I wear it out?"

"Certainly." Meg cast a glance between the two of them and a grin tugged at her lips. "I'll ring it up."

"Great." Holly grabbed her purse and bolted past Travis as fast as her high-heeled sandals could carry her. "I've got to go. I'll meet you later." But first she needed to clear her head and forget the crazy thoughts pounding at her sanity.

Like how there was more to Travis Braddock than met the eye and how she liked it.

How she liked *him*.

Crazy.

At least that's what Holly tried to tell herself. If only she actually believed it.

16

Travis barely resisted the urge to haul ass after Holly.

He wouldn't.

He'd pushed her a little too far tonight and now it was time to back off. He'd shown up at the dress shop, determined to tease her until she gave in to the need bubbling inside of her. She had. For a few precious moments. But then Meg had interrupted them. Reality had hit, and Holly had run hell for leather.

"I'll meet you later."

Fat chance. He came to that conclusion as he sat parked in front of the honky tonk later that night, waiting for Holly to show up.

Hours ticked by, but Holly didn't show.

He tried to tell himself that maybe she'd had a flat tire, maybe something had gone wrong. But deep in his gut he knew better. He didn't feel the unease.

The panic. The fear. Rather, he felt an overwhelming sense of disappointment.

Because oddly enough, he wanted to see her. To hear her voice, the steady beat of her heart and the deep, soft whisper of her breaths. He liked being with her, and she liked being with him. She just didn't want to admit it.

That, in itself, should have been enough to send him inside, in search of another female to bide his time with until Cody came home. He didn't do *liking* any more than he did monogamy. It was the nature of the beast. He was compelled to seek out women.

Oddly enough though, he didn't feel compelled at all as he watched a group of single women walk into the bar for girls night out. Any one of them would have wanted him.

The thing was, he didn't want any of them.

He wanted Holly. Her arms wrapped around him, her lush body open and inviting beneath his, her sweet blood flowing into his mouth.

He slammed the door on that last thought and headed back to the motel, and straight into a cold shower. He stood under the icy spray for several long seconds, trying to clear his head and cool the fire blazing inside of him.

No such luck.

He toweled off and stretched out on the bed. His muscles felt stiff. His body ached. The ceiling fan whirled overhead and the air whispered down the length of his body, over his bare chest, his abs, his stiff cock.

Desire knifed through him, cutting him to the quick and he growled. He was hard to the point that his teeth literally hurt. Frustration welled inside of him and he barely resisted the urge to go over to her house. To pound down her door, throw her onto the nearest horizontal surface and sate the hunger raging inside of him.

She wouldn't have stopped him.

No, she would have given herself to him because, hey, she owed him. He was helping her and so she intended to pay up. But while she would be willing, she would also convince herself she was doing it to keep her word. Not because she wanted to.

Because she wanted him.

He'd vowed to hold back until she gave herself to him, free and clear. And he meant it.

Just because he'd backed off, however, didn't mean he had any intention of letting her stand him up. She was acting on an *out of sight, out of mind* policy, and so she was keeping her distance. It was a strategy that would have worked with the average guy.

But Travis was far from average.

They'd had sex—*great* sex—and forged a connection. Not as strong as that forged with blood, but still, it was viable. If he chose to use it.

He never had before. In fact, he'd always run the

other way, moving on, fortifying the distance until the link between vampire and human weakened and ultimately disappeared. That's what would happen with Holly, as well.

But until then, Travis meant to use it to his full advantage.

He closed his eyes and thought about the way she'd felt in his arms tonight. How warm and soft and trembling. He could still smell the lush scent of her arousal. Hear the frantic thud of her heart in his head. Feel the silkiness of her skin against his...

The feelings shifted, until he wasn't just hearing her heartbeat. He heard the rush of water and the sound of a radio playing softly in the background. The sweet aroma of strawberries and cream filled his senses and soap bubbles tickled his skin.

He saw her then, standing in the shower, her hair streaming wet down her back, her body slick and naked.

And then he touched himself.

WATER PELTED HOLLY, running in rivulets over her heated flesh. She turned her face toward the hot spray and tried to clear her head. She needed to stop thinking about what had happened in the dressing room. About the way Travis had looked at her. As if he'd never seen a woman he wanted more.

As if.

Women were his thing and Holly was just another

in a long, endless line. She didn't mean anything to him. She never would because he wasn't sticking around. And even if he had been, she wasn't about to make the same mistake she'd made three times already.

She wasn't falling for him.

She turned the temperature up a few notches and steam fogged the air around her. She put her back to the spray and let the water soothe her exhausted muscles. She needed to relax. To sleep.

She had a full day tomorrow with Darla and the myriad of changes they were still trying to execute in time for Saturday's event. They were changing the menu from a buffet to a sit-down dinner, not to mention they needed new table linens and china and place cards and...

The list went on and on and the only way she was going to keep her sanity would be if she got some much needed sleep. That meant no tossing and turning and thinking about Travis Braddock.

His name stuck in her head and conjured all sorts of lustful thoughts. She saw herself naked and panting on her back, Travis between her legs, plunging into her over and over until she cried out. Travis below her, grasping her hips, helping her ride him fast and furious. Travis standing in the shower right in front of her, reaching for her...

She shook away the image and grappled for the soap. Steam thickened the air and water burned her eyes. Her fingers wrapped around the bar and she concentrated on lathering her hands. The feel of wet, slick soap made her palms tingle as bubbles squeezed between her fingers. Sliding the bar back into the tray, she ran her soapy hands up and down her throat, over her shoulders. But she didn't feel her own fingertips, she felt his. Trailing over her skin, circling her nipples, grasping the ripe nubs and twisting until she felt the pull of desire between her legs.

Her hands stilled and she drew a deep, steadying breath.

She wasn't doing this. She wasn't fantasizing about a man she'd made up her mind not to fantasize about. No fantasizing, no dreaming, no planning.

No getting her hopes up.

That's where she'd gone wrong in the past. She'd looked to each and every man in her life, thinking 'this is it.' The one. The future.

She'd been wrong. Just as she was wrong now.

Travis wasn't her future. She hardly knew him. Sure, they'd talked and she felt more connected to him than she had any man in a long time. *Ever.* But that didn't mean anything.

Even more, it didn't change anything.

Travis Braddock was temporary.

So give it a rest, will ya?

She focused her attention on reaching for the shampoo bottle. The sooner she finished, the sooner she could pile into bed and forget everything. She popped the push-up lid and was about to squirt the creamy liquid into her palm when the hard, smooth plastic brushed the ripe crest of her nipple. Lightning zapped her and her nerves buzzed.

She wasn't going to do it.

That's what she told herself, but her hands seemed to have a mind of their own. Her fingertips slid around the bottle, circling and grasping as she rasped the edge against her nipple. Once. Twice. *Yum.*

The cool hardness was a stark contrast to her soft, heated skin, and sensation saturated her senses. She moved the bottle again, slowly at first in a soft, seductive motion. Pleasure rippled through her body and her heart pounded. She played with the ripe nub a few more seconds before touching the edge to her other nipple. It sprang to life immediately, greedy for attention.

She meant to stop. Really she did. But it felt so good and she'd been so on edge and so damned needy after the encounter with Travis in the dress shop. And maybe, just maybe, if she did this now, she might be able to satisfy the lust burning inside of her and forget him long enough to sleep.

The edge of the bottle slid down, following the underside of her breasts, the sensitive skin of her belly. The hard coolness trailed over her belly button and lower until she reached the vee between her legs.

Hunger spurted through her when she felt the edge

of the bottle ruffle the damp curls that covered her mound. The sensation moved lower still. The hard, cool edge teased the slick folds and rasped her clit. Her lips parted on a gasp and her knees trembled. The air seemed to thicken even more, the steam fogging the shower glass and cocooning her in a thick blanket.

She blinked and just like that, Travis was there with her, right in front of her, steam edging his tall, powerful form. He was completely naked, his broad, powerful chest covered with a sprinkling of dark hair. His penis was hard and thick, the base surrounded by a swirl of dark hair. The same hair sprinkled his hard, muscular legs.

The water sluiced over him, running in rivulets down his tanned skin and she couldn't help herself. She reached out, touching the slick muscle.

She blinked, thinking he would disappear, *hoping*.

He didn't. He was still there. Right in front of her. Wet and naked and real.

"I missed you tonight." The words whispered through her head, so clear and distinct that a ripple of anxiety went up her spine.

Followed by a rush of excitement as he took the shampoo bottle from her hands and touched the edge to her nipple. He rasped the edge back and forth, teasing, taunting. She caught her lip between her teeth as pleasure spurted through her and the pressure tightened between her legs. The sensation grew, wringing a frantic whimper from her. She was so close to the edge. Another glide of the bottle and she would plunge straight over.

But then the bottle disappeared and she felt his hands. Cupping her breasts. Teasing her nipples. Swirling down her abdomen. Slipping between her legs. He rubbed her, teasing and taunting before sliding a finger deep inside.

Sensation bolted through her and a delicious orgasm gripped her body. She caught her lip, fighting back the cry that worked its way up her throat, the same way she fought back the strange sensation coiling inside her.

A feeling that something wasn't right.

That he wasn't right.

Real.

She reached for him then, sliding her hands around his hard, pulsing shaft. She moved, slicking her palms up and down, tracing the ripe purple head until he growled so low and deep that she felt the sound pulling between her legs.

He caught her lips in a fierce kiss, plunging his tongue deep, devouring her with his mouth as he thrust his erection into her grasp, over and over, letting her work him into a frenzy.

A growl vibrated the air around them and he pulled back. She opened her eyes to see him through the thick steam. He stared down at her, his gaze pulsing a hot, vibrant purple as he plunged deep into her hands one more time. His lips parted and she caught a flash of white as he bared his teeth—

She blinked and just like that, the image disappeared, fading into the steamy mist that filled the shower and leaving her with an odd sense of emptiness.

As if he'd left her.

As if he'd ever been there in the first place.

She stared down at her empty hands clutching the shampoo bottle and gave herself a mental shake.

Shoving open the shower door, she stepped out into the bathroom and reached for a towel. She rubbed at her body, eager to dispel the memory of his hands.

Her own hands, she reminded herself. This had been a one-man show, no matter how it had felt otherwise.

It was as if Travis wasn't just in her memories, but he'd crawled deep down inside of her head. Her heart.

She hadn't just felt him surrounding her in the shower. She'd felt him inside of her. His passion blazing through her body. His need mingling with her own.

Wait a second.

What was she doing? Losing it, that's what. That explained the purple eyes and the fangs. Seriously? *Fangs?* There were fantasies and then there were fantasies. She'd definitely crossed the line into the land of the looney.

On top of that, the old Holly was rearing her ugly head, making more out of the situation than what was actually there. Imagining a connection when really, it was just her own wishful thinking.

That's what was happening.

She was sliding right back into her old ways.

Sliding, but she hadn't gone completely down the drain. She could climb back up. She just had to remember how miserable she'd been after Chad. And the others before him. If she could focus on those disastrous relationships, she'd be okay.

Burying herself under the covers, she closed her eyes and tried to conjure an image of Chad's lying, cheating face. Nothing came. It was the same for Ben. And Allen.

She saw only Travis staring down at her in the shower. Travis's reflection in the dressing room. Travis sitting in her living room. *Travis.*

Holly blew out an exasperated breath, climbed out of bed and headed downstairs to the living room. A few minutes later, she flipped on the TV and cranked up the volume, determined to distract herself and ignore the truth niggling in her head.

That like it or not, she was falling for Travis Braddock.

17

HOLLY SPENT THE next few days neck-deep in making the changes for Darla's wedding. All of her other brides got put on hold until she could breathe the following Monday. Until then… It was all about Darla.

Thankfully.

With her week so swamped, Holly barely had time to think about Travis, much less see him.

Except in her dreams.

He came to her every night in the most erotic fantasies.

Erotic and vivid.

Dreams that had her waking up in a feverish sweat, her body damp and pulsing, her lips swollen and bruised.

Dreams.

She held tight to the thought and tried to concentrate on Darla who stood in the local catering kitchen of Millicent Dupree, Skull Creek's equiva-

lent of Rachel Ray and the culinary genius responsible for Saturday's formal sit-down dinner.

"But it's Thursday," Millicent was saying. "You
can't make anymore changes at this point. The wedding is the day after tomorrow."

"I know, but I want filet mignon."

"I already have prime rib au jus in the works for
five hundred people." Millicent stared at Darla as if
the bride-to-be just asked her to sacrifice her first-
born. "What am I supposed to do with all that meat?
And there's only three days before the event. It's impossible to get enough filet delivered here in time."

"We're smack dab in the middle of ranch country," Darla countered. "We've got beef coming out
of our ears."

"Fine then. Why don't you head on down to
the Circle B and see how many you can round up,
butcher and package for me? And of course, you
know that the filet has to be aged a certain amount
of time before I will even consider cooking and serving it."

"Holly," Darla said, turning to her. "Do something."

"She can't do anything," Millicent said. "Because
this is not going to happen."

Darla cast imploring eyes on Holly, but all she
could do was shrug. "Millicent's right. This is one
detail you're going to have to bend on. It's impossible
to get that quantity of meat delivered here in time."

"Meat is meat," Shelly chimed in, fingering the handcuffs hanging from her belt as if she were seriously considering using them on her sister. "Why are you making such a big deal about this? Can we go now? I really have to get back to the station. Matt's given me so much time off for this wedding that I want him to take the afternoon off before the craziness really gets started." Sheriff Matt Keller was fairly new in town. He was married to the local salon owner and ex-beauty queen. They'd both caused quite a stir a year or so back when Sheriff Keller had been caught in some racy photographs, or so everyone had thought. But since then, he'd proven that the pictures were bunk and he'd won his first election with a landslide.

"But my bachelorette party is tonight?"

"I'll be there. I might be a few minutes late—"

"But you're in charge of it."

"There are plenty of people to cover for me for a few minutes."

"But Sam's sister will be there."

"And?"

"And what will she think?"

"That I have a life. She can serve cake until I get there. Don't sweat it." She motioned with her hand. "Let's move this along. We'll take the prime rib."

"No, we won't," Darla argued.

"Perfect." Millicent waved them out. "Now get out of my kitchen. I'm doing cannollis for the Bachman Birthday party tonight and I need to get into my pastry zone." She turned her back, effectively dismissing Darla who looked ready to explode, and left the room.

"But—"

"Darla, why don't we go see what the baker came up with for the cake?" Holly offered.

"I don't want to see the cake," Darla insisted. "I want to settle this."

"It's settled," Shelly said. She murmured a few words into her walkie talkie. "I've got to go. I'll see you later." And then she disappeared in a blur of beige.

"We can't have prime rib," Darla whined once her sister had left. "We just can't."

"I happen to like prime rib. So do a lot of people I know."

Darla shook her head. "The entire wedding is going to be ruined because the reception is going to be ruined because the food is all wrong."

"It's a small detail in the big picture of things. I'm sure you'll see that once it's all said and done. Millicent makes an excellent prime rib. I know you don't like it, but—"

"I do like it. But Tom's favorite is filet mignon."

"But this wedding isn't just about Tom, is it? I'm sure he'll understand—"

"I *have* to have the filet." She turned desperate eyes on Holly. "It has to be right." *I have to be right.*

The truth gleamed in her gaze and Holly couldn't help herself. She had to ask again.

"Darla, are you sure you're in love with Tom?"

Anxiety stretched across her expression as she seemed to search for words. "He's a great guy," she finally said. "The perfect man."

"Yes, but do you love him?"

"I love everything about him."

"But do you love him?"

A strange light flickered in Darla's gaze and Holly knew the truth in an instant—that the young woman didn't love Tom so much as she loved the idea of marrying someone like him. She wanted a Prince Charming. A Mr. Perfect.

"I can't get married without filet mignon." Darla's voice drew her from her thoughts. "I just can't."

No problem. That's what Holly should have told her. She would call every supplier from here to Dallas if she had to in order to find enough and get it here in time for the wedding.

That's what Darla's wedding planner would have said. Particularly a wedding planner who didn't receive the last half of her fee until after the event.

But at that moment, Holly didn't care about money. She knew what Darla was going through. She'd felt it. She just hadn't had the courage to step up and stop it. Instead, she'd been so obsessive that she'd pushed Chad away until he'd called it quits.

Holly knew because she'd felt the exact same way.

The truth crystallized as she stood staring at her distraught bridezilla. Travis had been right about her. She *had* been more in love with the idea of being in love than with the man himself.

The moment when Chad had broken off the engagement, she'd actually felt relief. A quick feeling that had lasted only a few heartbeats until she'd had to face the world with her failure and mourn the carefully planned happily-ever-after she'd mapped out for herself. But she hadn't been miserable because she'd loved Chad. She hadn't.

Not like she loved Travis.

The thought struck and she pushed it back out and slammed the door. She barely knew him. Several days was not long enough to fall for someone. Even for a woman with her record.

She didn't love him. Not yet.

And she was keeping it that way.

"So don't get married," she heard herself say. "Postpone the wedding for a few months. Just until you can get everything right," she added when Darla looked shocked. "Take your time," she continued. "That way, you can get everything just perfect." *Or realize what a big mistake you're about to make.*

"Extra time would be nice," Darla said as indecision danced across her expression. But then her cell phone beeped with a text, drawing her from her thoughts and she shook her head. "The prime rib is fine," she muttered, staring at the screen on her phone. "We'll just go with that. I've really got to run. The party is in a few hours and I still have to meet Tom to sign the pre-nup." She left the caterer and Holly headed next door to the baker to check on the changes to the wedding cake.

By the time she got back to the office, it was almost six o'clock.

"Quitting time," Evan announced, powering off his laptop. "Our last evening off before the craziness starts. Bob's treating me to dinner." He arched an eyebrow as Holly closed several files and straightened up her desk. "What about you?" His gaze twinkled. "Are you seeing Mr. Tall, Dark and Luscious?"

She'd been avoiding any mention of Travis, but she knew it was truth time. She averted her gaze and busied herself packing up. "We're not seeing each other any more."

"Oh, no," Evan squealed. He reached her in a heartbeat and threw his arms around her shoulders. "You must be a wreck!"

"I'm fine." She hugged him back for a second before pulling free. "Really. It's no big deal. I told you it was nothing serious. He's only going to be in town for a few more days." She shrugged. "But it was fun while it lasted."

Evan eyeballed her a split-second before reaching for the phone.

"What are you doing?"

"Cancelling with Bob. You need someone to talk you off the ledge."

"I'm not on the ledge. I'm not even close. Seriously."

"That's what they all say. But the next thing you know, they're drowning in a gallon of Ben & Jerry's Chunky Monkey." He shook his head. "I won't let you do this to your hips."

"My hips aren't exactly small."

"That's what I'm saying. You can't afford even an ounce." He started to dial. "I'll just call Bob and then you and I can pick up some sushi and have a girl's night—"

Holly punched the button and broke the connection. "Thanks, but no thanks. I'm fine. Really."

"You can't go home alone."

"I'm not going home," Holly added. She wanted to forget Travis. With Evan playing twenty questions all night and trying to console her, that would be impossible. "I'm going out."

"Bingo with Aunt Tootie is not going to cheer you up."

"I'm not going to Bingo. Besides, Aunt Tootie doesn't play Bingo on Thursday nights." She hardly played Bingo at all. When Holly had talked to her yesterday, Tootie had said she'd had an alright time on Sunday night but that it wasn't something she wanted to do again. She needed excitement. "They're having their pool tournament at the honky tonk tonight. It's part of the in-door rodeo. No way would she miss it."

"Tonight's the weekly pot. Tootie's in contention for the grand prize. That's what Bob's friend's cousin said. She said Tootie is the reigning Bingo champion. She played twenty cards last night and won three pots."

"*My* Aunt Tootie?"

"You know another eighty-one-year-old in blue eye shadow and zebra print pants?" Evan wiggled his eyebrows. "He also said she was sitting next to Buck Gentry the entire time."

"She hates Buck Gentry."

"Just like she hates Bingo?" Evan shook his head and gave her another concerned look. "I'm calling Bob—"

"I'm going out," Holly blurted, "on a date." *What?* "Yeah, a date. Tonight."

Evan's hands stilled. "With who?"

Good question. "Just a friend of a friend of a friend. We're going to dinner. And dancing. So, you see, there's no need to worry."

He eyed her for a long moment, as if searching for some sign that she was about to go on an ice cream binge.

"Well, all right," he finally said. "But I'm doing a drive-by later tonight and you'd better not be home."

Not a problem because the last thing Holly wanted was to fall into her own bed. She knew what waited for her in her dreams. As exciting as that was, she was too mixed up inside to deal with it tonight. She needed to get out. Live it up. Forget.

Besides, it was time to test out the new Holly.

Her one outing with Travis at the honky tonk had actually done some good. Tommy Peterson had tipped his hat to her at the diner yesterday. And Jim Mitchell had given her a wink when she'd gone into the pharmacy. Both men were die-hard cowboys known for their escapades with women.

Holly had never been on their radar except when Jim had asked her to plan his parents' fiftieth wedding anniversary last year. He hadn't winked at her then. Instead, he'd called her ma'am and barely looked her in the eye. No long, leisurely treks up her body with his hooded gaze. No wicked thoughts. Nothing.

Until now.

He'd been with Susie that night at the bar and he'd seen the new improved Holly with his own two eyes. And obviously he'd liked what he'd seen.

There was only one way to find out.

Her mind made up, she packed up her things and headed home to change.

_18_

SHE WAS WEARING the dress.

His gaze zeroed in on the woman currently boot-scootin' her way across the dance floor.

She wore the short, black spaghetti strap sequined number she'd been trying on that night at the dress shop. Add a pair of black stilettos that emphasized her long legs, and Holly Simms looked like the hottest ticket in Skull Creek.

But it wasn't just the skimpy clothes that made her so sexy. Her hair, slightly mussed from all the dancing, flowed down past her shoulders. Her skin was flushed and glowing. Her eyes sparkled with excitement and wonder, as if she couldn't quite believe she was here and this was happening.

Every man in town was falling all over her. She was on her fifth dance partner in as many songs and Travis could see at least two more guys sizing her up, wanting a turn.

Initially, when she'd first presented her cockama-mie idea, Travis had had his doubts that a little face time with him could dirty up her image. But damned if she hadn't been right. The men in this town had eaten it up.

Including the cowboy she was currently dancing with. He looked ready to take a great big bite out of her and damned if she didn't seem to like it.

Travis took a deep swig of Coors, but the liquid didn't ease the tightening in his gut or sate the thirst that clawed at his throat. He needed to feed in the worst way.

While he'd been communicating telepathically with Holly and they'd had some of the hottest sex ever, he hadn't actually satisfied his hunger. Sure, he felt every moment and he'd enjoyed the experience. But to actually soak up her energy, he had to touch her with more than just his mind.

Hunger gnawed at him and he forced his gaze away from her, to the multitude of women milling around him. There were plenty. All his for the taking. One glance and he could be in the nearest bathroom, getting it on with anyone who caught his fancy.

He would.

Just as soon as he finished his drink.

He took another swig and watched as the cowboy holding Holly bent her backwards in a dip before pulling her back up and into his arms. He twirled her, then pulled her back against him.

Travis downed another gulp and barely resisted the urge to cross the room and throw her over his shoulder. Hell, he'd taught her that last move, for Christ's sake. And here she was, doing it with someone else. Where was the gratitude?

That's all he wanted—for her to be a little bit appreciative and remember how she got here. She ought to be throwing her arms around *him* and thanking him for all he'd done.

Her arms looped around the guy's neck instead. A smile curved her full lips and she stared up at the cowboy with smoldering eyes, as if he were the answer to her most erotic dreams.

As if he'd been going to her every night, touching and stirring and tasting her, instead of Travis himself.

Not that he cared.

Hell, he didn't give a rat's ass. It was time to call it quits and move on. He knew that. This was too hard. Besides, he was leaving in a few days. What the hell difference did it make anyway? He could have any other woman in the world, so why worry over this one?

Sure, she had a great smile and a nice laugh. And he actually liked talking to her. But so friggin' what?

Any woman would do.

He forced his attention to a tall, leggy brunette and smiled. She smiled back and he knew in an instant that she would gladly abandon the schmuck sitting next to her. She turned, said a few words and excused herself. A split-second later, she slid onto the bar stool next to him.

"My name's Nicole."

He nodded. "Travis."

"So where are you from, Travis?" she asked, starting with small talk, licking her lips suggestively every now and then, her gaze hooded. She leaned into him with a comment or two and stayed there, her arm against his, her hand resting on his thigh. It was too easy.

And everything with Holly was too damned hard.

He was too hard.

His groin twitched and his muscles tightened when he glanced at Holly again. Their gazes collided for a brief moment and excitement jerked through him. Followed by a rush of *what the hell?* when she didn't so much as smile.

There was no wave or nod of acknowledgment. Nothing. It was as if she wanted to forget him as much as he wanted to forget her.

Fat chance.

He could feel the steady thud of her heart, taste the excitement in her mouth, hear her breathless "Yes," when the cowboy asked if she wanted to leave.

The song ended and they headed for the nearest exit.

Travis clamped his hand around his beer and tried to resist the urge to go after her. He damned well would NOT. She was a grown woman. If she wanted to sleep with every damned cowboy in the place, it was her business.

What did he care?

He didn't.

That's what he tried to tell himself. At the same time, he stayed tuned into her. The crunch of gravel echoed in his ears as she followed the guy out to his truck. He felt the rush of *uh-oh* as the man reached for her and hauled her close.

Wait a second.

Uh-oh.

That wasn't the thought of a woman ready to jump into the sack.

He focused and sure enough, she wasn't half as anxious to get up close and personal with this guy as she should have been. Rather, she dodged his kiss and twisted away. He caught her arm and then—

The connection shattered as a bolt of pain zapped Travis and shook his entire body. His gut tightened as fear rushed up his spine.

And for the first time in his life, he didn't try to tell himself that he was overreacting or that it was nothing or that he was certifiable because he suddenly knew—*he knew*—that something was wrong.

He pushed to his feet and went after her. And he could only hope that this time he wasn't too late.

HOLLY CAUGHT HER breath against the incredible pain gripping her ankle. Her eyes watered and she blinked frantically. She wasn't going to cry over a sprained ankle. Even if it was two days before the biggest event of her career.

"Get your hands off of her." The deep, familiar voice sounded a split second before she heard Cal's surprised "What the *fuck?*" and a fierce thud as he landed on the ground beside her.

"It's okay," she said. "He didn't do anything. He tried, but I gave him a knee to the groin. When I went to turn, my heel broke and I twisted my ankle—" The words trailed off as her head snapped up and she saw Travis towering over Cal.

His eyes blazed bright and intense and bloodred. A growl vibrated in her ears and his sensuous lips drew back, revealing a pair of lethal-looking fangs.

Her heart pounded, echoing in her head, drowning out the music drifting from inside and the *crrrunch* of gravel as a car pulled into the parking lot. She blinked once, twice, but it didn't erase what was right in front of her.

What she'd known all along.

Travis was a vampire.

Her brain fought against the truth despite the memories that rifled through her head. The way his eyes had seemed to change colors and how he'd touched her without really touching her. *And the dreams.*

"No," she murmured, fighting against the truth.

The one word seemed to yank him from the angry rage he'd been caught in and he turned toward her.

Immediately, his eyes cooled into a dark, vibrant green and his fangs retracted. He was on his knees in that next instant, reaching for her, his touch gentle, possessive.

"You're mine."

His voice whispered through her head and she knew it wasn't her imagination this time. The words were clear. Distinct. Undeniable.

Shock jolted through her, followed by a wave of panic that crashed over her, tugged her under and tried to suck the oxygen from her lungs. She scrambled to her feet and tried to move. To get away as fast as she could. Not from him, but from the crazy feelings whirling through her. Because despite the truth, she wanted him.

As much as he wanted her.

Mine.

It was her own voice she heard this time. In her head. Her heart. She turned and tried to move. White hot pain ripped up her leg. Suddenly, it was all too much to take in. Her vision blurred and she stumbled. The ground seemed to shake and she pitched forward.

And then she fell head first into a pit of nothingness.

19

ANOTHER DREAM.

That's what Holly told herself when she opened her eyes to find that she was snuggled deep in her own bed, her favorite T-shirt tangled at her waist. She tried to move, her ankle throbbed. And she knew in an instant that it had all been real.

As real as the vampire stretched out in the chair beside her bed.

He sat, his legs stretched out in front of him, his arms folded, his eyes closed. He looked like any other handsome, sexy man keeping watch over his woman. More so with the tiny crease in his brow, as if he wasn't sleeping quite as good as he should have because she was hurt.

A man, she told herself, trying to ignore the sudden rush of memories.

She saw him that first night in the back parking lot of the honky tonk, his eyes gleaming a hot, bright purple as he'd loomed over her.

The image faded into yet another and she saw him standing on her doorstep, insisting that she invite him in properly. The way he'd stood in the shower with her, touching and stirring. There one minute. Gone the next. *Impossible.*

It would be if he was just a man.

But he wasn't.

She closed her eyes, desperate to deny the truth niggling at her. There were no such things as vampires. Such creatures only existed in movies and books and the fantasies of millions of young, *Twilight*-loving teens. It was hype. Not reality.

Still, the memories kept nagging at her. The eyes. The way he seemed to read her thoughts—

"It's part of what I am." His deep voice jarred her from the mental examination and she opened her eyes to find him staring at her. "When I look into a person's eyes, I can tell what they're thinking. I can also levitate and move faster than the average human. I can even lift an SUV if I feel like it. I can see myself in a mirror just like anyone else. But I am allergic to sunlight. Stakes are bad, too, if they're through the heart. Otherwise, I'm pretty invincible. Garlic and crosses don't bother me. Holy water, either."

"But you work with horses. Aren't animals afraid of vampires?"

"I had a knack for horses before I turned. Once I became a vampire, those characteristics became magnified. Horses spook a little at first, but they sense more friend in me than foe. My brother Brent was good with a gun before and now he's unbeatable. Likewise for Cody. He always could hang on for the full eight seconds. And his balance and endurance only magnified once he turned." He stared at her and she knew he saw the multitude of questions swimming in her brain. "I sleep during the day," he added, "which means I work horses at night."

"Isn't that hard to explain to a rancher?"

"Not really. Really good horse trainers have almost a mystical connection to the animals. Ranchers just think it's a quirk in my personality."

She tried to focus on his words, letting everything he said sink in. But every answer drew another question. "Do you really drink blood?"

He nodded. "But vampires don't just feed off of blood. We also crave energy. Sexual energy. The more lusty the woman, the better."

"That's why you followed me into that closet at the wedding?"

He nodded and a grin hinted at his lips, easing the frantic beating of her heart. "That and I liked the way you filled out that black skirt."

A warmth stole through her and she stiffened. So what if he liked the way she looked? She didn't care. She shouldn't care.

His grin faded as he regarded her. "I usually

like sex and blood at the same time. You're the first woman I haven't bitten."

"Lucky me." It was a sarcastic remark, but she couldn't help but think that maybe, just maybe, it did make her lucky. Like maybe there was something different about her. Special. "Why didn't you bite me?"

"I meant to, but then you rushed out of the closet so fast that I lost the chance. I still can't believe you walked away from me. Usually I'm the one walking away and it's the women who are begging me to stay." He ran a hand through his hair and stared at her as if he'd yet to figure her out.

Crazy, she knew. He could read her thoughts. She was practically an open book.

At the same time, she had the distinct feeling that she wasn't nearly as transparent as she should have been, and that he didn't like it one bit.

"When I look into a woman's eyes, she's powerless," Travis continued. "She'll do whatever I say, whenever I say it. But not you. You've got a stubborn streak that I can't touch."

"So no reading my thoughts?"

"Oh, I can read your thoughts. Right now you're not half as afraid of me as you are of yourself. You're afraid because you're not afraid. You're still madly attracted to me."

She wanted to deny it, but then he looked at her, into her, and lust stirred, fierce and quick and far more powerful than the throb of fear keeping time with her frantic heartbeat.

"Stop doing that."

"Doing what?"

"Influencing me."

"That's the trouble, sugar. I can't influence you. I've been trying for days and damned if I can do it."

She shouldn't believe him. It would be so easy to write off her aching body as a reaction to his vamp charm. Yet, there was just something about the frustrated look in his eyes that hinted he was telling the truth. He couldn't influence her at will and it bothered the hell out of him.

Ah, but he could influence her other ways.

His scent—raw and male and oh, so intoxicating—filled her nostrils and created the most damning thoughts of two bodies tangled together, touching and twisting and kissing. Sex at its most primitive level, but even more savage.

An image of him, fangs bared, popped into her head. And where she should have been afraid, she found herself wondering what they would feel like.

"It doesn't hurt," he said, reading her thoughts. "In fact, it's a pretty incredible sensation. Better than sex. It'll definitely make you forget your sprained ankle."

But other than a dull throb, she'd already forgotten about it. She was too focused on him. Her body trembled, urging her to turn, to reach out, to touch him and see for herself.

She wanted to.

She'd been denying herself for so long and suddenly playing it safe and keeping her distance didn't seem nearly as important as reaching out and seizing this one moment.

This one memory to add to all the others.

Because vampire or not, Travis Braddock was still temporary with a great big capital *T.* Their time together was running out. It was already after midnight, which meant Friday had officially arrived. He was leaving tomorrow. He'd said it himself.

Which meant she could either make the most of their time together or run the other way and live with the regret.

She shoved back the covers and struggled to the side of the bed, ignoring her throbbing ankle.

"What are you doing?"

"What I should have done a long time ago." She pushed to her feet and then she reached for the hem of her T-shirt.

TRAVIS WATCHED AS the soft cotton slid over her head. She wasn't wearing a bra and the first whisper of air against her nipples brought them to throbbing awareness. She hooked her fingers in the waistband of her panties and shimmied them down her legs. She stood there, naked and beautiful, offering herself to him. But it wasn't enough. He wanted to be sure. He needed it.

"I want you," she murmured as if reading *his* thoughts.

A sense of urgency rushed through him and he was on his feet in a split-second. He grasped the hem of his shirt and pulled it up and over his head before he reached for her.

He lifted her, taking the pressure off her ankle as he held her close, dipped his head and drew one sensitive nipple into his mouth. She tasted every bit as good as he remembered and he couldn't seem to get enough. He suckled her, holding her tight against his growing erection, cradling her, loving her.

The thought struck and damned if he could push it away. Even though he knew the feelings he had for her wouldn't last. They never did.

Still, he couldn't help himself. He held tight to the emotion rushing inside of him, pressed her down into the mattress and then proceeded to make love to a woman for the first time since he'd turned vampire.

His woman.

For now anyhow.

20

HOLLY CLOSED HER eyes to the wonderful pull of Travis's mouth on her breast. He sucked her so hard and so thoroughly that she moaned. Wetness flooded the sensitive flesh between her legs and she trembled. He drew on her harder, his jaw creating a powerful tug that she felt clear to her womb. An echoing throb started deep inside, more intense with every rasp of his tongue, every nibble of his teeth…

His *fangs*.

There was no mistaking the razor-like sharpness against her hyper-sensitive flesh. She stiffened.

His muscles tightened and he stopped his delicious assault on her breast.

She opened her eyes and found him staring back at her, his face only inches away. He looked at her, into her, his eyes hot and vivid, his fangs fully visible. He looked as if he'd like nothing more than to throw her down and sink himself and his fangs into her body, but he didn't move.

Instead, he waited, his hold on her firm and secure, his muscles stretched taut.

Are you sure?

His thought echoed through her head, sending a rush of amazement through her. The connection was so fierce between them. So intimate. So special.

She cupped his face, felt the rasp of his stubble against her palms and smiled. And then she leaned forward and touched her lips to his.

She kissed him slowly, deeply, tangling her tongue with his, drinking in his taste as if he were a tall glass of water and she desperately needed a drink.

He let her lead for a few tantalizing seconds before taking control as if he couldn't hold back. The kiss grew more intense, his lips nibbling at hers, his fangs grazing the fullness of her bottom lip. She grasped his shoulders and held on for dear life as he tore his lips from hers and licked a tantalizing path down the side of her neck, nibbling at the spot where her pulse beat frantically.

But he didn't bite her.

No matter how much she suddenly wanted him to.

His mouth moved lower as he dipped his head, licking a path over her collarbone, down between her breasts before catching one nipple between his teeth. He bit down just a little and pleasure bolted through her, pulsing along her nerve endings, heating her body until she felt like she would explode.

He didn't touch her with his hands. Just his mouth. He worked her until she moaned long and low and deep in her throat and her nipple practically screamed in ecstasy. Her legs trembled. Her tummy quivered. Goose bumps chased up and down her arms.

"Now," she murmured, but he didn't give in to her demand.

He seized the other nipple and delivered the same delicious torture. She grew wetter, hotter, her body shivering with each movement of his mouth. Heat clawed at her and lust beat at her senses.

And then his mouth was on hers again, his hot fingers rolling and plucking her damp nipples. She felt the sharpness of his fangs against her lips, and the sensation sent a shiver of excitement through her. He clamped down on her bottom lip just a little and she tasted the salty sweetness.

The growl that vibrated up his throat sent an echoing shiver through her body and she knew he was feeling the same pleasure she felt.

He urged her legs up on either side of him, pulling her flush against his crotch, his hands trailing down her bare back, stirring every nerve ending along the way. He rubbed her against the massive erection straining beneath his zipper and the friction sent delicious waves of heat through her.

Suddenly she couldn't get close enough. She grasped his shoulders and clawed at his shoulders. His erection rubbed against her slit and she moaned. She couldn't get enough of him, kissing him with all of the passion that she'd held back for so long.

She needed more. Now. *Please*.

His hand slid between them and played the slick flesh. His thumb grazed her clitoris, rasping back and forth, over and over. She bucked and arched as delicious tremors racked her body and she exploded in his arms.

She was so lost in the throes of her orgasm that she didn't even notice that he'd laid her down until she felt the soft mattress at her back.

She glanced up in time to see him unfasten his jeans. He shoved the denim down in one smooth motion, his erection springing forward, huge and hot. A white drop of pearly liquid glistened on the tip and she leaned forward, catching the drop with her tongue before sucking him in, greedy for more.

He groaned, long and low and deep, his fingers catching her hair and holding her to him as she sucked and licked and tasted.

"Not yet," he finally murmured. "I want to feel you all around me when I come." He pushed her back onto the mattress and followed her down. Urging her legs apart, he settled his erection flush against her sex.

He kissed her then, licking her lips and sucking

at her tongue before he caught her legs and bent her knees just enough to open her wider. He slid his hands beneath her bottom to tilt her just so and with one powerful thrust, he slid deep inside her.

She closed her eyes to the rush of pleasure.

"Look at me, Holly," he murmured and her eyelids fluttered open. "I need you to look at me." *To want me.*

He didn't say the words, but she heard them anyway because they were connected on a level that went much deeper than anything she'd ever experienced.

This was what she'd dreamt of. This meeting of the minds. Of the souls.

Hunger blazed hot and intense in his gaze and while she knew he'd looked at every other woman in his past the exact same way, for some reason it felt different. She felt different.

"You *are* different." His fangs glittered in the moonlight as he poised above her.

He didn't move a muscle for a long moment and she knew he was waiting on her. Giving her one last chance to refuse him. She was the one woman who could. Because as much as he wanted her, he couldn't make her want him back.

He'd admitted as much and the knowledge sent a rush of empowerment through her. She'd spent her entire life looking for that special someone, wanting to be that special someone.

And at that moment, she was.

She tilted her head, baring her neck, offering it to him. Not because it was what he wanted, but because *she* wanted it. She wanted to connect to him, fully and completely. She wanted to take all that he offered and give everything she had in return, not because it gave her some payoff in the future, but because she wanted him now. Right here. Right now.

Regardless of what happened later.

He dipped his head. His mouth closed over the side of her neck where her pulse beat a frantic rhythm. He laved the spot with his tongue, stroking and tantalizing before he sank his fangs deep. So deliciously deep.

True to his word, it didn't hurt. Rather, she felt only a slight prickle, followed by a rush of intense pleasure that made her gasp.

He thrust into her, pushing deep with his body, all the while sucking with his mouth. He drove her mindless, pushing and sucking, giving and taking, in a frantic rhythm that pulled the air from her lungs.

The pressure inside of her built, climbing higher until she couldn't take anymore. This was it. He was it. *Now!*

She cried out, bursting into a thousand pieces.

He quickly followed her over the edge, his entire body tensing, vibrating. He trembled, drinking in her blood the same way he drank in the sexual energy that rushed from her body.

His mouth eased and he leaned back. A fierce groan rumbled from his lips as he thrust one final time and she felt the spurt of warmth deep inside.

His body shook with the force of his climax, then he slumped on top of her, his face buried in the crook of her neck.

A few frantic heartbeats later, he rolled onto his back and fit her firmly against the side of his body. He held her close, as if he feared she might slip away from him.

He didn't have to worry. She could barely move. She felt weightless, floating, as if she didn't have a care in the world. And while she knew that wasn't true and she would have to open her eyes soon, right now the only thing she wanted to do was stay right here in his arms.

She rested her head on his shoulder and drank in several deep breaths of air. A tiny trickle of warmth slid down her collarbone and she reached up. Her fingertips brushed the two tiny pinpoints where he'd bitten her and a sharp burst of heat sizzled through her. She jumped.

She was surprised. Startled. And turned on.

"Easy, sugar." His hand came up to soothe the area. Not that it worked. It only served to stir her up even more. Her nipples pebbled and her thighs clenched. She closed her eyes as warmth bubbled between her legs and sizzled through her. She felt his smile even before she saw it. "I told you it would make you forget about the ankle."

"What ankle?"

His warm chuckle vibrated along her nerve endings as he slid his hand down the length of her body, stroking, soothing, lulling.

She snuggled deeper into his embrace, rested her head in the crook of his neck and went to sleep.

TRAVIS LISTENED TO her deep, steady breaths, relishing the sound until the shadows outside the window seemed to shift and the veil of blackness lifted just enough to tell him that it was close to dawn.

He pulled her arms from around his neck and slipped from the bed, careful not to disturb her. He pulled on his jeans and T-shirt and then reached for his boots. Snatching up his hat, he plopped it onto his head and turned back to survey the woman stretched out on the bed. He tucked the blanket up around her, his hands lingering at her hair for a long moment, relishing the silkiness.

She was so damned beautiful. And stubborn, he reminded himself. He hated that about her. And loved it.

Love?

Hell, no. He didn't love her. Sure, he liked her a lot. A helluva lot. Unlike most women he came into contact with, he'd taken the time to get to know her. He knew that she had two left feet, that she liked pink and that she loved her job. He knew she liked fireworks, that she ate ice cream when she got stressed, she used strawberries and cream shampoo and that she loved her aunt more than anything in the world. She was determined and loyal and strong, and he liked it. He liked all of it.

Still, the foundation of their attraction was still based on lust. That's what had pulled him to her in the first place, what had made him agree to her plan. He'd wanted her body *and* her blood. And now he'd had both.

That meant it was time to walk away for good this time.

He gave her one last lingering glance and then he turned and left.

21

"I REALLY THINK you should wear your hair down." Wanda Lancaster added yet another swipe of red lipstick to her lips as she eyed her daughter in the mirror. "It looks lots better, sweetie."

"That's *much* better, Momma," Darla corrected, "and I already told you, I like it up. It looks more sophisticated. All the major brides are wearing their hair like this." She indicated the bridal magazine sitting open on the table not far away, the model on the cover showcasing an expertly coiffed updo. She cast another glance at her mother. "Do you have to wear so much red lipstick? That went out ages ago. Try some lipgloss."

"I like red lipstick and I'm wearing red lipstick," Wanda insisted. "That's what you need." She held out the tube to Shelly who stood in a floor-length silver and black dress, white gloves to her elbows. Her hair was pulled up just like Darla's and she looked as if she was nursing a major migraine. "You need some color. You're pale."

Darla touched her own updo. "That's because these bobby pins feel like they're piercing my brain." She waved away the tube. "That stuff gives me the hives."

The hustle and bustle went on for several more minutes as Darla checked over everyone's dresses, flowers, hair and make-up while Holly went over her checklist with Evan.

"I think we're just about ready," she told her bride.

"That's right, pigskin. Ten minutes and you're getting married."

"Mom, please don't call me that. I hate that name."

"But I thought you liked pork rinds."

"About a hundred years ago. And while I liked to eat them, I don't appreciate you calling me that name."

Wanda shrugged. "I think it's sorta cute."

"That's sort of, Momma. There's no such word as sorta." The door opened then and an older woman in her fifties waltzed in wearing a floor-length blue sapphire suit with rhinestone buttons. Her expertly colored blond hair was done up in the latest style, her make-up immaculate.

"There she is," she declared, a wide smile on her face. "My soon-to-be daughter-in-law."

Darla smiled, but Holly didn't miss the flicker of apprehension in her eyes.

"Well come here and let me look at you."

Darla stepped forward and the woman took her hands. "Why, you look lovely. My son is a lucky young man. You've got such beautiful skin. And that hair…" Her smile faltered just a little as she took in the hairstyle.

"What is it?" Darla blurted. "What's wrong?"

"I just didn't realize that you were going to wear your hair up."

"I thought it would be more flattering to the veil."

"She always did like wearing ponytails," Wanda offered. "Why, we would have called her ponytail if it wasn't for the fact that she was always munching on all those pork rinds."

"Not now, Momma," Darla whispered. "You really don't like it?"

"It's fine, dear. I just think it would be more flattering down. That's all. It's your choice." She waved it off and turned. "I'd better get out there. I've got a handsome young usher waiting to walk me down the aisle."

"Me, too," Wanda said, heading for the door. "See you out there, sugar."

"I'm sending the maid of honor out," Holly said into her headset. "Get the rest of the bridesmaids ready."

"10-4," Evan said.

Holly motioned to Shelly and sent her out the door and then she turned to Darla. "Are you ready?"

"What do you think about my hair?" the bride asked her pointedly.

Holly saw the indecision, the uncertainty, the fear and her heart went out to Darla, regardless of what a bee-yotch she'd been lately. She knew what it was like to want something so badly that she would do anything to get it. Even convince herself she was marrying the right man.

She also knew what it was like to want something so badly that she would convince herself she was turning her back on the wrong man.

But Travis wasn't wrong for her. He was so right that it made her teeth ache. Not that it mattered. He obviously didn't feel the same way. He'd left before dawn on Friday morning and she hadn't seen him since. She'd spent the entire day listening to Tootie talk about Buck Gentry and how he wasn't such a bad fellow after all, on account of he'd turned her on to Bingo. Heck, she might even like him a little. Not that it was any reason to get excited. It wasn't like she was going to marry him.

At least that's what she'd said, but Holly had seen too many brides over the past few years to believe her aunt. She had the same anxious light in her eyes. And while she would never have thought it in a million years, she was starting to think that even Aunt Tootie might take the leap and head to the altar.

It was now Saturday evening and Travis would be leaving in a matter of hours. She'd heard from one of the hairdressers that Cody and Miranda were ar-riving at seven tonight. Travis would get his chance to talk to his brother, and then he would leave.

"So?" Darla pressed.

"I think it doesn't matter what I think. It matters what you think." As she said the words, realization dawned. Travis might be all wrong, but when she was with him, he made her feel right. He was right.

Not that she was telling him. She'd rather spare herself the embarrassment.

Darla turned and stared in the mirror. For a split-second, Holly thought she would actually leave her hair as is. But then she started yanking bobby pins until her hair hung around her shoulders. She shook out the curls, worked at the veil for a split-second and then she turned. "Let's get this show on the road."

"Bride walking," Holly murmured as Darla hauled open the door and headed down the hallway.

Darla refused to listen to her heart and Holly didn't blame her. She would be giving up so much. Comfort. Safety. Her future.

It wasn't about embarrassment for Holly. She was scared. Scared of the way Travis made her feel. Scared of what might happen tomorrow. Scared that it wouldn't be the comfortable little future she'd mapped out for herself.

That's why she refused to take the initiative and call him. Take a chance.

"I can't do this," Darla's voice pushed into her

thoughts and she saw her bride standing in the entry-way outside the main ceremony area. "I don't want to do this. I like Tom, but I don't love him." The minute she said the words, a weight seemed to lift from her expression. Panic quickly followed.

"What do I do?"

"Go find him. I'll take care of everything else." Holly sent Darla off to the holding area for the groomsmen and then she told Evan what was happening. "Explain it to the parents and then let everyone else know," she told him as she pulled off her headset and handed it to him.

"Where are you going?"

"I need to talk to someone." And then she went to find Travis.

It was time she took her own chance, no matter what the future held.

"WE'RE ALL HERE," Travis said, motioning around the dining room table where all the Braddock brothers gathered for the first time since that fateful night. While they were all called back to the place of their turning every year on the anniversary, it was different. They'd been spread out at the ranch, one on one side, another over here, another over there. Together, yet alone. But they were all here now.

Colton, the oldest, sat next to Travis looking as somber and as quiet as ever. He'd walked in a half hour ago just before Cody arrived home. He hadn't

said much. He didn't have to. His eyes said it all. They glittered with an anger that Travis had never seen before. Colton was hurt. Betrayed. And even God wouldn't be able to help the woman responsible once he caught up with her.

Brent and Cody sat on the other side of the table. Miranda sat next to Cody, her hand in his while Brent sat with his arm around Abby. And despite the subject matter, they didn't look half as tense as Travis felt. Rather, they seemed relaxed. Happy. Loved.

A pang of envy shot through Travis and he couldn't stifle the thought that maybe he was wrong. Maybe he could have the same happiness with Holly if he just gave it a chance.

He'd been so damned convinced that the lust would drive him straight into the arms of another woman, but he wasn't so sure anymore. It had been twenty-four hours and he still couldn't stop thinking about her. He'd spent all night working with the wild black mare and he'd managed to break her. But all the work hadn't been enough to distract him from thoughts of Holly. She was under his skin. In his head. In his heart.

He hadn't wanted to believe it, but seeing his brothers, seeing how happy they were, suddenly he wanted it. He wanted it more than anything.

Even more than the revenge he'd been so deadset on for so many years.

Not that Holly wanted him. She hadn't made a

move to contact him any more than he'd tried to contact her. She wouldn't. She'd taken her Love Buster vow. And while she'd fallen off the wagon, she would climb right back on. She was a stubborn thing. Too stubborn for her own good.

"So where is she?" Colton demanded. "Just give me a location and I'm on my way."

"Sit back down."

"Why?"

"Because she's right here, or she soon will be. We have something she wants. There was a prisoner transferred to the jail a few days ago. A young man about twenty-two."

"And what does this have to do with Rose?"

"He's her last living relative. I had a private investigator do some checking once we found her. It seems she's been helping this guy out, keeping an eye on him. I'd be willing to bet she's on her way to Skull Creek right now—"

The ring of a doorbell drowned out his words.

A minute later, Holly appeared in the doorway. She took one look around the room and Travis saw the flash of recognition. Even so, she wasn't the least bit intimidated by a roomful of bloodsuckers. She headed straight for him.

"I love you," she blurted out. "I know you might not love me, but I love you anyway. There it is." She put her hands on her hips and stared him down. Waiting. Worrying. "I know you're a vampire and, well, it

presents a few problems. But I'm willing to deal with them. That is, if you want to try. I know it won't be perfect. No daytime wedding or anything like that. That is, if we even get that far. But I'm willing to give it a shot and see where it goes." When he just kept looking at her, she added, "Well? Aren't you going to say something?"

"It's about damned time." Travis was on his feet in that next instant, pulling her into his arms.

"Is that all you're going to say?"

He stared down into her eyes and saw the emotion he felt deep inside mirrored in her gaze. There was so much they would have to work through. At the same time, with her in his arms, it seemed like there was nothing he couldn't do. *Nothing.* "I love you, too, but only if I get fireworks instead of birdseed."

She grinned and then she kissed him.

* * * * *

& A sneaky peek at next month...

Blaze®

SCORCHING HOT, SEXY READS

My wish list for next month's titles...

In stores from 16th September 2011:

❏ Shiver – Jo Leigh

& Private Sessions – Tori Carrington

❏ Northern Exposure – Jennifer LaBrecque

❏ Hold on to the Nights – Karen Foley

Available at WHSmith, Tesco, Asda, Eason, Amazon and Apple

Just can't wait?